Only Human

The Targon Tales

Chris Reher

Chris Reher

The Targon Tales

Sky Hunter

The Catalyst

Only Human

Rebel Alliances

Delphi Promised

Quantum Tangle

Terminus Shift

Entropy's End

also available in eBook and audio format

www.chrisreher.com

Copyright © 2012 Chris Reher
All rights reserved
ISBN: 978-0-9916985-3-0

the pilots passed along to their planes using the microscopic sensors buried in their brains. Again, the Kites performed as hoped for, handling their tasks with ease, obedient to their flesh and blood masters.

"All right, looks good," O'Neill said much too soon. Nova heard a few groans from the other pilots. "We've got enough. First one back at the tower gets the point. Go!"

Nova launched herself at the distant horizon, waiting not another nanosecond for the others to process his command and pick up the chase again.

"Nice reflexes, Whiteside." She heard a smile in O'Neill's voice. "We'll have to—"

"Lost you on that last bit, sir."

There was no reply.

"O'Neill, come in."

Nothing.

An orange light flashed among the controls, indicating another plane nearby. The others were closing in. "Did any of you lose the tower?" she asked.

No one answered. The orange blip continued to eat the distance between them.

She felt her heart beat high in her throat and cursed herself into calmness. Medical sensors taped to her chest, head and neck fed her vital signs back to the control center for analysis as this test unfolded. Not just the planes were under scrutiny.

"Keta? Dylan? Is that you back there?" Nova muttered unfine endearments to herself as she tried to identify her pursuer. By now it was obvious that he was pursuing her, dangerously close, and not just sharing her flight path. Her mechanical sensor faithfully reported a Union-issue fighter plane. He moved above her and began to lose altitude.

Her alarm systems screamed at her.

The Kite continued to drop, forcing her to do the same. Where were the others? She varied her speed, hoping to slide out from under him. He reacted to her maneuvers as if anticipating them.

Nova smiled grimly, having met her match. Few of her

peers flew with such precision. She decided to stay in the neural link and play him along, her plane twitching the way a rabbit runs before a predator. Perhaps she could still outfox him. Surrender did not occur to her, nor did the repeated warnings of the instructors not to risk the expensive Kites needlessly. This might be fun. She began to maneuver, pushing the machine to decide between her unspoken commands and the safety parameters of the plane's design.

"Hey! What the…?"

He had opened fire! She saw projectiles tear into the ground below, flinging up clods of red mud in twin rows running after her shadow.

"Are you crazy?" she hissed into her microphone. "What are you doing?" She raised her visor to get a better look at the plane above her.

The hunter answered with another round.

"Identify!" Nova's voice shook. Fear sliced into her gut like the blade of a cold knife. Rumors of rebels on the base were now widely accepted as fact. Could one of them be on that plane? She brought her gun controls online and prepared to return his fire, knowing that there was still a chance that one of her overzealous colleagues was simply playing the bad guy. But how long could she wait?

Then something grazed along her hull to send her Kite into a wild spin. The ground rushed toward her at a sickening speed, and sky changed places with earth in a kaleidoscope of red and blue. Out of instinct, she reached for the steering bars of the plane but then recalled her direct link with a far more precise steering system than she could ever hope to be. She allowed it to follow her mental commands to steady the ship, gaining control by sheer, teeth-grinding determination.

And just when her Kite recovered, another missile streaked past her dome.

Anger now pushed her fear somewhere into the background where she didn't have to deal with it. "Bastard," she breathed and forced the Kite into reverse. The plane obeyed, held together by little more than its shields, less

successful in protecting its Human cargo. She was thrown hard into her belts and felt her helmet collide with the steering bars.

The hunter swooped over her head, firing rapidly.

"Control, Whiteside under fire," she reported, forcing a calmness into her voice. "It's live and not what I signed up for today!" A bright signal on her dashboard reported further trouble. "I've lost my left neural tap. Come in, Control!"

Still, no reply.

Her pursuer had banked into a tight turn and now came head-on, his fire barely missing her Kite. She continued her evasive tactics, now relying on only a single neural link to her machine.

This game had turned into a mindless bid for survival. And now, although she had not taken a direct hit, her displays signaled yet another malfunction, this time in the crossdrive system. Her velocity dropped steadily.

Cursing, Nova stopped the plane and hovered into a passable emergency landing on a clear patch among the tall grasses and pools of stagnant water that made up most of Myra's surface. She disengaged from the sensors in her helmet to break the neurolink, retracted the canopy, and freed herself from her belts and parachute. She slid across the plane's triangular wing to land on spongy ground, taking her gun and a small backpack containing medical supplies and emergency rations.

Her actions were automatic, a list of priorities ingrained into her since the day she walked into basic training over a decade ago. Her only conscious thought now was to abandon the plane before the enemy's missiles turned it into a deadly storm of shrapnel. She ran toward a gully, slowed by the surface mire, tearing through brambles and reeds until she found a hump of moss-covered rocks among the fronds of fern. She gasped for air, her lungs on fire.

Had he given up? Nova listened for the other plane, hearing nothing. Had he landed, too? She raised her arm to activate the sensors on her data sleeve and found the whole thing offline. Was anything working correctly today? She

waited through uncounted minutes, letting the insects of this bog find her. Her head throbbed. She knew that the people back at the base would be shaking their heads over her erratic vital signs. She forced her breath to slow, tempted to remove the wireless sensor that still stuck to her chest beneath jacket and shirt.

Something trickled along her cheek and when she touched it her hand came away bloodied. Gingerly, she prodded her neural interface node and found that it had torn.

"Oh, Noooova," a contrived falsetto sing-songed behind her. The barrel of a gun stabbed into her nape. Startled, she spun to raise her own weapon. A heavy boot came down on it, pinning it along with her hand against the rock that was supposed to have hidden her.

"Interesting reflex there. I could have taken your head off."

Nova wrenched her hand free. She rubbed it, glaring at the lieutenant, angry at herself for having allowed him to come up behind her. "You're a pig sometimes, Fynn."

"Whatever that is." He looked at the blood on her face in thoughtful fascination. "I've caught myself a prisoner."

"Good for you. Let me up." She pushed his leg aside and stood up. Her uniform dripped with swamp water and her boots were probably ruined. "Why are you even out here? How dare you shoot at me! If O'Neill finds out you'll be demerited into oblivion." She jammed her gun into its holster and turned to march back to her plane.

"Hold it," he said. "Didn't you hear me say that you're my prisoner?"

"Yeah, so?" Nova said irritably, the terror of the chase already receding in her memory. She had lost the contest!

"I'm playing a Rhuwac today. Big mean Rhuwac rebel wants to play with his prisoner."

"You're not funny."

He gripped her arm, rougher than necessary, to turn her around. "Good, because I'm not joking."

"Just really very creepy."

He leered unpleasantly. "This is turning me on."

"And you're pissing me off, Fynn." Nova stalked away. "You probably damaged my plane, I've hurt my head thanks to you and you've used your guns. You better figure out a way to keep O'Neill calm when he sees you."

"I had orders to shoot."

Nova halted. "You what?"

He caught up with her. "Command told me to force an emergency landing. They know it'd take guns to make you land. They fabricated your malfunction when you weren't about to give up. Nothing wrong with your plane. Don't worry about them finding out how easily I tracked you down here. The game was over for you the minute you left the cockpit. That's all they cared about."

"And you let me run for my life and scare the hell out of me for nothing?"

"Fun, wasn't it?"

"Jerk." She slapped his arm with the back of her hand.

He caught her wrist and twisted it until she winced in pain. "We could have some more fun, if you like."

Nova recognized the half-angry, half-excited glint in his eyes. She was tempted to reach for her gun. "Let me go," she said evenly, in no mood for a fight today. "I need to see a medic."

Fynn hesitated, disappointed with her reaction. He released her.

Nova walked ahead of him back to the ships, her anger smoldering. Why did she allow him to bully her like that? And why did she keep going back for yet another taste of his abusive nature? He was unpredictable in his moods and could be downright nasty when the wrong mood was upon him.

When Nova took leave from active combat for retraining on Myra, what seemed a lifetime of dangers and discomforts already lay behind her. The squad she had left behind consisted of seasoned career pilots who expected her to shoulder her load under any conditions. And conditions on Ud Mrak were miserable. Fynn had been quick to realize this and had claimed her attention, soon marking her as his own. He showed her how to have fun on this base where there were only tests to worry about and superior officers to elude. Adept at the latter, Fynn made a game of ignoring curfews, breaking rules for the sake of breaking them, and infusing as much recreation into his stay here as possible.

Nova joined in his games at first, enjoying the relative freedom of Myra for a while. But her nature and upbringing did not allow her to defy authority or create new rules for herself. Growing up on one army base after another taught her the value of order and routine that did not vary from one post to the next.

She knew it would not be long before she would end this. For all the technical skill she admired in him, Fynn was a danger in combat. She would never be able to accept his disregard for others from which not even she was exempt. In bed he was as fierce as in battle, but away from her cot he had the social skills of a Rhuwac.

Nova had a sudden mental image of a hulking, leather-skinned Rhuwac monstrosity holding his own at a cocktail party, and she snorted with laughter. Then she caught a glimpse of Fynn glowering in her direction as he stomped toward his own plane. He no doubt suspected that she was laughing at him. In a way she was, she supposed, and decided not to bother to explain her sudden fit of giggles.

* * *

Nova landed her Kite directly into the hangars of the base. She had no wish to hear her squadron mates' snide remarks about her 'capture'. Some of them hadn't clocked even half of her flight hours and damn them all if they thought the forced landing embarrassed her.

She relinquished her plane to one of the hangar jockeys and turned into the hall leading to the residential wing and her own room for a change of clothes. Her boots squelched with every step and the drying fabric of her uniform was chafing her into renewed irritability.

Her head, too, demanded attention. She changed her

direction and entered the base clinic, cursing Fynn under her breath.

"You're a sweet mess today, aren't you?" the medic, someone with whom she was familiar enough to know by name had she been able to pronounce it, greeted her. He, however, was fluent in Union mainvoice, accompanied by a whistling sound originating somewhere in his throat. "Whiteside, isn't it? Captain Nova Whiteside." He did not bother to confirm her identity when her touch on his screens displayed her file. "I shall soon need to ask for additional staff if you continue to lacerate yourself."

She followed him into an examination room where a nurse began to clean the blood and grime from her injuries.

"You've been here for what? Eight months? And in that interim we've seen you six times. I'd hate to see how you fare in active combat."

"I was transferred here out of active combat," Nova told him. "And there I rarely had the need for a doctor. It's the boredom here."

He sniffed disapprovingly. "Many soldiers would welcome eight months of retraining here on Myra. It's an excellent facility."

"Ouch!" Nova frowned at the nurse swabbing her abraded hand. "Maybe so, but I'm a Hunter class pilot. I don't know what I'm supposed to learn here."

"Modesty, maybe." He motioned her to follow him to a diagnostic station. "Or perhaps the mechanics involved in keeping a helmet on your head. You jarred your node almost completely loose. Any local pain there? Dizzy? Vision fine?"

"No, no, yes." She let him inspect the triangular interface module embedded in her temple. He winced when he peered through a probe to look for damage. His wince was for the abused technology, not her face.

"I wish you pilots would take a little more care with the taps. Do you have any idea how expensive they are? Not to mention the minor fact that they lead directly into your brain." He attached a filament to the nodes on both sides of her head and consulted his diagnostic displays. "Follow that light. Good. Now run the simulation. So you are between orders?"

She obeyed his instruction and directed the computer to build a complex geometrical shape out of smaller components. A simple undertaking compared to using the neural link to operate her plane or weaponry, but every single synapse was analyzed and charted during the short exercise.

"I am. I didn't apply for a transfer and my past commander wasn't thrilled when I got one anyway. I don't even think he knows where I am now. If he did, I'm sure he'd request to get me back. My time is wasted here."

The doctor regarded the bedraggled warrior in front of him, ready with a suitable comment to put her into her place. He realized that he could do no such thing. She was wasting her time here, he agreed. He tugged the connectors from her nodes and fused the loosened edge to her skin. "Try not to collect any more injuries in your boredom. Come back in five days for follow-up."

Nova thanked him and continued on to her room. The doctor had been right to chide her, she thought. She only recently visited after dislocating a finger in hand to hand combat training. Two previous injuries, both minor and caused by Fynn, were not the type of accident one easily came to in combat.

But here she was, playing war games with junior officers while the real battles were fought elsewhere. For what seemed to be the millionth time, Nova wondered why she had been transferred to Myra and then forgotten.

Moodily, she rounded a corner, now only a few minutes away from her room and a clean uniform.

"Nova!"

She groaned inwardly and slowed her steps to let Fynn catch up.

"Yo, kid, I've been looking all over for you." He had changed into his usual fatigue trousers and a black shirt meant to show off his powerful torso.

She held up her bandaged hand, shaped into a fist. "Where

the hell do you think I've been?"

"Don't be cross. O'Neill sent me to find you."

"I'll get down to the test center as soon as I've changed my suit. He'll have to wait a while if he wants to tell me how badly I did today."

He took her arm and turned her around. "Walk this way, and quickly. Colonel wants to see you."

"The colonel?" Nova wondered why the commander of the base wanted her.

"Yeah, and you better hurry. He's been looking for you for a while, I hear."

"I can't see him like this!" She pointed to her sodden boots.

But Fynn was already propelling her along the hall, shouldering aside anyone of lower rank and smaller size. "You got to. He's got everyone looking for you."

"What's so urgent?"

Fynn stopped dead and spun her to face him. "Listen, you won't say anything about my live fire on you today, huh?" He pressed her arm as if to squeeze an answer from her.

She pulled out of his grasp. "I thought O'Neill sanctioned that. Didn't he?"

"Well, in so many words. You know how the colonel is. Wouldn't put it past him to demerit me because of a bit of roughhousing."

Nova laughed humorlessly. Roughhousing! "Someday they'll throw you out, Fynn," she warned. "Transfers are coming up. We've got a hundred recruits coming in and some of us have to leave."

His features rearranged themselves into an expression of apprehension. As much as Nova ached to leave this playground, he wanted to stay. Here he showed off his skills in friendly competition without any real danger to himself. Out there, he thought correctly, was only hard, dangerous work among pilots equally or more skilled than he. He dreaded the day that would bring his next assignment.

He looked truly miserable and Nova relented. "Don't worry; I won't mention it. I'll see you later."

She left him to hurry along too-slow conveyors, struggling to untangle a few strands of copper-colored hair that had escaped its clasp, patting ineffectively at her wrinkled uniform. A pleasant thought had struck her. Was she, finally, to be transferred back into serious work?

* * *

The colonel finished another revision of his speech and replayed the recording. This was not the first time he would deliver it to a troop of new pilots, but he still polished it like a treasured memento. It was also a good way to pass the time while waiting for the overdue officer. The other option would be to return to the window and waste more time glaring at the ships that waited on the tarmac below.

Voices outside announced Nova Whiteside's arrival. She was out of breath when she finally stepped into his work space.

"Hello, Father." Nova went to his desk, her stride unmistakably military. "You were looking for me?"

The colonel's welcoming smile faded as he regarded her silently and for an uncomfortably long time. Her uniform and boots were mud-splattered, and strands of hair floated loosely around her head. He did not miss the fresh bandage on her hand and the swollen skin around the newly repaired interface node. "I did," he said at last, rising to his feet. "I see that I caught you unprepared for this interview."

Nova blushed and fussed over her rumpled sleeves. "The race..."

"I know. I just spoke to Major O'Neill. You seem to have had some difficulty with your emergency landing."

"I did," she said simply.

He waited for more, pleased when she didn't budge. "We know how you were forced to land. And we know that you held it together and stayed in neural link until you landed. Laudable, Captain." He did not mention that he had hung on every second of the transmission until the moment she left the plane safely, fearing that she would try to take manual control of the craft. "I'm less pleased with Bridger's deportment. I will be glad to see him shuttled off my base and onto someone else's."

"Fynn? Why?"

"His time here is up. And Major O'Neill and I, among others, now agree that the best place for him is on Targon. We're sending fifty of your group there in a few days."

"Targon?" Nova gasped.

Colonel Whiteside nodded. Targon represented the heart of the Union's military activities in the Trans-Targon sector. The highly modern, highly disciplined Air Command base on that planet also included hospitals and research facilities as well as one of several military academies. Nova had visited the base on a few occasions and often enthused about being stationed there someday. Most Air Command pilots did.

"Lieutenant Bridger will be stationed on Isora, the patrol detail cruising the Targon-Feyd corridor. A fighter plane and some strict discipline should make repairs of whatever it is that drives the young man. He is lucky that Targon is requesting able pilots rather than valiant characters. His record does not make him one of the better soldiers sent out from Myra."

"Father, he's only..." Nova sprang to Fynn's defense but then seemed at a loss to find words to describe any quality that would endear him to the colonel. "Well, he's a little careless sometimes, maybe," she mumbled instead.

Whiteside shook his head in dismissal, wondering why he was using that worthless pilot to stall for time. "He will be given a chance aboard the Isora. It's up to him to make it there."

"What about me? Will I be transferred to Targon?"

"Not directly."

"The Magra base?" she asked hopefully.

"No."

"A transport, then," she said, sounding disappointed.

Whiteside shook his head and wandered to the large window that dominated the room. He observed the activity on the airfield below with the same expression he reserved for facing his most difficult recruits. Staff and mechanicals scurried from hangars to planes, from planes to service stations. Most of the craft belonged to the academy, representing a variety of shuttles, old cargo frigates and retired Kites now used for training. Even a few captured enemy Shrills were used here to teach maneuvers.

There were two very different cruisers down there now, blocking one of the fueling stations. A third of that class was due to arrive soon. He stared at them with loathing. They were fine ships, possibly the best ever engineered, but their presence here was costing him too much. Costing him everything.

"You know," he said, "I have often wondered if bringing you and your mother to Trans-Targon was fair to you both. Although, I am sure, you do not feel like a stranger here."

"Stranger?" Nova said. "Most of the people here are Human."

He shrugged. "Here, yes. A small planet in the safest sector of the Commonwealth territory. A good place for Humans. But this war belongs to the Centauri and to the Shri-Lan rebels. I have sometimes thought of taking you back to Terra, our Earth."

Her eyes widened. "Back? That reach takes years to cross! The jumpsites are so far apart that you'd be in deep sleep for most of the way. Why would I want to go to Terra? I don't belong there." Nova could not have sounded more indignant if he had actually asked her to return with him.

Whiteside had to agree that she didn't belong there. Nova had never known the peace and prosperity that her mother had missed so much. So green and so rich, that place where she might have come of age not knowing the heft of a gun or the face of a Rhuwac. But instead of growing up in a gentle world to become a gentle woman, Nova had turned from army brat into warrior. A fairly deadly warrior, according to the reports of her superiors.

She looked so much like her mother, he thought. Red hair forever escaping whatever bonds she tried to devise for it, pale skin that saw the sun too rarely. Her green eyes missed nothing and no one escaped her broad smile without echoing it. But

Nova's hands were trained to kill, while her mother had used hers to create with paint and music. He sighed, feeling old. "Since your first trip aboard a shuttle I've known it would come to this."

"Come to what?" Nova's brow furrowed.

His gesture invited her to join him at the window. She looked over the afternoon routine below, searching for whatever he had pointed out.

The cruisers perched ready for take-off near the small craft hangars. They looked out of place here on the base where civilian planes had no business. One was a Feydan transport of some age, the other seemed to have been cobbled together out of spare parts. They were small, likely carrying a crew of no more than three or four with a little room for cargo. Inconspicuous ships designed for long distance flights far beyond the groomed runways of civilization.

"Multi-terrain landing gear. Those are dual crossdrive intakes." She raised an eyebrow. "Expensive. If they're ours, I'm guessing covert ops."

"Eagle class."

Nova gaped, stunned into silence. That class was a feat of engineering that allowed them to traverse normal space as fast and efficiently as any of the massive Union Commonwealth transports that moved among the allied planets. It had taken the fine mind of a Delphian to rethink the cumbersome crossdrive system and, at tremendous cost, fit it into a ship of minute proportions.

"Vanguard," she said finally. "That has to be Vanguard."

He nodded. "You qualify."

Nova grasped the window's narrow ledge, so overwhelmed by his announcement that she had missed the regret in his voice. "Me? Vanguard?"

The colonel regarded his daughter carefully, wishing he could reverse these orders that would take his only child into places and dangers that he doubted he would ever willingly face himself. He had lost his wife in this war and, although Nova had flown a fighter plane for years now, seeing her join that cadre filled him with misgivings. The life expectancy of a Vanguard member was not among the best statistics he had studied lately.

"You are an able pilot, but your talents go beyond that, as you've proven in the past. You belong with the scouts and recons. Today's performance confirmed what we already know. It was a demonstration of your abilities for your new commander." He cleared his throat. "I have to say that your choice of language in that situation was less admirable."

Nova stared into the middle distance, musing. "You know, I have dreamed of this. I never told anyone; I was afraid they'd laugh at me. I thought maybe in a few years I'd have a shot at it and that would show them all, wouldn't it? But now..." Her eyes wandered back to the crafts below.

"There are three Vanguard teams here on Myra right now," Whiteside told her. "All need new crew members and will take over your field training. It's time for you to return to active duty." He paused, not liking the expression on her face. He, who tolerated weakness in no one and least of all his own child, almost wished that she would express some sort of doubt. If she showed the least bit of apprehension about joining the Vanguard, if she asked him if he thought her capable, he would consider it enough to disqualify her from this duty. But her confidence was true; he saw no fear of failure, as much as he tried to read it into her features. She was ready for this assignment. "I have met your new commander," he said.

Nova did not miss the expression of distaste that crept over the colonel's face. "And you don't like him."

Whiteside raised his head, surprised by her insight. After a moment he shrugged. "When did you start reading me so well? He has an excellent record."

"But?"

"Ah, regulations had to be bent. You are, after all, female. Long journeys can be a trial for the most..." he cleared his throat. "Long journeys can be lonely..." he broke off again, embarrassed by his inability to say what he felt must be said.

"I think I can control myself," Nova said, amused by his discomfort.

"You were teamed with the one with whom there would be the least risk of, well, circumstances..."

"He is not Human," Nova interjected.

"The major is Delphian."

She pursed her lips. "They don't like us much." She didn't have to add that the sentiment was reciprocated by Humans and Centauri alike.

"Perhaps not," Whiteside said. "But they don't hate us, either, so I suppose that's a blessing. Sometimes I think that this war between us and the Shri-Lan amuses them. We're just some nuisance to them."

"At least they're not hostile," Nova said. "We have enough on our hands."

"And, unfortunately, we need them. Without their mental abilities, we'd still be paddling around in real space. They are valuable navigators."

While genetically nearly identical to their interstellar neighbors, evolution had broadened the Delphian mental capacities without the pharmaceutical aids or gene manipulations most other species relied upon. Their ability to focus their resources when needed made them better pilots, better doctors, better engineers than their Commonwealth allies. This, perhaps, as well as the tight-lipped isolationism imposed by Delphi's government, often led to resentment even among closest associates.

"At least the ones they allow to leave Delphi. As if we weren't spending huge resources to keep the rebels off their doorstep. Arrogant bunch of—"

"You will keep that to yourself, Captain. Arrogant or not, they are valuable and they are allies. Maybe you can use this assignment to improve your understanding of them."

"Nobody understands them, sir."

"Then be the first." The colonel consulted his screen. "Major Tychon," he read and shook his head in disapproval. "These people change the rest of their names with the weather.

We just list Tychon."

"Is he the navigator?"

He nodded. "Level Three spanner."

"Three? That means…"

"Uncharted jumpsites. Deep space work. And if you're lucky, a little exploration as time allows. Most certainly the most attractive part of this assignment for me. Being Delphian is a terrific advantage at that level and they're not known to be cowboys. We need more spanners and I'll expect you to learn much from him. You've shown the aptitude. These three commanders need new pilots and we're giving them the best we have."

"Now? Today?"

"Indeed." He glanced at his timepiece. "Congratulations, Nova, but there is no time to celebrate your new assignment. Although now you know why I insisted that you join me for dinner yesterday. The major wishes to leave immediately. You are expected in the smallcraft hangars."

Nova embraced the elder Human. "I will see you soon," she promised.

He watched her go, not believing it.

* * *

Nova reached a vacated hallway on her way to the hangars before she let out a joyful whoop that would not be contained any longer.

Vanguard! Racing along the concourse, she thanked each of the currently popular gods, regardless of origin, for bringing this day so soon. She would be part of Air Command's most valued division; she would visit places previously restricted, whole worlds to be seen under the protection of the Union emblem. It wasn't just a dream anymore!

She skidded to a halt when she rounded the corner to the vast parking halls, startling the guard at the doors. She nodded coolly in his direction and proceeded into the hangar at a more sedate pace. There, dispatch told her that she was expected in one of the ready rooms.

She picked up speed again to jog across the prelaunch byway which couldn't possibly be prohibited on a day as exciting as this.

"Nova, for pity's sake!" someone called to her. "I've been looking all over for you."

"Dylan! Have you heard? Isn't it amazing?"

"Yeah," he grinned. "It is. I got Vanguard, too. Eagle One. And now we're both late."

Nova followed the lieutenant to the lounge where they received an icy glance from her superior. A major had prepared a speech for the occasion and was now delivering it with all the long-winded formality he could muster. It dealt mainly with the rigors of teamwork and the dangers of reconnaissance and was punctuated by references to their glorious Union Commonwealth and the protection thereof.

While the officer droned, Nova studied the other people in the room. Dylan was a good friend, but she knew the other chosen one only through training sessions. Both of them stood at attention, like Nova still trying to understand their sudden good fortune.

The only people in the room not impressed by the occasion were the Vanguard officers. Since they were not required to wear a uniform, their clothing was an assemblage of off-world items, mismatched and comfortable-looking. Their weapons were also not Air Command issue. While their new pilots, the instructors and the brass stood in stiff formality, they perched on the arms of chairs or leaned casually against the far wall. None of them was actually sitting. It was a study of indifference in which the relaxed slouch had nothing to do with laziness. It didn't seem to be coincidence that their backs were turned neither toward door nor windows. No one stood behind them and no angle of body or article of clothing came between them and their side arms. Nova wondered if they even had to think about taking such defensive positions. Irrationally, she was tempted to unsnap the safety of her own gun. It seemed to her that, should an alarm sound, these men and women would be on their feet and battle ready before she could even begin to reach for her gun.

She recognized her new commanding officer easily. He had hitched a hip onto a table near the back of the room but looked far from restful. While the other two commanders were accompanied by a few crew members, he was alone. His clothes, as casual as those of his peers, were well-fitted, and the only visible weapon was a laser hand gun sporting a wide flash.

More than his neatness and lanky frame, it was his hair that set him apart from the others. Most of the men and some of the women here followed military convention by shaving their pates, but the major's hair grew as it would. A glossy cascade hung freely to the middle of his back in the manner of Delphian males. That style was of some cultural significance more than fashion, but Nova had always thought that it gave their severe features a dash of much-needed charm.

The nails of his long fingers, his eyes, brows and the mass of hair were of a deep blue color. Blue shadows played over thin, unsmiling lips—he looked cold.

Their speeches finally delivered, some of the officers began to file out of the room. Nova took a few moments to thank a senior officer who had been one of her mentors and then approached the major now standing by the door.

He was speaking to Adachi, Vanguard One's captain and Dylan's new commander, using the drawling inflection of a Centauri dialect. Nova joined them and found that, although people often asked her how the weather 'up there' was, he towered over her. His sharp features might have looked harsh and unforgiving except for the remarkable blue eyes and the slate blue mane. Delphians also grew a thin line of hair along their spine and he would have no other hair on his body - if one believed the gossip in the pilot dormitories. Her eyes found the neural implant at his temple, disproving the rumor that they did not need an interface to communicate with their machines.

"Are you paying attention?"

She snapped out of her reverie. "Yessir."

His long upper lip twitched. "What is it, then, Whiteside? I asked you a question." His speech was unaccented, but it was clipped, tightly controlled and seemed as lacking in warmth as the rest of him.

"I'm sorry, sir. I am not used to..." She bit her lip.

His eyes traveled to her rumpled uniform and mud-splattered boots and back up to take note of the recently patched interface node. "I suppose that you meant to say that you are not used to saying your good-byes in five minutes, because that is all you have."

"What?"

He motioned her along. "I am now hoping that your skill as pilot is better than your ability to listen. Collect your gear and then meet me on the liftplane launch."

She looked up at him, bewildered. She would have to watch her step around this one. Somehow she felt as she had years ago, before joining the Union's Air Command, whenever she was faced with a particularly stern instructor.

"Collect my gear? We're leaving already? I haven't even..." she fell silent. Hadn't he made it clear that he had no interest in good-byes and farewell parties?

As she hurried to her quarters to pack her few belongings and to jot a note to her roommate, Nova was surprised by a sensation of loss at the thought of leaving this place, almost certainly forever. Her transfer from active combat to this drab training base had not been an easy adjustment. But at some point these Spartan halls had become home to her, the instructors had become mentors, friends. The long, uneventful months that she had spent here and often complained about had not been completely devoid of fun and companionship.

Nova thought of Fynn, her lover. He would be angry to find her gone. She did not dare to take the time to explain to him, grateful for the excuse to avoid yet another fight. He would know soon enough where she had gone. Nova did not bother to examine her complete lack of regret over leaving him.

She made her way through halls and stairways, stopping only to requisition and receive a few new uniforms. The people passing her on her errand saluted or not, as their ranks dictated; unaware that she would not be part of tomorrow's flight schedule and training sessions. Already they seemed like strangers, bland faces in an unmemorable crowd.

* * *

The major waited for her outside his ship, a hulking and patched model that looked in need of a good mechanic and perhaps a fresh application of paint. She saw repairs made without bodywork to hide the scars and a few scorch marks that could only have been sustained in battle. All of it very nicely hid the sheer power and up-to-the-minute technology tucked into every millimeter of its construction.

He said nothing when she approached but turned to climb a narrow ladder into the pilot hatch rather than bother with the cargo bay door. She followed, encumbered by her travel bag until he reached down and pulled it up into the ship.

"Thanks," she said once aboard. She looked around. "I've never been on an Eagle. I'm familiar with the specs, though."

She peered into the cockpit, down a few steps to her left. A bank of outboard gun controls was currently positioned out of the way but did not look different from the cruisers she had flown. A row of screens presented various angles and scales showing their surroundings in real-video, holograms or graphics. The pilot couches, each equipped with a neural interface headset, looked well-made and comfortable in contrast with the rest of the interior.

The cockpit angled from the communications console into the main cabin. Multi-functional out of necessity on a ship this size, it served as bridge as well as main living quarters. A wide lounger along one wall topped storage drawers and faced another bank of compartments. Two doors in the small space leading to the cargo bay likely led into the crew's sleeping quarters. Near the small galley, a round table seemed to double as workspace. A closer look into its reflective surface confirmed that the table converted into a projector for both two and three dimensional displays. The cabin's ceiling was softly illuminated to give the illusion of space where there was none. The major's head nearly brushed against it.

Every centimeter of the ship was used for either storage or instrumentation, without waste, without luxuries. The cabin was precise and neat.

"Where is the crew?"

"You're it for now." The major went down into the cockpit. He gestured to the co-pilot's bench. "Take us up."

"What? Me?" she gasped. "Now?"

"I was assured that I was taking on a pilot. Are you not a pilot?"

"Well, yes. I mean…"

"So can you fly this? Or are you staying here?"

She hurriedly slid into the seat he had pointed out. He said nothing while she went through pre-flight, held his silence when she stumbled over a few protocol errors before receiving clearance, and barely raised an eyebrow when she awkwardly strapped herself into her bench while already taxiing to the launch. She thought she saw him roll his eyes when she waved to one of the jockeys on the byway. All of this gave her enough time to assure herself that she understood the control panel configuration and learn a little bit about the ship's maneuvering quirks.

When she finally launched the Eagle and reached escape velocity, he nodded to himself, his eyes on the shield monitors. But she took them out of Myra's atmosphere with barely a shudder, and soon they had left the red planet behind them. She let out a breath of pent-up air, pleased with the take-off.

His congratulations were not forthcoming. "Is there a reason why you decided to launch manually?" His gesture indicated the headset behind her that would link her neural interface directly to the central processor of the ship.

She peered into his face and saw little there but sharp angles and a pair of watchful blue eyes. His tone held neither criticism nor complaint. What answer was he looking for?

"Because I *like* flying manually."

He rose from his seat and went back into the main cabin.

She followed, too curious about the ship to speculate over his approach to 'training' his new crew member. He sat on the lounger to watch her prowl about.

"You live here all the time?" She peered into the tiny food preparation area, realizing that she had not had dinner. She hoped that he was a better cook than she was, as much as cooking aboard a cruiser usually involved knowing which packages of lumpy gray nutrients to combine into something edible.

"Mostly. We are stationed on Targon, which is a formality." He answered her unspoken question by pointing out some of the storage units along the wall. "Weapons, weather gear, camo, air."

She opened the bin he had identified as camo. Inside was a tangle of clothes chosen for being nondescript and unidentifiable, head covers, boots, boxes of colored lenses, currencies, masks, tattoos and dyes for temporarily changing skin and hair color. "You have a Greval vest! That's a big thing on Myra right now. Worth a fortune."

He started to say something, paused, and then shook his head. "No one sent weather gear for you. You can request a set when we get to Targon."

"You step out that often?" she asked, referring to occasions when leaving the ship without a complete and sealed enviro-suit would be hazardous. She bounced a little on the balls of her feet to test the ship's near-perfect gravity. That, along with what felt like healthy air quality, was a desirable feature on long-range cruisers. She had spent time on vehicles either half afloat or weighted down for hours and days at a time. "No need for extra padding in here. I'm impressed."

"I'm glad."

She perched on one of the stools by the map table. "You don't approve of me."

"My approval is not based on first impressions."

Nova hesitated. How did one converse with a Delphian officer? Why had that not been taught anywhere? There were few Delphians working for Air Command and it had been a long time since she had even talked with one of his people. "You don't seem to welcome my presence here."

"I don't find it necessary, even if Command thinks it is." He tipped his chin toward the cockpit. "The Eagle's neural interface is the best ever engineered. There is no real need for a crew. And I'm not a teacher."

"You got something against people?" She waited for him to ponder whether she meant 'people' or if she meant 'Humans'.

He did not rise to the bait. "Machines are a lot more dependable. They tend to last longer, too. And use up less oxygen."

"So it's not something you have against me personally."

He arched an eyebrow. "I do not know you well enough to hold anything against you."

"We're supposed to work together. We have orders to work together."

"You are a subordinate officer. How I deal with you is up to me." He leaned back and picked up a computer screen. His eyes remained on his fingers while he tapped in some commands. "I have orders to train you. And so I will. But I have work to do. I am in the middle of a difficult assignment that will not allow me time to wet-nurse a greenie."

"Greenie!" Nova exploded, leaping from her chair. "I've been flying planes of one type or another since the day I lost my diapers. I came out of three years of Academy as wing commander. Three more years of combat and Flight to make Hunter class pilot. Did a tour outside Pelion and then two on Ud Mrak before I got stuck at Myra. They don't exactly accept just any shuttle pilot in the Mrak system. I've got all weapons certs, five base languages, including yours, hand to hand and three grades of ground combat training. I'm a qualified chartjumper. If you'd read over my records you'd know all that makes for almost ten years of active duty. How can you call me a greenie?"

"It doesn't take a genius to jump a charted site." He turned the screen in his hands toward her. The text was too small to see from where she stood, but the image it also displayed was of her. "I am aware of your records. You've never been outside of Union domain. Yet since you lost your diapers, you've destroyed Tamotsu Comori's main lab on Drar Drogh, you blanket-bombed what was probably the biggest rebel ammo dump on Bala, you managed to kidnap one of Tharron's favorite wives and hand her over for questioning, you stole an atomic destined to take out Skyranch Nine by pretending to be the transport pilot. On an Arawaj rebel ship."

Nova grinned.

"Your name is attached to two classified files and last year you bailed out of your Kite to let it ram a freight skimmer carrying two hundred breeder Rhuwacs on Ud Mrak."

"That hull was tough. I didn't have the weapons to take it down."

"Your plane was worth more than two hundred lizards."

"What else does it say in there about me?"

"Plenty. So much so that Air Command decided to take you out of active duty until you cool down. I doubt there is any single Union officer more loathed by the rebels than you are. The concept of staying low when Tharron is counting heads hasn't occurred to you. And now here I am, on covert assignment, and they give you to me like a great big shining beacon."

"Oh," she said. "Well."

He rose from the lounger when a tone from the cockpit interrupted them. "I do not think that Tharron has forgotten about you. Learn to duck, Whiteside. There will be no grandstanding here, am I clear?"

"Yes, sir," she said, deflated.

He leaned over the controls in the darkened cockpit. "We have cleared Myra space. Go for jump."

"From here? We're not taking the jumpsite?"

"That'll take us to Targon. We're not going to Targon yet. We're going to keyhole out of here."

She took her place beside him and reached up to settle the headset onto her interface node. Her sensors connected smoothly and a bank of indicators came to life on the display before her. The major also engaged his system.

"Do nothing," he said. "Just catch us on the other side. This span is awkward and I want to push it to Callas if I can find the right exit."

She felt a giddy shiver of anticipation when he reclined in his couch and closed his eyes. His opinion of the skill required to navigate a charted and stable breach, although arrogant, was probably warranted. The mental fireworks needed to work in tandem with a computer to open a 'keyhole' in space, calculate and detect its terminus, preferably somewhere near the desired location, and emerge without being crushed was something else entirely. She shifted her attention to the controls, prompting the plane to approach the coordinates he sought.

Both of them felt the Eagle's emitters wind up.

"Going negative," she reported needlessly.

He did not reply. She felt him direct the ship, suddenly aware that they now shared a connection not only to the plane but also to each other. Using the enormous complexity of their brains, augmented with the physical capacity and protection of the ship, he tapped into subspace to expand the anomaly and looked for a way out again. She allowed herself to be swept along, awed by the precision with which he calculated the span that would bring them to Callas. He moved deeper and farther, searching, measuring, almost feeling his way through the endless nothing until he seemed satisfied with what he found.

She gasped when they surged into the fissure and then there was nothing. No lights penetrated her closed lids; there was no sound, no sensation of even touching the couch on which she lay. Her moment of panic was quickly subdued when she felt the Delphian's calm presence reach her like a steadying hand on her shoulder.

Then they were clear. Nova's attention snapped to their external sensors, assuring her that no one and nothing was nearby to risk a collision. She took control of the ship from him and throttled their velocity to run a quick systems check. All was in order; the major's skill with the aperture had landed them safely in the middle of nowhere.

"That was just… just neat!" she declared, opening her eyes. "I don't think I've ever jumped this far." She checked their coordinates. "Nice work! You hit that terminus perfectly. We're less than five hours from Callas."

"Whiteside," he said.

"Sir?"

His eyes remained closed. He reached up to pull the sensors away from his interface nodes. "Be… quiet."

She grimaced. He remained in his couch for uncounted minutes, recovering from the tremendous strain on his mind and body. At last he stirred and moved his long limbs with some effort to sit up on his couch. He swung his feet to the floor and found her watching him intently.

"You were scared," he said finally.

"Was not!" she protested with a laugh.

"Was." He stood up. "You have some talent. If we can get you to achieve a measure of stillness, you could even learn to span on your own. Some day. I'm going to sleep. Wake me when we reach orbit."

TWO

Nova shifted restlessly in the small alcove housing various real-video screens as well as thermographic and acoustic surveillance sensors. No matter how diligently designed and well-padded, after four hours this chair felt like it was stuffed with sawdust. She tried to loosen and relax each cramped muscle in turn while keeping her eyes on the glowing sweep of the sentinel system in front of her.

Could one die of boredom? On the other side of these bulkheads was only darkness. No moonlight ever revealed the shapes of the trees she knew to be there, as there were no moons over Callas. This was her third night of passive surveillance while Major Tychon was doing things never fully explained. She knew that he had made contact with rebels, but he seemed uneager to let her join the operation.

Whatever he was doing, it seemed to be more demanding than her lonely boredom. She was able to sleep when necessary, trusting the ship's sensors. He, however, battled fatigue in coping with the short nights here, returning in the gray dawns to drop onto the lounger in the main cabin, not bothering to find sleep in his own bunk. Nova passed her time in long games of strategy with the computer, studying, and tiptoeing around the major until she realized that he did not wake easily. He slept motionless, rarely turning or shifting in his eerie, silent rest. Delphi's peaceful evolution had not taught its creatures to remain alert even while in repose. Eventually, she adjusted her own sleeping habits to his. His taciturn presence when awake was still far more interesting than the games his computer offered.

The Delphian spent several hours each day in showing her his store of data to help her understand the nature of their work. Much of it was dry material, geography and environment of places they were to visit and also the laws, dialects and politics of sentients found there. But he was an interesting teacher possessed of great patience. She found that she enjoyed her studies until it was time for him to leave the ship again.

And so her last few days had been spent. Reading, staring at screens, reports, chores aboard the ship. Tychon was quite obviously trying to keep her occupied.

The Eagle's alarm system startled her out of her mood on the fourth day. A life form other than Tychon and his contacts appeared on the screen, man-size and moving stealthily around the ship. She reached for her gun and opened the pilot hatch to investigate. Once on the ground, she crouched by the landing structure, her gun aimed at the edge of the clearing. She saw nothing until her eyes adjusted to the little light shed by the stars above.

A shadow slipped from the far edge of the clearing and moved noiselessly toward her, neither humanoid nor any other sentient she recognized. Nova used her data sleeve to engage the ship's parking lights. The intruder was a Class Three resident who, after a fierce display of fangs and claws, moved on to easier prey. Nova laughed silently and extinguished the lights.

She was reluctant to return to the confines of the ship. What could Tychon possibly be up to on this outpost planet? Perhaps he came to gamble and carouse the night away. Nova stifled a snicker at the thought of the major in a carousing mood. After some hesitation, she holstered a second sidearm and walked in the direction of Tychon's rendezvous. The sensor on her wrist array, along with that of the ship's system, showed her the way in nearly absolute darkness.

She followed her mechanical guide through a stand of massive trees, so straight-boled that they seemed like a forest of stone columns holding up some vast canopy in the sky. Nothing but strangely luminescent mushrooms grew around their feet.

Eventually, Nova emerged into a meadow where she found a low building made of local materials and plastic modules commonly used by off-worlders when putting up temporary shelters. A dim light shone above the door, allowing her to see a few battered ground vehicles and a skimmer nearby.

She crouched close to the hovel and ducked past filthy windows until she heard voices. She watched from the cover of the undergrowth, resolving to spy for just a few minutes and then return to the Eagle.

The major sat with a few others in a dim room that was no more presumptuous than the outside of the building. Currency of various denominations was scattered on a table that seemed barely sturdy enough to support its own weight, let alone the elbows of those seated around it. Tychon fit well into this group. His hair was disheveled, the loose clothing dust-covered and ill-used. Nova saw that all weapons had been placed on a stool near the only door into the room. The motley group spoke in low tones, their language foreign to her. One of them, a female Caspian, laughed in a high-pitched whistle and clapped Tychon's shoulder.

Nova nearly missed the sound of more voices behind her. More by reflex than calculation, she dove deeper into the bushes.

Three figures walked past her. One of them turned briefly in the doorway and peered suspiciously into the night. Rhuwac! Small eyes within leathery folds of skin seemed to bore into her and it sniffed the air, perhaps sensing the enemy she represented. She knew that this creature's sense of smell was its keenest. Would it recognize something foreign here? Nova's hand tightened on her gun. Every last Rhuwac walking the surface of any but their own planet belonged to Tharron's army of foot soldiers. If this one discovered her, she would not die quickly.

The Rhuwac squinted myopically into the gloom, sniffed again, and then sneezed. It was an insignificant huffing sound, like that of a small mammal. It scratched something under its tattered coat and ducked into the building. Nova offered a brief prayer of thanks to whatever had induced the Rhuwac's allergy. She returned to the window in time to see the newcomers enter the room.

The initial greetings were sharply interrupted when one of the strangers spat a cat-like hiss and pointed at the blue-haired member of the group. He snarled something and pulled a weapon from beneath his vest.

Nova rose out of the shrubbery and smashed the window with the butt of her gun. The sharp beam of her weapon sliced across the room to pass between the still-seated confederates to find its target.

Tychon was the first to break out of the motionless second of surprise that followed. He leaped out of his seat and shoved one of the newcomers back to fall over the smoldering body near the door. A projectile tore into the wooden wall by his head. He turned and dove through the broken window, landing hard beside Nova. The look on his face when he saw her was almost comical.

She passed him her gun and drew another from her belt. They chased through the dark without stopping to return their pursuers' fire. Suddenly, ahead of Nova, Tychon stumbled and pitched to the ground. She turned to fire into the blackness behind them, holding the rebels back until Tychon regained his feet. He adjusted his gun to serve as a torch and moved forward again, more slowly than before. To Nova, it was an eternity before they reached the Eagle and he heaved himself up and into the ship. More of the solid projectiles ricocheted off the hull, and she barely ducked a tracer slicing the air just above her head.

Once inside the Eagle, Tychon took the controls and launched into an unbalanced vertical take-off that threw Nova off her feet. She grasped the fixed legs of the map table and hung on until he stabilized the ship. His movements were quick, impatient, but he took the time to complete pre-acceleration checks before leaving the atmosphere.

"You think we'll be followed?" Nova said as she picked herself up again, spoiling for a fight, perhaps a chase.

"No, they don't have a decent plane among them. There is a charted jumpsite at E 26 399 6 that reaches to Feyd. Set course for that. I've already programmed the receiver."

Disappointed, Nova took the helm from him. His taut expression cautioned against argument. She watched him move to the communications console and signal a request for contact. After some delay, he received a faint reply without video, indicating that a relay station was ready for his message packet.

"Targon, Vanguard Seven for Colonel Carras. Tight band." He paused a moment while the message priority was changed and scrambled. "Nebdan grain vessel *Begiad* BT3222 is heading for Magra carrying arms. Bound to show up at Aram Gate any moment and jump from there. I would file a proper report, but I thought that you might want to intercept. No one important on board. I had hoped to get a location on Tharron today but his underlings remembered me from some past affair." He felt beneath his shirt and swore when he saw blood on his hand. His clothes were torn in several places, likely from his flight through the broken window. "Sorry, that wasn't directed at you, Tal. I'm sure your parentage is impeccable. I have good news, too. I think we've got a bead on Anders. I'll report later. V7 out." Tychon shipped the packet to the relay at the nearest jumpsite, from there to be transferred into Targon space.

Nova made the final adjustments to their course and hurried to find the ship's medi-kit. "Don't pull your shirt over your head. You got glass stuck in there."

He raised his hands while she carefully cut what was left of the rough-spun fabric and let it fall to the floor along with a shower of splinters.

"When did they hit you?" she asked when he dropped onto

the lounger with a grunt. "Move your hand." He stretched out and lifted his arm out of the way. A ragged wound oozed dark blood just below his ribs. Nova was glad to see that the projectile had only grazed him. "Your friends are living in the dark ages. I haven't seen that kind of raker wound in years."

"What is darkages?" He ground his teeth when she slipped a painkiller under his skin and used a fine beam of light to clean and cauterize the tear. "I think it happened when I was down. Could not see a damn thing." He did not watch her tape the wound. "I didn't see Field Medic on your record."

She shrugged. "I only have Basic. I picked up the rest during six months on Bellac. I learned fast."

"I heard about that. Tough conditions. Took years to get the rebel activity under control. Could not have been a pleasant tour."

Nova shrugged and kept her eyes on her work. "There. You're new again," she declared. "Sort of. Lean toward me." She checked a few cuts on his shoulders and removed a splinter or two. When she pushed his hair out of the way, she saw the thin line of blue strands that grew along his spine. Carefully, she used her nails to extract a few shards.

"Captain, I think I should tell you that, as is the custom among my people, you are currently engaged in a sexual act."

Nova jerked her hand back. "Oh, sorry!" She blushed, glad that he had spoken before she could comment on the silken texture of that particular hair – likely a transgression of spectacular proportion. "I didn't mean to…"

He sat up. "I would not expect you to know about such things."

"You'd better shake out your hair," she said, suddenly aware of their close proximity. "I think there's glass in there, too." She handed him a moist towel to wipe the blood from his hands and where it had pooled at the waistband of his trousers.

He came to his feet to follow her advice. "It is never totally dark on Delphi with all those moons. We do not see well on nights like this. My visor is still back there in that shack." He peered at his injury before sitting back down, wincing. "I don't know whether to reprimand you for leaving your post or to thank you for bringing me out of there."

She packed up the medical supplies, her movements sharp and efficient. "Don't do either. I'm not doing you any good playing sentry on a ship that none of those people could even begin to break into. Quit treating me like a greenie."

He raised an eyebrow.

"That was Tal Carras on Targon there, wasn't it? You are insubordinate to bloody colonels but you expect me to stand at attention every time I see you. Gets pretty tiresome on a ship this size. I am not a cadet."

He smiled. It was a warm, open smile that involved his whole face and one she had not seen on him before. Delphians had convoluted social taboos against showing their feelings to strangers, and most of their facial expressions were merely calculated communication. She could not even recall when last she had seen one of them smile so genuinely. "You are probably right," he said.

"Of course I'm right," she mumbled, inwardly astounded by his admission and pleased by the smile he had given her. "Anyway, what was that all about down there? Unless they have no sensors, going in there with an Eagle is like waving a big Union flag at them."

"That was the point. They thought I wanted to sell a stolen ship." He rose and headed for his cabin for a change of clothes. "Delphian rebels are unheard of, but we do have the odd thief among us. We're about to make the jump to Feyd. Charted jump. You'll be taking us in."

"Humans can't go to Feyd!"

"You rely too much on your manuals. You will be fine as long as you avoid Feyd's flowering plants. We will not be there for long. Unless, of course, you want to stay in orbit."

"Not likely!" she exclaimed before realizing that he was teasing her. It wasn't exactly clear from the tone of his voice or his expression, but she was beginning to notice that the deep blue of his eyes changed in intensity with his mood. It was a useful discovery.

"I think you'll like the planet. Interesting people. We're meeting an agent and then I have a stop to make, but you can look at this as a day off. Pick up some clothes while we're down there. Something suitable for desert climate. Cold desert. If my hunch is right, we're going to take a trip to K'lar Four. I think you should wean yourself off your flight suits. You are Vanguard now." He did not seem to notice her joyful smile when he said that.

"What stop do you have to make?"

He paused by the door to his cabin. "Going to visit my son."

"Your what?"

"There is a school for officers' children on Feyd. Obviously not something we advertise. I'd like to visit with him for a few hours before we go to the lower city. You can use the rec center if you want. It's an excellent facility."

"Can I meet him?"

His brow twitched, more in surprise than a frown. "Yes, of course, if you wish."

* * *

Nova had not been on this planet before. It mattered little in wartime strategies, still out of reach of overt rebel incursions and used mainly as a commercial and recreational destination by Commonwealth members. Although most Humans suffered allergies here, Feyd offered a playground of lakes and rivers to those who tolerated the sweltering temperatures. The planet provided some of the most valued produce in Trans-Targon, and the Commonwealth's primary commercial organizations headquartered here.

The Eagle landed among a steady stream of traffic coming and going to Talan An, the planet's oldest city. They parked on a public airfield and boarded a shuttle that took them across tracts of arable land, dotted with modern farms, to the school property. The transport stopped near a complex of what looked like colorful, glass-fronted cubes scattered over the side of a hill. Covered walkways connected most of them.

The two pilots moved slowly in response to Feyd's high gravity as well as the torrid heat that felt much like wading into an oil slick. Humidity enveloped them like a hot bath and no breeze moved to cool the sweat on their bodies.

Children of all ages and many species played in the gardens between the buildings, oblivious to the heat. Some of them likely wore coolers under their loose clothing and Nova wished she had slipped into one before leaving the ship. She craned her neck at the windows of nearby buildings, seeing bits of colorful paper stuck to the panes.

Tychon led her into one of the buildings, through a security check, and into a bright commons room. Nova smiled tentatively at the unfamiliar sight of young children at play. The noise was deafening although the children were loosely organized into groups, each led by an adult. Verbal expression was obviously a valued part of the curriculum.

The pandemonium of sound and moving bodies ebbed when Nova and Tychon were discovered. Some of the children forgot their play and edged closer, staring at the newcomers with varying degrees of shyness.

"Dadda!" A small boy raced across the room to fling himself into Tychon's arms.

Tychon lifted the child high and kissed him loudly. "Kiran," he sighed and tousled the tightly curled hair. "Are they turning you into a soldier yet?"

The boy began to prattle about the school, his playmates and himself, seemingly wanting to fit all of this information into one endless sentence. Nova listened to his exclamations, her eyes on the soft expression that had stolen over Tychon's face as he knelt in front of his son, listening to the words pour from the child in delightful confusion.

She sat down on a low table, willing to listen for hours. But, although she had moved soundlessly, the child halted his bright monolog in mid-sentence to study her quizzically.

"Oh, Cadet Kiran, this is my senior officer, Captain Nova Whiteside," Tychon introduced.

The child saluted, eyeing her suspiciously. Nova returned the gesture. "At ease, Cadet," she said, smiling at the smaller version of Tychon.

He sent the boy to change his clothes and took a few minutes to question the staff about Kiran's progress. Nova heard that the boy excelled at most of his tasks and was no disciplinary problem. He showed aptitude for engineering skills and languages. One of his teachers voiced her concern that Kiran seemed withdrawn at times, even inattentive. It was not something that was a common problem among Delphian children.

"Of course," she added, "we're only now receiving a larger enrollment of Delphian children. We have applied for additional staff from Delphi to help us understand them a little better."

Tychon accepted this, eager to continue his visit with his son. When Kiran rejoined them they strolled back to the waiting shuttle and Nova saw her commander discard his cold remoteness as he gave all of his attention to the child. She heard him laugh at something Kiran said and even engage in a tickle fight. He seemed almost relaxed.

The shuttle brought them from the lovely countryside to a large, precise square of soaring buildings arranged around a long, artificial lake. Elevated sidewalks and pedestrian bridges teemed with well-dressed people, most of them Centauri and many of those in uniform. The whole quarter seemed swept clean, as new as it looked, built with Commonwealth trade currency. Nova was torn between liking it for its newness and loathing it for its newness.

Tychon stepped onto the sidewalk with her when the shuttle had come to a halt in front of a towering edifice of glass and metal.

"This is the rec center I told you about. They have everything you can possibly want here. You can use your insignia to pay for what you need."

"I haven't shopped for clothes in years," she said, already eyeing the displays through the street-side windows. "Aren't those pretty? Oh, shoes!"

"Women!" he scoffed.

"Yes, yes, I'll get desert gear, too."

He gestured toward the shuttle. "I will take Kiran for our usual outing. Meet me back on the airfield in four hours."

"Beautiful child," she said.

Tychon turned to observe him fondly. Kiran waved to them through the window. "Like his mother."

"I didn't know you were partnered."

"I was married," he said. "Delphians have strange customs."

Nova tried to read his expression, not sure if he was joking this time or just cynical of currently popular mating habits. "You're not, uh, married anymore?"

"She's dead."

Nova bit her lip, a dozen well-meant platitudes forming in her mind. They got no further when she saw the blank look on his face. He had made a statement, nothing more; her sympathy was neither wanted nor appreciated.

She waited as he boarded the shuttle, beginning to realize that, with each day that passed, her early impression of the controlled, disciplined Delphian commander was crumbling away to show her someone who wasn't so very different from anyone else she knew. Just as the highly decorated pilots of her former squadron on Ud Mrak had turned out to be no more than rough, tired and fed up soldiers, so this man was beginning to show himself as something that was almost Human.

Still musing, Nova turned her attention to the center. It was, indeed, a handsome piece of luxury. Part hotel, part commerce center, it offered anything its visitors could want with charmless efficiency. She visited a spa for a long and very hot bath and then shopped for clothes that were either practical or entirely decorative. Before heading back to meet Tychon, she sent a message to her father and ordered a few supplies to be shipped back to the Eagle along with her purchases.

* * *

She found the major near his Eagle where a few mechanics were busy with the landing gear. He cocked his head when she joined them, his eyes on her clothing.

"You like it?" She touched her freshly styled hair and turned to show him one of her finds, a low-cut tunic of a breezy fabric worn over snug breeches.

"Did you get suitable clothes for K'lar Four?"

She nodded, a little disappointed by his reaction, and then berated herself for her vanity. What did it matter what the Delphian thought of fashion? "Did you enjoy your time with Kiran?"

"Yes," he said and closed the ship's door. "Let's head to the meeting."

They left the busy, modern side of the city for the busy, ancient quarter that still went about its business much like it had for hundreds of years. Despite the discomforts provided by Feyd's weather, Nova enjoyed their stroll. She had spent many years either on a military base or on a mobile station where holidays were things that other people enjoyed. Walking through these narrows streets that had never felt the heavy hand of a city planner felt like a welcome adventure.

The houses were open and airy, large windows allowed a view of whole interiors, and top stories often had no walls at all but only a roof supported by stone pillars and curtains for privacy. Livestock, too, occupied some of the roof rooms.

It was wonderfully disorienting to walk through these crowded, ancient streets and then to look to the horizon where graceful skyscrapers rose above the Commonwealth-built sector, the air whirring with arriving and departing traffic. In the distance hovered cloud-swathed volcanoes, their slopes covered in jungle growth.

And everywhere she looked, people went about their business of shopping, selling, strolling and thieving, threading their way through alleys and stifling heat, oblivious of the wonder in which Nova observed them all. It was difficult to distinguish native from Human or Centauri here. They looked so very much alike that Nova decided that the individuals wearing the warmest clothing and who did not seem to fight gravity with every step must be native Feydans. They also seemed to have an appreciation for elaborate tattoos, which seemed to cover every bit of exposed skin. Tychon attracted some attention, Delphians still being a rarity in this sector.

Eventually, the street led to an open market where they joined others along a tall shelf where people stood while enjoying their meals. Someone brought a bowl of dumplings floating in a red sauce, served with a sticky hodgepodge of shredded meat and vegetables wrapped in a sheet of what appeared to be bread. A tankard of warm, spicy ale completed the menu, which did not vary from one table to the next. Both of them passed on a platter of roasted insects.

"Archaic," Nova commented. "But so, so very good."

They were served by a mute Chayko male, a slave mark livid on his thigh. Nova furrowed her brow. As a Union planet, Feyd had to adhere to Commonwealth rules forbidding the use of sentient slaves. Had she been in uniform she would have confiscated this one and arrested his owner. But then, had she been in uniform this Chayko would not have been sent to serve them.

She passed the jug to Tychon before remembering that most Delphians did not impair their minds with spirits.

"Be careful," he warned. "I imagine that you have not had anything but canteen slop in a long time."

"I haven't had a lot of things in a long time," she replied.

He tilted his head. Amusement lit his eyes.

She blushed. "I meant, well, I've been on a base for so long..." She frowned defensively. "Where is your mind at, anyway?"

He grasped her wrist.

"Hey!"

"You cannot eat that." He took a piece of fruit from her hand. "Only cooked food for you here, Human."

"I should have thought of that!"

"No harm done, Greenie." He looked past her shoulder to greet a short, squat woman who had come to their table. They spoke too rapidly for Nova to make out more than the gist of their conversation. Apparently, a Union liaison had been abducted by the Shri-Lan rebel faction and was to be traded back for a spy held by Air Command.

Not a chance, Nova thought.

Tychon turned to her. "I have to go with this one for a while. She doesn't want to be seen with both of us. Meet me here in one hour. If I am not back, return to the Eagle for clear air or, better yet, find a place where they sell respirators and pick up a supply. We will need to visit Feyd fairly often."

Nova grumbled at this but agreed. The market outside with its fascinating people made up for being excluded. No doubt he would brief her later.

She strolled among the stalls, stopping often to chat and examine the wares imported from any place accessible to traders who were often willing to take an uncharted jumpsite in their search for profit. In that way, they were the Union's best unpaid source of explorers.

There were fine costumes in rich fabrics made on Pelion and Nebdan, intoxicating wines, pastes and tobaccos of Feyd itself and hundreds of gadgets and novelties from other worlds. Pebbles gathered in the Badlands were set like jewels in rings and headbands. Shaddallam leather, more supple than silk, went at outrageous prices to those who could afford it. Nova gaped like a child at tame grush cats and the colorful birds of Genen and smiled indulgently when she saw peanuts transplanted from Earth to Trans-Targon and sold here as aphrodisiacs. She tried not to stare at the many travelers from distant places who did not consider themselves part of the attractions.

A feeling of lightheadedness began to annoy her. It was probably time to return to the Eagle but she could not quite remember why. No one sold respirators here and nothing reminded her to buy one to filter the still, pollen-laden air of Feyd. It had not occurred to her to head uptown in search of a dispensary. The heat of the day made her drowsy and she slowed her steps, her eyes and thoughts flitting over the many strange things to be seen. Time passed as she watched an artisan create a miniature flower out of sugar and she would have stood there for hours had not a sudden commotion startled her.

"Dun uragla, ragla!" a man shouted after a thief. The boy, no more than ten or so, raced toward Nova, a smile of mischievous glee on his face. He knew he would get away, and Nova stood aside as he passed, watching his escape. The crowd was now either cheering or cursing the boy or the merchant, Nova did not know which.

Others joined the chase and Nova was pushed out of the way. Her hands found no hold as she sought to keep her balance. The high grasses of a ditch beside the road softened her fall and a heady scent wafted up, a sweet odor that carried with it a sharper taste of herbs.

Someone helped her to her feet. Nova looked at the grass stains on her hands and shirt and laughed. What a strange, amusing day! Still chuckling, she wandered on, away from the crowd. She seemed to have lost her parcels of purchases. That seemed funny, too.

It occurred to her that there might be something that she should be doing. The crowd soon thinned, and after passing the crumbled remains of an old wall, Nova found herself outside of town. She saw a few vineyards in the distance and a fork in the road that led into a small stand of woods. It would probably be cooler there, she thought, walking onward.

She came upon a stream that meandered through the little forest, deepening in this glade before it broadened on its way through the city. She sat down, delighted by the running water, the way it bounced off rocks and glinted in the filtered sunlight from above. The day seemed to grow even hotter as she dreamed quietly, occasionally rubbing her skin where the irritating dust of the roadside flowers had adhered. No one was near and she felt very sleepy.

Then someone called her name. Perhaps she should

answer. What was his name again?

* * *

"Nova!" When she had failed to appear both at the food seller and the airfield, Tychon had looked for her in the market, soon very worried. Nearly six hours had passed since they had arrived on Feyd, and unless she was using a respirator she would by now be in great danger. His hails to her com band went unanswered. Luckily, her height and the deep red of her hair made her easy to describe and remember to the people he had asked. Some of the locals had seen her wander off toward the distant vineyards.

Lying there, she seemed asleep, one arm trailing in the water. The long hair had come loose, as brightly reflecting the dappled sunlight as was the surface of the brook. Her usual, intent expression was gone, replaced by a gentle smile that softened her features.

"Captain!" he called, more concerned than annoyed by her lack of response. "I told you to stay nearby."

She raised her head, opening dilated eyes. "It's so much prettier here."

Tychon knelt beside her. "What are you..." He saw traces of the shimmering powder on her blouse and hair. "I told you to stay away from the flowers!"

"You're always telling me things. Who can keep track of them all?" She sank back and closed her eyes. "Wake me when we get to Feyd."

He shook her arm. "Come now, back to the ship."

She did not reply.

Tychon pulled the bottom of his shirt over his face and inhaled deeply, several times, filtering the pollen-rich air through the fine fabric before rolling her onto her back. Covering her mouth with his, he forced his own breath into her lungs.

Nova opened unfocused eyes. "A strange kiss to say hello," she murmured. Strands of his hair had fallen over her face and she touched it thoughtfully.

He cursed, knowing that there was humor in this somewhere and hoping that he'd find it pretty damn soon. He continued to give her his air, all too aware that her hand had dropped onto his thigh.

At last she squirmed away from him. "Stop it! Enough!"

"Take your shirt off," he breathed.

"Are you out of your mind?"

"You have spores all over yourself." He pulled his own shirt over his head and tore one of the sleeves from it. He ripped a seam and then tied the fabric around the lower part of her face to fashion a filter of sorts.

"I fell down back there," she mumbled and followed his direction to remove her blouse.

Tychon averted his eyes from the thin shift that was all that covered her now. "Is that army issue?"

Nova slipped into what was left of his shirt. She swayed on her feet but remained upright. "You know, I always thought Delphians would be blue all over," she said vacantly. Her fingertips touched his bare chest. "But you're not. You just seem cold, Ty. Can I call you Ty, Major?" She watched her fingers touch a long strand of his hair. "When do we get to Feyd?"

Tychon moved out of her reach. "Damn!" He continued to mutter curses while they made their way back to the road into town.

"I don't feel very good," she said, stumbling. Her feet seemed too big for the ends of her legs and kept getting in the way as she tried to keep up with his long strides. He finally flagged down a passing skimmer to take them back to the ship.

Back at the airfield, Tychon half-carried her up along the Eagle's short cargo ramp and into the main cabin where he placed her onto the lounger. She closed her eyes once he had fastened an oxygen mask over her face.

The xenobiologist at Feyd's largest clinic took an unnerving amount of time to be found. When she finally appeared on Tychon's screen, she seemed to take pleasure in instructing the

Delphian about managing his Human staff on Feyd. She glanced at the vital data he transmitted and assured him that the spores Nova had absorbed would soon be out of her system. Before also assuring him that the tab for her services would be sent directly to Air Command's finance department, she forwarded a directive to have an additive to the oxygen he was already giving Nova sent to the ship.

Relieved, Tychon closed the connection and returned to where Nova lay sleeping. He observed her for a while, recalling the lovely sight of her in the pretty and somewhat revealing slip now hidden by his shirt. He shook his head and resolved to drop in on a friend at their next destination. Until then a cold shower would have to do.

THREE

This was a hopeful day on Shaddallam, likely the day that would blast through this uneasy tension like the first crash of lightning at the end of a summer's heat wave. Tharron's foul mood would break, finally, although some of those gathered here doubted that it would be for the better. The rankless officers of Tharron's inner guard whispered among themselves, daring to speculate on what was about to happen.

They had cursed the day on which their K'lar commander had learned of the legend. Since then, he had focused all of his attention and most of the few good agents he possessed on finding the truth of the myth. While they had carried on Tharron's smuggling and extortion operations, no progress had been made in their fight against Union dominance. They had lost their foothold on Aram for good this time, and negotiations with Pelion had stalled. The Targon scheme would end in disaster unless Tharron, their figurehead, was there to turn their advice into orders.

They all agreed, although the thought would not pass their lips in fear of Tharron's spies, that the Shri-Lan leader was obsessed with a fairy tale.

Since hearing the legend, Tharron had passed but one order: Capture alive someone to confirm the story. Not a difficult order until one considered that the only person who could answer Tharron's questions would have to be Delphian.

There were no Delphians among the Shri-Lan. Tharron's warriors were Rhuwacs, his pilots were traitor Centauri. His agents, spies and advisors were Human, Feydan and a very few K'lar. His household staff were Shaddallam slaves. Delphians barely cooperated with the Union and would certainly never consider Tharron's employ.

Tharron had fumed for weeks, taking his ill temper out on his servants and advisors alike. It had proven impossible to capture a live Delphian in combat. During the skirmish on Aram, one fighter plane had been taken but the pilot had turned out to be Centauri. At last, to appease Tharron, a detail had set out for Delphi. Pe Khoja had landed in a rural area and simply captured a farmer alone in his field.

Tharron's men were confident that this prisoner would answer to Tharron. Their leader would finally realize that the legend was, after all, just a legend. This madness would end and Tharron would return to the business of reaping great profit from war-torn Trans-Targon.

There were a few among his staff, so very few, who did not share the others' disbelief in the story. Pe Khoja, the Caspian, was one, Tamotsu Comori, the Human, another. It was they who had decided to abduct the hapless farmer, not because of the truth he would tell but because someone like him would not *know* the truth.

So today, all hoped, their troubles were over. Self-satisfied, Tharron's men stood in a loose semi-circle around their leader, who sat expectantly on a raised bench as if on a dais, the focus of everyone's attention. As always, he wore a long, simply cut robe reminiscent of those worn by his nomad kinsmen on K'lar but made of far more luxurious fabrics. Broad bands of precious metals adorned his massive arms, and his hairless head was painted with intricate designs calling upon the gods of his K'lar people. In a fine mood, he had ordered everyone outside and the prisoner brought to him there.

A good day, Tharron thought, letting his eyes roam about the garden. The old man and his family that he had evicted from their stately home had created a lovely oasis of eternal spring deep within the jungle of Shaddallam's lowlands. Outside the stone walls of garden he could hear his men, a comforting sound. The entire town had been evicted to make room for them. Shaddallam was an ideal planet on which to establish headquarters. It could be months before the Union's scouts found them here.

By that time, Tharron suspected, a change of climate would not be objectionable. The trouble with his Rhuwacs was that they tended to foul their own nests, murdering, vandalizing and destroying until they started to turn on themselves. Then it would be time to pack them all up again into huge freighters and ship them to another place. Like restless children, Tharron thought indulgently, whining and squabbling until allowed to go play.

He chuckled to himself, rubbing his large hands together. "Bring me the Delphi!" he roared.

Two silent Rhuwacs approached, shoving before them the prisoner. Tharron grinned when he saw that someone had taken a knife to the blue hair and hacked a long tress from it. To a Delphian, the height of humiliation. Bound at the wrists, the prisoner stood before Tharron, his expression impenetrable.

The K'lar leader observed the man with surprise, having expected a cowering and bedraggled petitioner for mercy. This specimen, however, stood before the most despised rebel in all of Trans-Targon without a trace of fear, his arrogance blazing. He had been handled by the Rhuwacs, his long vest was torn and he bled from a fresh cut on lips already swollen from previous blows. Still, the blue eyes shone with defiance.

Tharron shifted uncomfortably. He motioned to his guards to force the Delphian to kneel before him. It made little difference. Kneeling, the man still seemed to tower over them all. Tharron hated Delphi and all that prospered on her lush soil.

"Do you know who I am?" he said in a low voice.

"Yes." The Delphian did not give him the satisfaction of

reciting his titles and deeds.

Tharron's hands balled into angry fists. Pe Khoja had advised him that these people were able to feign an outer calmness through a trance of inner meditation. He curbed an urge to smash that tranquil face. "Do you know why you're here?"

"No."

"I have asked you here, my friend, to tell me a story." Tharron leaned forward, his hands gripping the chair's armrests. "Tell me what truth there is to what you call the Tughan Wai."

The Delphian recoiled as if slapped. Tharron's men nodded to each other, confident that all would be revealed as a children's tale. It was almost embarrassing that Tharron would go to these lengths to hear it. But then, this Delphian would not live to tell others about their leader's gullibility.

"Well?" Tharron prompted.

A small smile played over their captive's cold lips. "It is a legend."

"I have heard that it's a legend!" Tharron snapped. "And I don't believe it for one minute. Talk or you will die. I will hand you to my guards for amusement!"

The Delphian glanced at the Rhuwacs. Some of them sneered, showing their teeth. "The Tughan..." he began haltingly, as if afraid to pronounce the name. "The great Tughan Wai is the protector of all Delphi. He will guard our people against the evil wrought by you and that which the Union brings. His powers will shake the mountains and boil the seas..." he faltered.

Tharron had propped his chin into his palm and his other hand tapped idly on his armrest, bored. When the Delphian had interrupted his tale, Tharron bent closer to him. "Boy, I believe that I told you I know the legend. I am not interested in your borrowed prophecies and doomsday visions. You see" —he leaned back and stretched out his arms to encompass his entourage— "we would all like to find out the real story." He turned to his men. "Would we not?"

Those assembled nodded half-heartedly. Real story? Comori directed a nervous glance at Pe Khoja. Pe Khoja shrugged but, as usual, did not look particularly concerned.

Tharron faced the Delphian again. "Talk."

"He will destroy your armies and fling your ships from the sky—"

Tharron struck the Delphian with a force that would have killed a lesser man. He snapped his fingers. "Comori!"

The small man, heavily robed despite the midday heat, hurried forward. His movements were quick and the Delphian, stunned by Tharron's blow, was slow to react. The doctor's instrument forced a pale liquid into his veins, heating his body from within, at once dulling his mind.

Tharron smirked. "Nothing like a bottle of wine to loosen your tongue, eh? Except, perhaps, for a little something from Mr. Comori." His harsh laughter chased what remained of peacefulness and tranquility from the garden.

The others waited, some apprehensively, for the drug to take effect. Not even Comori knew how his truth serum would affect a Delphian.

"Now, Delphi, hear me," Tharron said companionably. "Talk or die, it's up to you. Tell me of the Tughan Wai."

"Of course," the Delphian said, his unfocused eyes seeing into the middle distance. "As you know, we Delphians have mental capacities that never developed in your own races. We have limited telepathic abilities, as you call them, and we can attain several distinct levels of awareness. Most of you differentiate only between the conscious and the subconscious. Waking and sleeping."

"Get on with it."

"Yes. There is among us a sect called the Shantirate, something for which I, too, am being trained. My initiation took place two years ago."

Pe Khoja heard a groan escape the doctor beside him. He winced at the grim justice of having taken a country bumpkin only to have him turn out to be a Shantir novice! Karma, my dear Mr. Comori, he thought. He turned his attention back to the prisoner.

"Shantirs are those that have attained a deep understanding of how we may use our minds. They are our physicians, healing without surgery or medication. The mind cannot just heal itself but also the body that supports it. The Shantirs are at once our doctors, our seers and our religious leaders. It is all very complex—"

"How does this affect the Tughan?"

"The Tughan Wai is an experiment. Many generations ago, the Union Commonwealth was a threat to us. As we saw it take hold of the part of our galaxy which you call Trans-Targon, we needed a way to defend ourselves. Traditionally, we do not bear arms. The Shantirs set out to create the Tughan Wai." The Delphian halted his monotonous narrative. An uncertain expression stole over his face.

"Comori?" Tharron murmured.

"He'll go on," the little physician said.

"Continue, boy," Tharron prodded.

"The Tughan is a person. It is also a weapon. We do not make guns and warplanes, but the Shantirs can direct a mind to suit their purposes. Shortly after birth, a young mind can be influenced through a procedure called a *khamal*. Behavioral patterns can be created by the more powerful mind of a trained Shantir. I, too, was thus influenced at birth; my destiny was dictated to me. I will be a Shantir. Moreover, I *want* to be a Shantir. You are fortunate to have captured me, as only the Shantir guild knows of the Creation. Others know only of the legend, which, of course, is nonsense."

"What did they do to the Tughan?"

"The Tughan Wai is our ultimate ambition. Many experiments failed, killing each candidate. There was too much power, too much knowledge..."

"Go on, what is the purpose of the Tughan?"

"Er, the Tughan is... The purpose of the Tughan is to destroy... things, people. Thought energy channeled in ways I do not yet understand. Terrible power... planets burning... worlds exploding..."

"We're losing him," Comori warned.

"Worlds exploding!" Tharron scoffed. "Keep talking, Delphi, and skip over that apocalyptic nonsense. This is the last polite warning you'll get from me."

"But the children died," the man continued. "They died from the collective powers given to them by the Shantirs. Some went mad. Then it was discovered that such powers could remain hidden, lying dormant until the young mind reaches maturity and has been trained. New experiments showed promise..." The Delphian closed his eyes.

"Give him another shot," Tharron ordered.

Comori shook his head. "It will not be effective. We can try again later. This drug was not designed for a Delphian."

Tharron stood up, looming over his captive. "Did they complete the experiment?"

"There were some successes." The Delphian's voice seemed strained, far away. "But more out of curiosity than any real need. Our leader, Phera, ordered the Shantirate to stop their experiments. The Union is no threat to Delphi. It protects us against you..." the man's body convulsed and the muscles of his face clenched to keep his lips from speaking.

"But they didn't stop, did they? Does he live?" Tharron roared. "Does the Tughan exist?"

"...the Tughan lives."

"Does the Union have him? Air Command? Do they plan to use him? How can I find him?"

"Sire," Comori warned.

The Delphian farmer tensed his entire body, his mind frantic in its efforts to overcome the drug and remain silent. "No Tughan for Tharron!"

Tharron lifted the youth to his feet and shook him like a dust rag in his insane desire to know the name of the man chosen to be the Tughan Wai. "Who is he?"

The Delphian hung weakly in Tharron's grasp. A whisper escaped him. In the tense silence, everyone heard the name he revealed. The name of the Delphian who would bring the entire Union Commonwealth to its knees before Tharron!

Tharron dropped the limp body, satisfied. "Bring him around. Feed him. I want him on his feet." He paced, grumbling. "I need to know where this Tughan is. Can he be bought? I'll need one of those Shantirs to deal with him. I need..." He turned to the doctor now kneeling beside the prisoner. "I need him on his feet! I have a thousand questions!"

Comori looked up from his examination of the youth. "The Delphian is dead, Sire."

Tharron was speechless. His first urge was to tear the physician to pieces. Had the man been anyone but Tamotsu Comori, he would have done just that.

"Dead?" he said finally, his voice hoarse. "How could you have made such an error?"

"This drug does not kill, Sire. This Delphian killed himself."

A startled murmur passed through the small crowd of onlookers. Those more cowardly and those more experienced with Tharron's ire began to move toward the building, out of the immediate range of his wrath.

None expected Tharron's raucous bellow of laughter. "Excellent! If this peasant can just will himself to die, imagine, all of you, the power of the Shantir. And then consider, all of you, the might of this man called Tughan Wai!"

His entourage drifted back together, nearly applauding in hysterical relief.

Tharron sobered. "I want him found! Pe Khoja and his crew will leave for Delphi at once to find out where he is. Is he working as one of those Shantirs? Is he loyal and to whom? Can he be bought? If not, find his family and use them as leverage. Go, all of you!" He waved them away to their collective errands. "Find me a Shantir!"

Comori remained hunched beside the dead Delphian. How he wished to have been able to study the fine mind. A farmer! He would never understand these people. He glanced up at his bellowing leader. Find me a Shantir! Get me the Tughan! Comori knew that it would take more than an army of

Rhuwacs to bring the Delphian to Tharron. But didn't Tharron always achieve what he set out to do? Didn't he know when and how to use people? He even knew exactly how much each of his men hated him and how much each of them needed him. He made men powerful and wealthy. Regretfully, he could make them dead, too.

They had all left the garden now. All, that is, except Pe Khoja. The Caspian lounged in Tharron's chair, a sacrilege no one but him would dare. He had turned his golden, densely furred face to the sun, but his eyes were on Comori, unaffected by the intense light. Ah, that one, Comori thought. That one was different. Tharron did not own him as he owned everyone else here. The scholar, the poet, the murderer. Pe Khoja was, perhaps, the only rebel here that truly was a rebel.

"Looks like we botched that one, eh?" Pe Khoja said, his yellow eyes alive with humor that so far escaped Comori. He had hooked his legs over the armrest of the chair, dangling large three-toed feet so endowed with fierce claws that few Caspians bothered with shoes. In contrast, his six-fingered hands were delicate and nimble. Many Caspians were courteous creatures who enjoyed the company of other species. Pe Khoja was not.

The doctor glanced around to make certain they were alone. "We can still stop it," he hissed.

"Why?" Pe Khoja said. He stretched and scratched the striped hide of his chest. "This is beginning to interest me. Don't tell me you wouldn't like to spend a few long hours in conversation with this Tughan thing."

Comori looked at the Delphian's crumpled body and nodded. "Of course. But I'm afraid that..." he cleared his throat. "I'm afraid."

"You? Afraid that Tharron'll blow up another skyranch or two? You've done that much yourself." He chuckled over some unseen joke. "Not with your head, though."

Comori glared at the Caspian. Of course he was afraid. He was afraid because Tharron was dangerous and Pe Khoja was dangerous and neither of them needed another bomb to play with. Yes, he would have liked to meet this wonderful creation. But not ever while it was on Pe Khoja's leash. Because Pe Khoja just might find it interesting enough to let Tharron use it. "I am afraid that Tharron is too obsessed with it to be cautious. He could endanger us all."

Pe Khoja cocked his head. "He's already done that, Mr. Comori. It's what's making us all very rich, isn't it? You'd just as soon work for the Union as you do for him, wouldn't you? But *he*" — Pe Khoja nodded toward the mansion— "he lets you do *things*, doesn't he?"

Comori closed his eyes, willing this man to go away. Leave, take his murderous habits and knowing, ever-knowing, eyes and go away so that he, Comori, could take the Delphian body to his lab and dissect its brain.

"I must be going." Pe Khoja sprang lightly from his perch. "I'll leave you to your doctoring, doctor, and see to my piloting. I need to figure out where they keep this awesome personage. I seem to remember hearing something somewhere about Delphi's Phera. It'll come to me, I'm sure."

FOUR

Neither Tychon nor Nova was in a particularly good mood when the ship's system woke them on the next morning. Nova was unsure of how she ended up on the lounger instead of her own cabin and had only a hazy memory of the previous day. He told her most of what had happened on Feyd, and she felt angry at having come through it like a greenie. Not only that, but he had made another subspace jump unassisted and without even jarring the ship enough to wake her, making it clear once again that her presence aboard his ship was unnecessary.

Tychon was more taciturn than ever. He flew the Eagle manually and barely glanced at her while she sought to keep herself occupied during the long flight. No doubt her stupidity irritated him. Her disregard for his orders and her own safety could have delayed their mission, perhaps even endangered it. She stayed in her cabin and out of his way as much as she could, feeling a little irritable, as well. He finally left the cockpit when she asked him if he wanted to eat, which he did not.

He dug through some bins. "I just got confirmation and changed course for K'lar. It's on. Going to bust out a friend who was kidnapped by Shri-Lan rebels. Make sure your guns are working properly. We will be running into trouble."

"So you do have friends?"

"What does that mean?"

"That someone will put up with your unpredictably fluctuating levels of rudeness," she said pointedly. "You haven't spoken to me all day. Then again, that isn't so very different from most days."

"I am not paid to be nice to you, Captain."

She glared back at him, refusing to yield. "And I'm not paid to be ballast around here, Major!"

His eyes narrowed, and for a moment Nova wondered if she had gone too far. She had never spoken to a superior officer like this. Well, she thought, not without good reason, anyway. But her limited experience with Delphian customs had taught her that outward courtesy was highly valued by all of them. Her sharp words weren't likely to gain his respect.

He took a deep breath and his tense shoulders relaxed visibly. The expression on his angular face settled into the usual calm exterior he presented to the world, an irksome trick that hid a Delphian's true feelings from even the most astute negotiator. "You are not heavy enough for ballast. And my name is Tychon. Do not use my rank when we're down there. In fact, don't use it at all."

"As you wish," she replied, barely mollified.

"Have you ever been on K'lar?"

"Once, briefly. Desert, isn't it?"

He nodded. "Gravity is a bit light but that will give us an edge."

"What is your plan?"

He motioned for her to follow him to the map table in the center of the room. The slide he selected was at once illuminated from below. A rough, hand-drawn map appeared on the surface of the table, altered here and there and marked with notes and landing coordinates. He bent over it, tracing a line with a long, blue-nailed finger.

"I hope this is still pretty accurate. If so, they are keeping him in one of these buildings. I am sure that I can get a few friendlies to create a diversion over here. With luck, we can do this quietly. Air Command is building an orbiting station over K'lar and we don't want Tharron deciding that he doesn't want it there. I don't know who is being more audacious: the Union for putting a base over Tharron's own home planet or Tharron for holding a Union delegate captive right under our noses."

"He probably hasn't been there in years," Nova said. "Nothing going on there. They might not even know what we're building over K'lar. I mean, look at the layout of this compound!"

"Not unusual for Tharron. What cities and airfields the Shri-Lan hold they took by force from either our people or neutrals. Most of Tharron's outposts are no more than garrisons. He does not care for niceties. It will not be difficult to find Anders."

"Anders?"

"Anders Devaughn."

"Devaughn, like the general?"

"His son. He works as a liaison on the Union base on Delphi. Xenologist and language expert, ranked captain. Any of that makes him valuable enough to be bartered."

"You think he's still alive?" Nova doubted that Tharron would bother to keep a hostage in good condition. All of his own people were expendable.

"He better be, or they'll pay for that, too."

She studied his face. "What else are they paying for?"

His shuttered expression cautioned her to mind her own business. She stood her ground.

"Kiran's mother," he said finally, finding some object of interest across the cabin to look at instead of her. "Back then we were both regular Air Command pilots. Escorting settlers to a new colony in the Badlands. Easy assignment. Practically a vacation. We had to stop over on K'lar Four." Tychon paused to examine his nails.

"Go on," she said softly.

"We'd been laid up by a sandstorm and when it finally cleared, Danaria took some of the civilians outside. Rhuwacs caught them. She held them off while most of the others got away. She took three Rhuwacs out, then she was cornered." His eyes focused beyond Nova and he spat out the last of his words. "The other two raped her. Right there among the dead. I found her body not long after. Or what was left of it. Took me longer to find her head."

"Gods, Tychon..." Nova whispered. She touched his arm, sickened by the images forming in her mind.

"I should not have taken her there," he said, now looking at Nova. His gaze took in all of her. "And now I have to go back and they give me another woman to take with me."

"Is that why you were against having me on board?"

He shrugged.

"I'll be careful, I promise," she said, but her words sounded meaningless even to herself. They were all trained to be careful. She knew well that being careful was not enough when faced with a sufficiently brutal enemy.

When she looked up, she found his eyes boring into hers as if there was more to be said. Of course he'd be acquainted with her records. The incident on Bellac had never been classified and it didn't take much more than a quick skim to figure out the real story behind the official phrasing. She dropped her eyes. The official record would have to satisfy him. She would not make herself his charge to be protected and worried about.

"Being careful is not always all it takes," he said finally and tapped the table surface. "Let's get back to this. I have some background about the rebels on K'lar."

Nova waited while he consulted with the data system. "How long ago did that happen?" she asked.

The hands on the screen paused their rapid motion. "Four years."

"Is this why you're still Vanguard?"

"And will continue to be until I drop dead or the last of the Rhuwac beasts is decomposing somewhere."

Nova looked at the screen he showed her and listened numbly to his explanations of the displayed information. But she pondered her own life up to this point, surely as exciting and eventful as she could make it, but had any of this really touched her?

She had killed and she had been wounded in this war. Someday, she supposed, it would kill her, too. She had seen mindless destruction caused by rebels and by her own people. Were these even her people? Trans-Targon was little more than a frontier in which the Centauri sought to establish civilized order as they did wherever they went. Their Union Commonwealth was above all a trade organization welcomed by most worlds ready to explore outside their own solar systems. Everywhere but here, in this tiny part of their galaxy.

When the Centauri stumbled upon this concentration of inhabitable planets, they had invited their Human friends along to help realize the vision of an expanded Union of allied planets. They found allies among the people of Bellac Tau, Feyd and Aram and, eventually, Delphi and soon would be allied with Pelion and the fiercely contested Magra Alaric as well.

What had led them here was not just the quest for new trading partners, but the certainty that here, somewhere in this sector, the answer to their very origin was to be found. No other area thus far explored by the Commonwealth was so richly populated with species that were not only like-minded but who also shared a common ancestry. Nova's own mitochondrial DNA could be traced back to several possible planets here.

Then they found Tharron. The small opposition he represented had turned into the Shri-Lan rebel faction and finally into a considerable enemy. The war had started when sabotage and assassinations escalated into the destruction of Union bases and colonies. Tharron did not distinguish between army personnel and peaceful settlers.

But what did this war matter to her? It was a job, nothing more. She was a Human who had never seen Earth, raised into the army by soldier parents and trained to hunt rebels. She did this willingly, followed orders blindly and asked no questions. She was playing warrior, never understanding the cities that burned and the worlds that were changed forever.

Nova thought back over the past ten years of her life and saw only a series of days and weeks and months spent in training, in police actions, in defenses and in offenses. She had never experienced civilian life and had only an abstract idea of what civilians did, if anything.

Through it all, Tharron himself remained a nebulous concept to her. Tharron, leader of the Shri-Lan, the great enemy, was an objective set up in this game, and she was one of the players whose aim it was to eradicate him and his rebel following. His Rhuwacs, to her, were little more than slow-moving targets. She felt no personal hatred for them, as Tychon did. Terrible things happened and people died somewhere, sometimes. It was her job to stop that, nothing more.

But now she was not so certain of that. If Tychon had more than just a scorecard to fill, did that mean that the rebel did, too? Had anyone ever really explained to her *why* their enemy insisted on fraying the edges of the massive Commonwealth conglomerate?

She was glad when the Eagle moved into a high orbit over the arid wasteland that was K'lar Four, forcing her to concentrate on less intangible matters and do what she was trained to do.

* * *

"Does this thing go on my head? It looks like a shoe."

Tychon looked up from adjusting his own desert gear and sighed at her attempts at arranging her burnoose. He showed her how it closed over her face to protect her eyes and skin, ignoring her protest when her ear caught in one of the folds.

Nova knew by now that nervousness was against his Delphian nature, yet she felt a sense of expectancy, a keen alertness as they readied their weapons and equipment. Her attempts to lighten his mood were met with only blank looks.

He took the helm and soon they were skimming the ship over the dusty surface of the planet, heading for the huddled sand igloos that made up the town of Gyan, its outskirts their destination.

There they walked into a tavern of sorts, and Tychon spoke in low tones to the barkeep who seemed to know him. Or had expected him. Nova sat by a narrow window, waiting and listening. She heard the cold desert winds drive sand in needle sharp blows against the stone building, widening the gouges and channels that already scarred the thick walls. Darkness descended without the preamble of twilight.

Tychon slumped into a seat beside her, his hooded eyes on their fellow patrons. No one spoke; only the eerie music of the ceaseless wind outside moved through the brooding silence. A shallow pit filled with dying coals in the center of the room was the only source of light here. They were all waiting.

Three men and a woman entered, slamming the door against the driven sand. They were native desert dwellers, their eyes mere slits within flat-planed and leathery faces. The bodies under their loose robes seemed dense, powerful. They would have been tall had evolution not taught them to walk forever stooped against the winds. K'lar had not always been a desert.

Tharron was born here, Nova reminded herself. But he walked upright, larger than any Prime species. The images she had seen of him showed a man looking more Human or Feydan than these unsmiling nomads. Perhaps sought to escape the hardships of this wasteland and found that there was more to existence than striving for the next drink of life-giving water. She had seen how much Tychon paid for the flask of liquid he now shared with these people.

The manner of conversation around this table fascinated Nova. Tychon, who never used two words where one sufficed, seemed almost chatty compared to these people. Long, thoughtful pauses seemed to be as much part of the conversation as slow gestures and monosyllabic answers. From what she understood, most people on K'lar had only a vague concept of what the Union Commonwealth represented. They did know, however, that whatever great unknown a future allegiance with the Commonwealth would bring, Tharron was by far the greater evil. Allowing a Union base in orbit seemed a small price to pay.

They were relieved to learn that the rebel base here was staffed almost entirely by Rhuwac and that no planes were kept here. Nova's suggestion that Tharron had not yet received word about the new Union station now seemed probable.

At last, two of the men left to head for the far side of town. Nova watched through the window as they mounted awkward, furry beasts of burden that moved unexpectedly fast when prodded.

The remaining group fastened their head coverings and prepared to leave. The other customers of this alehouse watched their exit silently, covertly. Nova was certain that she had seen approval in the weatherworn faces.

Others joined them outside and closed around Tychon and Nova on their way through town, hiding the more slender figures among their number. Moving in huddled groups through the ever-present squalls of sand seemed a sensible way to get around.

Nova saw that most of the buildings were single-storied with few narrow windows shut tightly against the abrasive weather. The roofs were sloped, almost completely round, and the airborne sand glanced over them in angry blows. There were no basins to catch rainwater. She bent low, buffeted by the fine grit.

"So you had to pick a storm to do this?" She wiped sand from her lips, shivering. The seeping, drifting stuff had begun to filter through her clothing and file away on her skin and already taut nerves.

Tychon whispered back to her, the wind snatching away all but something about 'normal weather pattern'. He tugged a fold of her burnoose up to cover her mouth and nose. She thought she heard the word 'greenie' through the whistling gusts.

Their companions had disappeared into the deeper shadows. Tychon gestured toward a cluster of low constructions at the edge of a wide, open square. Its designers had not learned from the native population - the stone buildings were flat-roofed rectangles. Deep drifts of sand embraced the walls facing the prevailing wind. A battered radio tower and sentries posted at intervals betrayed the rebels' presence.

"Gods, they're ugly." Nova observed the guards with interest. They seemed to be little affected by the cold and dust. The Rhuwacs topped well over two meters, their thick skin chitinous and red. Uneven patches of hair covered their heads and bare arms. Grotesque jaws jutted forward to show double rows of blunt teeth. Some of them carried guns, others little more than cudgels.

Tychon made a strangled sound, his hands balled into fists, when he saw the creatures. She could almost feel his need for revenge burn across the space between them. She cuffed him, deliberately aiming for the still tender wound at his side.

He shook his head as if to clear it, his eyes shut. She heard him murmur something in his native language before he continued forward. In the gloom of the day Nova saw him point toward a sentry to her left. She moved, halting only to await his signal to strike.

"What the hell...?" she whispered to herself when he crept toward another guard. Why didn't he just shoot it? She covered his progress with her pistol. Perhaps he sought to avoid detection by not using the telltale tracer of his laser. Nova watched anxiously, suspecting the real reason for the more personal attack.

His arm clamped around the Rhuwac's thick neck. The struggle was brief, almost pointless, and the beast fell dead without having uttered a cry of warning to his mates. Nova used her pistol to dispose of the other guard, less eager to attempt physical combat with the massive creature.

She scurried to where Tychon waited by the building he had selected. They huddled at its base, dun-colored shapes against dun-colored stone.

"How do we get in?" She peered along the windowless wall, expecting another sentry to round the corner at any moment.

"Up." He bent his knees, cupping his hands. "Lie down up there, wait for me."

Nova looked up with some doubt but put her foot into his hands. She felt herself catapulted into the air, almost too surprised to reach for the ledge of the roof. Seconds later Tychon landed beside her.

She rolled over to him. "I'm impressed by your brawn, but this low gravity probably helped you show off, Major."

His reply was obliterated by the roar of an explosion less than a kilometer away. Both instinctively covered their heads.

Nova blinked into the light of a fireball that rose before them, turning the whipping sand into so many snowflakes. "Your diversion, right?"

They crawled along the roof until they found a metal plate. Tychon pried it open and looked inside.

"Clear." He leaned back to let her lower herself into the building. She dropped to the stone floor and at once flattened herself against the wall. Tychon also dropped, crouching, his gun ready. There was no one there. It seemed as though everyone had run to investigate the explosion.

He gestured for her to move down the hall. While he watched her progress, she peered into two of the rooms and found them empty. They heard deep voices coming from the next. Carefully, she extended a telescoping wand from her wrist monitor and risked a quick snapshot of the room. After a glance at her screen she signaled Tychon by lifting two fingers and raising her hand high over her head. Two Rhuwacs. He nodded and drew a finger across his throat. She leaped into the doorway and fired at the two targets while he caught up and passed her along the hall, taking his turn to explore while she covered him.

"Whiteside," Tychon hissed, pointing into the next doorway.

They had found a small room furnished with outdated but doubtlessly workable communications gear. Even now incoming messages announced their presence with impatient persistence. She saw a barred door to her left and moved to throw the bolt back.

Suddenly, a thin beam of light cut the stone wall near Nova's head, flinging fine splinters into her face. She whirled to face a Rhuwac, headset clamped around the large skull and looking weirdly out of place. The beam of her own weapon dealt with his head as impersonally as it did with the machinery. Both nerve centers melted, twisted and disintegrated.

Tychon poked through the smoldering equipment. "No long range. Would not make it to the first jumpsite with this unless they figured out how to use our relays. They must have another base here. This will only reach other areas of K'lar. Did, anyway, before you got to it."

"Let's get moving before they come back," Nova said. She released the latch on the locked door, finding only darkness beyond it.

"Anders," Tychon whispered into the gloom, looking for a switch or a lamp beside the door.

Nothing came back to them until he tried again. They heard a groan. "Hullo? Who's there?"

Nova stepped into the room, adjusting her gun to emit light. The floor she expected to be there was nothingness beneath her feet. She stumbled down along a narrow stairway and landed painfully on her knees.

Tychon was beside her at once. "Are you hurt?"

She shook her head, looking around. "Bingo!"

"What's B—" He turned to where her light pointed. "Never mind." He approached a short row of cells at the foot of the stairs. "Anders?" He peered into the darkness, assaulted by the ripe smell of decay.

A very dirty hand passed through the rough bars of a cage. "Ty! Am I dreaming? Get me out of here!"

Tychon forced the lock with his gun. A Human in ragged dress uniform stumbled forward and fell into his arms like the long lost friend he was. "I can hardly stand up, man."

Nova checked the other enclosures for anyone else with the misfortune of having fallen into the Rhuwacs' hands. She found no one.

The filth-encrusted officer leaned feebly against Tychon, watching her. "I was wondering if someone'd come for me. Glad you did. It's about time someone kicked the rebels out of K'lar. Did you get them all? I heard there were more in the mountains. Did you take the town? It's pretty infested, but I wouldn't want to see the natives get displaced."

"What are you talking about?" Tychon asked. "We didn't take the town. She and I are the only ones here."

Anders stared at him, wide eyed. "Just you? You snuck in here by yourselves? Holy gods, how did you manage that?"

"We walked in. I intend to leave the same way."

Anders shook his head. "You didn't by chance notice the Rhuwacs here, did you? From what I've seen, there must be hundreds of them here. Thousands, maybe. Training or something. It's like he keeps his spares here but I haven't seen many high-ranking rebels, Shri-Lan or otherwise."

"A hatchery? That's what the K'lars were talking about!" Nova said. "They could have been a little more specific about numbers. We better get out of here before someone finds the Eagle."

Tychon ducked reflexively when they heard the stomp of heavy boots over their heads. There were shouts and curses and, suddenly, silence.

He nodded to Nova. She crept up along the staircase until she could peer under the closed door into the room above. She saw the feet of many soldiers on the other side.

"No way." She returned to the others, whispering. "Ten or more up there."

"Anders, is there a way out of this cellar?"

He shook his head. "If you're a rodent, maybe. For us, the only way out is that way."

Nova looked up, wondering how long it would be before the door would fly open to admit the bloodthirsty Rhuwacs.

"Nova," Tychon whispered, lowering Captain Devaughn onto the stone steps. "Remember where the door to the hall is?"

She nodded. When they entered the control room, the door into the prison had been on her left. Hinges on the right. She mentally retraced her steps and found that, if they could throw the cellar door open, the hallway was only an arm's length away.

Tychon went down the steps again to study the basement ceiling. Two stone pillars supported the floor above, made of some sort of composite. "The stairwell and the door frames will be sturdier than the walls and floor. You can jump from the top of the stairs to the hall door."

"Sure," Nova said, understanding his plan. Both of them dropped their heavy outer garments, no longer in need of disguise. "Should hold as long as we step only on the jambs. We'll be safe on the stairs when the ceiling comes down."

"Or maybe the whole building'll come down!" Anders exclaimed. "Have you thought about that, woman?"

"Probably," Tychon said. "But she knows how to take orders. Do you have another suggestion, Captain?" When Anders did not reply, he motioned Nova to go ahead. "Percussion charge. Let's not start a fire."

Nova switched her pistol to her left hand and retrieved a new weapon from her belt. She aimed at the bottom of one of the pillars; Tychon took the other.

"Mark."

Anders ducked when the supports exploded in a cloud of dust and flying bits of masonry. For a moment nothing much happened, but then the floor above began to groan under the weight of those waiting in ambush. Tychon scooped Anders off the steps and hefted him over his shoulder. He lurched drunkenly for a moment before finding his balance. They raced up the stairs as the ceiling caved in, bringing with it the startled Rhuwacs. Nova fired into the avalanche of bodies, feeling like she was poking into something nasty, like a nest of rats. She kept firing as she burst from the cellar door and leaped for the hallway, avoiding what was left of the floor boards.

Tychon followed, slowed by the burden he carried. Anders closed his eyes, wishing he had a gun and the strength to aid their escape. He felt like an enormous target fixed onto the Delphian's back.

In the hall, Nova stood against a wall to let Tychon hurry past, shooting at Rhuwacs huddled in doorways. She moved after him, stepping backward, her gun blasting into the rebels' hiding places.

Something whizzed by her head, lifting strands of hair in its wake. Nova glanced around to see a metal arrow embedded in the wall behind her. A Rhuwac now stood in the middle of the hall, fitting another quarrel into his crossbow.

"Flash!" she yelled in Delphi mainvoice, unsure if Tychon had made it out of the building yet. She slapped the butt end of her pistol into her palm. A quick twist of the barrel activated her wide flash. Her finger squeezed the trigger. A blinding flash of light ground into her eyes despite the hand she clapped over them. When she looked around, the Rhuwacs lay dead, dying or blinded forever. She whirled around to join the others in their retreat across the square outside. She heard angry shouts, could almost feel enemy fire bite into the stone walls around her. She kept her eyes on Tychon's figure, aware that from several points to the right and left, unseen allies held back the Rhuwacs that followed.

Ahead now some of the large, robed natives waited in the sandblasted alley, urging her to hurry. They held two of those furred mounts and, even from here, she could see the whites of the beasts' eyes as they pranced nervously amid the noise and confusion of the battle. It had apparently not occurred to anyone that she had never navigated a non-mechanical vehicle in her life.

Tychon slung Anders across a saddle, climbed aboard the skittish animal and galloped toward the waiting planes. Nova sighed. Well, today was a good day to learn to ride. She motioned for one of the men to help her. He lifted her quickly and threw a single rein to her before he slipped away into the murkiness to help cover her retreat. Desperately, Nova prodded the animal with heels and hands, glad that it was at least pointed in the right direction. With a squawk, the beast jumped forward and then picked up speed. Nova laughed out loud in fear and hope. She bent low over its neck to present a smaller target, wondering where the brakes were.

They made it out of the alley and into the open where the Eagle waited, obscured by gusts of drifting sand. Happily, she saw some of the locals run toward her, intent on stopping the galloping animal. She slid off its back and raced into the ship's open cargo bay.

* * *

Once aboard the Eagle and away from K'lar, Anders was stowed in Tychon's bunk, sponged relatively clean, and examined for damage. His nose was broken under a thickly swollen yellow and purple bruise but none of his injuries were particularly threatening.

"You'll be fine, Captain," Nova said. "You need sleep. And food. Sleep first."

He looked up at her, still edgy from the escape but basking in the sure safety of the Eagle. "When I saw you flying down that staircase I thought I had died and was seeing angels." He grinned at Tychon, who had entered the cabin with a drink in his hand. "You wouldn't know what an angel is, you heathen."

"*You* are calling *me* a heathen?"

"Who's the lady?" Anders took the cup, still looking at Nova.

Tychon frowned. "My senior and only officer, Captain Nova Whiteside, Hunter Class pilot."

"Aw, go on." Anders yawned. "She's much too pretty to be risking her neck with you out here." He sank back into his pillows. "What do you need a Hunter for on this bucket, anyway? Must be nice, having your own..." He was asleep.

Tychon snatched the cup from his hand. "That worked fast, didn't it? I may have put too much in that."

Nova gathered the medi-kit and returned to the main cabin. He found her staring vacantly into the cold storage compartment of the galley.

"Are you all right?"

She shrugged. "Tired, but wound up. Was a big day. I'm not exactly fond of shooting people, whatever their cause."

"They were only Rhuwac."

"Is that how you deal with them?" she said, thinking of the guard whose neck he had broken. "With your bare hands?"

He shrugged. "It did not feel as good as it should have. It never does." Tychon took Anders' unfinished drink and propelled her to the lounger. "Here, drink this. It will help you relax."

She followed his advice, knowing she would not find sleep without it. "Don't you ever get uptight? You never seem to be out of control."

"It's... unseemly for a Delphian. We try to keep our heads together."

She was silent for a moment, beginning to feel drowsy. "What'll you do when you run out of Rhuwacs? Will your mission be accomplished?"

He shrugged. "This is my life, Greenie. There is nothing I want on Delphi."

She stretched out on the lounger. "But it's home. You must miss it."

"Sometimes. My mother often complains that I'm not home enough."

"Home," Nova mumbled. "I've never had one of those."

He took the cup from her unresisting fingers and pushed her sleeping figure away from the edge of the bed. When he had covered her with a blanket, he retreated to the cockpit and programmed a course for Anders' base on Delphi.

Under his touch, Eagle Seven soared noiselessly, its converters absorbing the cold vacuum as a whale consumes plankton. As always, the dim silence of the cockpit soothed and, as always, he was amazed by the comfort that the thin shell of his ship provided against the dead emptiness outside.

Two people now slept peacefully in this shelter, uncaring of the power that hurtled them onward. Their trusting presence aboard made the vigilance of the Eagle all the more awesome. Tychon was happy to share this wonderful piece of machinery with them, this machinery that had been his home for years.

Tomorrow, the ship would awaken them as it had been told to do. Nova's cheerful restlessness would enliven the in-flight days when solitary comfort could otherwise turn easily into loneliness. Anders, Tychon knew, would bring laughter and a welcome break from routine.

Smiling, he wondered why he had preferred to fly alone for so long.

* * *

Anders had recovered enough after a long, healing sleep to join Tychon and Nova for breakfast. Nova chuckled when he entered the main cabin dressed in some of the Delphian's clothes. Both shirt and pants were too long in sleeve and leg while uncomfortably tight about the waist. But he looked rested, his blond hair cropped back to mere stubble, and a ready smile was on his lips.

"Are you laughing at my attire or my broken nose?" He bent over the reflective surface of the map table that also doubled as dining area.

"Your nose can be repaired," Tychon reminded him, sipping tea. "You will just have to live with that body of yours."

Anders turned to Nova. "And what are you doing with the friendly giant here? Us Humans not good enough for you?"

Nova glanced at Tychon, embarrassed.

"Space slop!" Anders exclaimed. "I never dreamed I'd ever be happy to eat freeze'n nuke again! No way did Ty cook this. He's inept. Will you marry me, Nova?"

"Eat slow if you want to keep it down," Nova warned, amused and concerned. "And Tychon did make that."

"You wouldn't believe the shit they serve on K'lar." Anders chewed slowly, savoring the precooked, nutrient-balanced meal. "Has sand in it. Seriously, they can actually digest the stuff. How's that for roughage? Can't say I liked it there much. Had a couple of cellmates for a while, but we didn't have any cards. And the Ruwwies aren't much for playing Lo-G ball, not like Tychon Of The Mighty Backhand here. Wasn't a total loss, though." He drained his cup and held it out for more. "Happen to overhear back there that they're planning an assault on Targon. Search and destroy, mainly. I doubt they have a definite target."

"Targon! When?"

Anders shrugged. "Didn't come up. Soon, I suspect."

"Do they know that you know?" Nova asked.

He shook his head. "Didn't let on that I understand their language." He leaned toward her. "I speak Grunt, you know."

"I'll send a report," Tychon said and left the table.

"So, tell me, Nova, how about taking up commission on my base? It's on Delphi, but we've got some Humans there. None as pretty as me, though, once I get my nozzle fixed. It'll be a party!"

She shook her head, smiling. "I like this work."

He leaned back and slapped the tabletop in mock exasperation. "Risking your butt every day with this madman? Not healthy at all. Come stay with us on Delphi. You can trade laser burns for politics. That's practically the same thing. It'll be a vacation compared to this."

"I hardly know you!"

He winked. "That's an easy fix."

Tychon returned from the cockpit. "Don't listen to any of his exhaust. He has more women than he can keep organized and I need an able pilot more than he does."

"Yes, but I'm out of Humans and your blue beauties won't come near me."

Tychon shrugged. "They have good taste." He lifted a hatch to the engine chamber. "I'll be cleaning sand out of my filters for a while. Try not to run off together."

Anders smiled after him affectionately and then leaned toward Nova. "So you two kids aren't playing nice-nice? Is that all you are to him? An able pilot?"

"Of course that's all. What are you suggesting?"

"The moment I saw you two together I thought you were making it."

She rose. "We're not making anything. He can hardly get his wife out of his head."

"Delphians mate for life." Anders shrugged. "But that doesn't make him a monk. You two might as well get cozy."

She cleared the table by stacking their trays in the recycler. "You are getting awfully personal."

He pointed at himself. "Do I offend? I am merely trying to be objective."

"And interfering."

"Is it because he's blue?" Anders' voice suddenly carried a nasty chill. For the first time this morning the smile had left his face. "Because he's Delphian you think I'm talking nonsense? Because his hair is blue? Because he'll live longer than you? Not on this job; you two are on a suicide ride. So they can play with their heads better than we can. What difference does that make? I've known Ty for a long time. He looks at you in a way he looks at few people. You must have done something to impress him."

She shook her head and went to fetch the weapons they had used yesterday. "I know how Delphians feel about off-worlders. He has no use for me, either."

He began to disassemble one of the guns, looking for traces of K'larn dust in the works. "If you're going to work with him, you'll need to stop trying to figure out what he's thinking. Delphians have a knack for hiding what's going on in their heads. You won't ever know what he's feeling if he doesn't want you to."

"Yeah, I noticed."

Anders leaned closer to her. "Tell you a secret," he said. "Outsiders keep saying that Delphians are cold bastards who don't feel much. Utter nonsense. They just hide it from people they don't know. So if they get moody around you, you know they like you." He sat back again to resume his work with the gun. "He tries to get along with off-worlders. More than most of them do. Probably because he's worked with us for so long. He's spent more time away from Delphi these past few years than on Delphi. I suspect he secretly likes Humans, even."

"And so you think he's interested in *this* Human? He's been around for seventy years. What could he possibly find interesting about me? He's not going to risk his commission with a subordinate officer."

"Seventy-two, but it's all relative. And don't cite me rules about fraternizing out here. That didn't stop the brass from making you bunkmates."

"Rules exist for a reason."

He shrugged. "Depends where you break them. It'll never be acceptable on Delphi. They would never greet one of us as equal, no matter how polite they are. The last thing they want is for a Delphian to prefer an off-world mate instead of choosing one of their own."

"Oh? Are they worried about half-humans overrunning Delphi?"

"Impossible, in any case. You've got the right parts, but not quite the right genes. Delphians are just a bit farther up the evolutionary scale."

"So *they* think."

"So they know. They're just as interested as we are about why so much of our DNA is the same. Centauri, Feyd, Magra and a whole lot of others, all piled into this tiny bit of the galaxy. But you'll never catch them admitting to the relation. 'Specially not since that also throws Rhuwacs into the mix."

Nova grinned. "That part must annoy them to no end."

"Well, I think the main reason they don't want us running off with their own is their weird reproductive cycles. For such an old civilization, Delphi has an amazingly low population, probably because they live so long. That's also the reason they don't want the Union around, taking their people off planet. They just don't have as many babies as other races to replace them all." He lowered his voice and leered theatrically. "That means they like to mate as often as they can. I hear they're extremely virile."

Nova snapped gun parts together with renewed efficiency. "I don't know why we're even discussing this!"

"Don't be angry. I am just pointing out the obvious." He

toyed with the flash modules scattered on the buffed surface of the map table. "I've known Ty all my life. Gave me my first ride on a solar cruiser. We had some big plans back then. He planned to do a couple of years for Air Command, get his wings, and then we were going to head into deep space. He's one of the best spanners we have - what's he doing chasing rebels? We were going to reach the end of the galaxy and then see where we can jump to next. I was going to find a new planet and start my own population with whatever space girls I'd find there." He smiled absently and found his way from his memories back to Nova. "Then Ty lost his wife to Tharron's damned Rhuwac lizards. He joined the Vanguard and we never talked about any of that again. I'd give a lot to see him care for his life again."

She looked toward the open hatch in the floor. "He told me about that day," she said. She pointed at herself. "But *I* am not looking for a lifemate. I am not interested in Delphian mating habits or whether he is free to take a second wife. Give it up!"

Anders scrunched up his face in a thoughtful expression. "I'm not talking about lifemates, Nova. The word means what it is. He won't ever take another wife. He enjoys women, but Delphians don't draw a straight line between bedmates and some deeply meaningful partnership. Not like us Humans do. Poetically speaking, they're free with their bodies but you won't catch their souls so easily. No matter how well he gets on with off-worlders, he is Delphian and his affinity is to the house of Phera. He has Kiran to think about. Nothing else matters."

She drew back. "I didn't know that. I don't know much about Delphi at all."

"I'll teach you. If you touch this spot on their lower back, they—"

"Anders!" She tried not to laugh.

He held up both hands. "Okay, okay, I'm sorry I brought it up. He'd be disowned, anyway. Forget I said anything."

Nova turned away. "Fine! Consider it forgotten."

He winked. "It's a long trip to Targon, though."

"You figured we'd head there, huh?" Tychon's voice reached them. He had overheard Anders' last words as he climbed up from the hold with a box of filters.

Anders was still leering at Nova. "Yup, just telling the captain how well I know you, Your Blueness."

Tychon glanced from one to the other, noting Nova's tension. He clapped his brother-friend's shoulder hard enough to be taken as a warning. "If he had two mouths, he'd talk with both of them."

* * *

Four standard days after Anders' rescue on K'lar Four, the Eagle descended on the sparsely populated, water-rich planet of Delphi.

D'Elph'Pi, the proud natives had proclaimed this small orb to the first Human-Centauri crew to land here. The unimaginative explorers were quick to spell the name in a more easily pronounced way. As with most off-world concepts, it was accepted by the blue-haired inhabitants with an indifferent shrug.

"It's beautiful!" Nova marveled during their approach, mentally comparing the image on their screens to what she knew about the planet of her own origin.

Large ice caps and vast oceans separated the landmasses, turning the planet into a colorful bauble fixed forever against the velvet backdrop of space. Bright cloud patterns abutted severe mountain ranges that, in turn, gave way to deeply colored lowlands. There were cold, flat polar regions but no deserts.

Tychon understood her thoughts. "Those that have been there say she reminds them of Terra. Too bad that we will not have time to stay long. Just enough to drop off our cargo."

"Cargo? Me?" Anders exclaimed from where he sat on the steps behind them. "Hey, Nova, is he calling me cargo? Cargo! I should tell you about how we once smuggled Ty through Aikhor Gate in a..."

"Shut up, or I'll make room for you in the bay." Tychon

grinned, happy to be coming home.

The Union base had been built over the initial objections of Delphi's Clan Council less than twenty years ago, by Targon's standard time. It was therefore small, no more than a token embassy. All foreigners lived on the base as immigration and settlement of off-worlders was discouraged outside the strict perimeters of the compound. What little trade existed was restricted to appointed agencies that rented space on the Union base. Few off-world Union members were granted visas and their visits were always closely monitored. Trespassers were subject to the strict Delphian penal system and tourism was nonexistent.

Nova was a little disappointed that the airfield here resembling any other Union installation. She had expected haughty, blue-robed natives to meet them. Instead, most of the ground crew was Centauri or Human. But even she knew that nearly all native recruits were quickly moved to other bases to train as pilots or engineers. It was the Delphian surety of eye and movement, as well as their inborn ability to channel stress into productive energy, that was coveted by squadron leaders as far away as Ud Mrak.

So far, Delphi allowed its own people to leave the planet as they wished, although grudgingly. Tychon had gone against convention by enlisting. When he had encouraged his wife to join him, he had enraged those who held with tradition. Delphians who had followed their example and entered the Union's military had, like Tychon, become able officers.

The Clan Council was increasingly anxious over losing so many of their young people to the military. The Union's presence on Delphi meant protection against Tharron's growing rebel force, but the Council cared little about battles fought elsewhere, nor were they interested in trade revenues and the free exchange of thought and friendship among the Commonwealth of United Planets. Their only interest was the preservation of D'Elph'Pi and its population.

But the people of Delphi listened to the house of Phera. That clan had long ago ceded its rule to an elected council, reserving only a few seats for itself. A fierce loyalty remained for Phera and his kin and when Phera expressed his opinions, the people listened. It was only because of his views that the Union had been accepted on Delphi at all.

Anders Devaughn, despite his sunny disposition and easy ways, had become an able ambassador. He kept the Council at bay, working hard to establish a sound relationship between the Union and Delphi, all the while spiriting gifted new recruits off to the academies as fast as they came to enlist. He was one of the few outsiders who had access to other parts of Delphi.

Today Tychon, as the only Delphian Vanguard officer, was received with enthusiasm. When the service shuttle delivered them from the airfield to the main administrative building of the base, a crowd of people surrounded him and his companions. There were, among the officers, a half dozen of the tall natives, some in uniform, some not, eager to have a word with Tychon or to welcome Anders back home.

Nova saw through the guarded expressions around her that even the civilian Delphians were glad to see him safe. She observed a blue-haired Lieutenant leaning close to Anders in conversation. Although his face remained carefully neutral, his hand rested on the Human's arm.

Colonel Jervada sent word that the base was to observe a day of celebration to mark Anders' safe return and to honor the Vanguard officers' presence on Delphi. Messages were sent from the base to the cities of Delphi and Phera's residence, requesting the presence of Tychon and Anders' civilian friends and the few pro-Union council members.

Nova wondered if their arrival here was just one of many occasions that called for celebration. More likely, she thought, there were too few reasons to enliven the segregated existence on this small base.

Colonel Jervada's suite already hosted a jovial crowd by the time Tychon and Nova arrived after dinner in the base mess hall. Most were Centauri officers and Delphian pilots, but Nova spotted a few of the red-skinned Bellacs and one or two Feydan natives, judging by their dark, tattooed skin. There was even an Aramese visitor, his furred body crisscrossed with a network of coolant tubes. The murmur of conversation blended the languages of dozens of regions from several allied planets.

After the solitude of space, the lively gathering was at once refreshing and a little overwhelming for Nova. She searched the crowd for Anders and was disappointed to hear that he had not yet returned from the base hospital. A stranger here, she remained at Tychon's side.

He seemed to know everyone. A tall woman, her silvery blue hair cropped to chin length, clasped a hand possessively on his arm. "Shan Tychon," she purred in a delightful lilt, her sapphire eyes barely registering the Human beside him. Most of her words were incomprehensible. She used a dialect foreign to Nova, who took the time to study this elegant creature carefully.

"I am based on Targon now," Tychon said politely, using Delphi's mainvoice for Nova's benefit.

The woman looked shocked and replied something that conveyed a mixture of affected sympathy and a little disgust. Nova felt offended; she had always liked Targon.

Tychon took Nova's arm. "Excuse us, Elder Sister. I see that Colonel Jervada is looking for us." He steered Nova through the crowd, accepting greetings and congratulations along the way.

"Wow!" Nova managed at last.

"What?"

"Are all Delphian women that beautiful?" Nova wore the gauzy wrap purchased on her visit to Feyd and had for once allowed her copper hair to fall unrestrained over her shoulders, but she still felt like a combat grunt compared to these Delphians.

"I suppose." He looked back to where they had left the woman with her equally stunning companions. "Those can't fly planes, though," he added with a smile.

Nova smiled back, glad for his attention among these strangers. It wasn't easy to ignore the suspicious glances and some outright calculating stares directed at her. She could imagine what thoughts passed through those finely honed minds and preferred not to know for sure.

"Major Tychon!" Colonel Jervada exclaimed when they found the base commander near a selection of refreshments that definitely did not originate in the mess hall. "Have I told you how grateful I am to you and your very charming crew?" He took Nova's hand in both of his. "They don't make soldiers like they used to! At least not on the outside. Young Devaughn tells me you freed him single-handedly from a horde of rebels."

"Well, just Rhuwacs. And Major Tychon was the—"

"This is how legends are made, Captain," the colonel interrupted with a chuckle. "The true stories are generally uninteresting. Or classified." His eyes moved beyond her. "Ah, there's our lost son now!"

Anders had arrived at the door. Someone started a cheer. Others applauded.

"Hey, Derry! Heard you took a Rhuwac mate!"

"Who had to pay to get you out?"

"Who paid Tharron to lock you up?"

Anders grinned, looking around the room for Tychon. There was more back slapping and catcalling as he made his way to them.

He presented himself to Nova. The last of his bruises were erased, the fractured nose repaired. "See? This is what I look like with my nose where it should be. Now will you marry me?"

Nova laughed and shook her head.

"Well, I tried," he sighed. "Colonel, if she weren't enslaved to the Vanguard, she would run off with me immediately. She practically told me so herself! I suppose the major is taking her to that Targon desert?"

Tychon nodded. "Targon is on alert and the Vanguard got recalled. The Shri-Lan rebel base on Magra Torley is mobilizing, just like you reported. We expect they'll take a few jumps so that we won't know from where they'll arrive."

"If they're not using stable jumpsites, they'll have to bring more than one spanner," Nova said. "This might be a good opportunity for us to take a few of them out. Tharron doesn't have many to spare."

Jervada frowned. "Was it explained anywhere why they decided to hit Targon of all places?"

Nova shrugged. "They may be aiming for the research center."

"So they attack the most heavily fortified base of the damn sector? Anything of any importance is too far underground to reach, even if they knew how to design an air strike properly."

"Rhuwacs are not known for their powers of reasoning," Anders said.

Jervada's face was surly. "It's not the Rhuwacs that are pushing the buttons. It's a priority that we cut off the supply of weapons and air power to the rebels on Magra. Is that not your assignment, Major?"

"It is," Tychon said. "We suspected they were sourcing them outside Trans-Targon. But the funds for that just aren't there."

"You know who's behind this, don't you?" The colonel's good humor appeared to have left him.

"As long as we can't move on Magra Torley, Tharron's man there is virtually untouchable."

Anders swatted Tychon's arm. "Come now, I thought this was a party! I'll introduce Nova around. Maybe if she sees how normal people live she'll hand in her combat boots."

Tychon and Jervada watched them disappear into the crowd.

"She is competent?" the colonel asked.

"I think so."

"There are a lot of people here that don't approve. You are a very prominent entity, Major. They say you're setting an undesirable precedent and flaunting Delphi's traditions, if not outright taboos. And if that's not enough, there is speculation on what merits she made Vanguard. She's young."

Tychon snarled. "I am aware of that. She'll prove soon

enough that she didn't make Vanguard because of who her father is. And you know that only my clan complains about me, uh, consorting with a Human, which, by the way, I am not." He hesitated briefly. "Isolation of Delphi isn't possible anymore. Not with the Union's Air Command the only thing between Tharron and Delphi's wealth. Your people didn't get here by pointing out differences between Human and Centauri."

Jervada regarded Tychon as the Delphian watched Nova move gracefully through the gathering. He saw many things in the way this man looked at her, but they had nothing to do with politics or race relations. "I have confidence in your judgment. I'm also glad you're on Colonel Carras' staff and not mine anymore."

"Targon isn't Delphi."

Jervada decided to change the subject. "Have you heard that we may have a rebel problem on Delphi?"

"Here?"

The colonel nodded. "Strange things have happened. First, Anders' commuter plane is hijacked en route to Targon. Then we spotted an unidentified craft entering Delphi space, landing and taking off again within minutes and before we could investigate. Of course, the Council is accusing us of ineptitude but we can't really question outside traffic. This is not a Union planet. If our base is ignored, it becomes a Delphian matter. We assume the trespasser was a rebel ship. Any other would have landed here on the base out of courtesy. And most recently, someone used one of our satellites here to pry into Delphi's archives. They were shut down, of course, when they did not present an access code. The curators were rather tight-lipped about that incident but the intruder could not have been a Union member. We've never been denied access to your library."

"As long as you don't try to access the wrong files," Tychon amended. "What do you think is happening?"

"Wish I knew. Tharron's never been interested in Delphi before. At least not so far. It's too close to Targon."

Tychon shook his head in puzzlement. "Do you have more bad news?"

"I sure do. Shan Velani wants to see you."

Tychon sighed; he had expected this. "I don't have time for him. It can wait, whatever it is. I'm sure he'll track me down eventually."

* * *

The party drew to a close much later. Delphian nights were longer than the cycles to which Nova was accustomed, but she felt far from tired when they prepared to leave the base residentials. Much of the food and drink had been new to her and Anders had encouraged her to try a little of all that was offered.

She felt giddy and lightheaded and agreed when Tychon passed the airfield carts and suggested a walk back to the Eagle. The crisp air at this altitude would help to evaporate this evening's indulgences.

Tychon strolled silently beside her as they neared the far end of the airfield, slowing his steps to suit hers, clearly enjoying the feel of Delphi beneath his feet.

"What a wonderful staff on this base! I talked a bit with Captain Griffin and he absolutely agrees that I need to stay out of Callas entirely. But then he got into an argument with Cillian Rafe about Humans on Callas and so I left them to it. Did you have some of that orange noodle stuff? Not noodles at all…" She laughed. "I am babbling! You can stop me, if you like."

"Not at all. I don't often see Human civilians. You are very civilian tonight." He smiled in anticipation when they reached the end of the runway. "Look," he said.

Nova stared at the panorama before them, speechless. Her hands gripped the metal links of the high fence surrounding the base to take in the spectacular view.

The ground on the other side of the enclosure dropped gradually to form a deep, vast valley. The moons of Delphi poured their light over dense forests, exposing the taller trees in stark relief. Thick streams of mist edged the meadows and obscured the lights of faraway settlements. The mirror surface of lakes shone everywhere on this cloudless evening. The valley narrowed in the south, where she saw the only large city of Delphi, Chaib Psa, its graceful skyline bordering the rustic lowlands without the preamble of suburbs. All of this was ringed by snow-tipped mountains whose fringes formed the site on which the base had been built.

"It's so much like Earth! I've seen video that showed places like these. You grew up here?"

He inclined his head toward the foothills of Chaliss'Ya, Mother Mountain.

"And you left?"

He turned toward her with a sudden movement that startled her. Whatever he meant to say did not seem to want to pass his lips, and she peered up into his face, desperate to understand his mood. The moonlight had softened his features and Nova realized that he was no longer the unsympathetic officer she had met on Myra. Probably hadn't been for days. The hand he now placed on her bare arm sent a rush of sparks through her body. His eyes touched her lips for an eternity and for some reason she felt that all the way down to her knees. Then he blinked, as though awakened from a daydream. He looked once more down into the valley, and then he turned away, toward the Eagle. "I am a pilot, not a farmer. Maybe someday I will be back."

FIVE

The Eagle screamed into the well-guarded landing bays of Targon, the Union's military headquarters in Trans-Targon, after general quarters had already sounded.

Even through the limited range of their real-vid screens, Nova perceived the high-pitched tension as the base personnel prepared for the impending attack. Normal, efficient routine was put aside; all hands on deck, pilots and ground crew racing against time to ready planes and weapons.

The base was a hulking gray complex of airfields, hangars and administrative buildings, all connected by covered roads, tunnels and conveyors. Constructed in what was essentially a combat zone, few buildings exceeded a height of more than a few floors. Most of the more sensitive areas were located well below ground level. Even the fighter planes launched from tunnels deep inside a towering cliff at the edge of the main installation.

Beneath the dismal surface of the planet sprawled a spongy layer of mostly unexplored tunnels, shafts and caves ranging from small chambers to vast, vaulted caverns. Although thin, Targon's atmosphere was livable, but the native inhabitants were cave dwellers that rarely sought the light of day. The surface water had seeped underground thousands of years ago and they had followed it, learned to hunt the white, fish-like creatures and to harvest algae and subterranean mosses for sustenance. When the Union arrived there had been room to share, or perhaps the natives simply did not care.

What made Targon a suitable base was its central location, the hub of Trans-Targon. From here, space and time was measured, distances between planets charted into neat sectors, and jumpsites accounted for. Targon was Terra-Centauri's embassy, its capital in the New Domain. That it was also its largest military base seemed only prudent.

Tychon and Nova slipped into Air Command uniforms before leaving the ship.

"Is that what you're supposed to look like?" Nova asked.

He looked imposing in the dark gray jacket festooned with emblems and marks attesting to his achievements as a pilot and Vanguard agent. His hair was brushed back over the crown of his head and caught in a tight braid at his nape, robbing him of anything that might soften his severe expression.

He snarled, pulling at the stiff collar. "How can you stand these soldier suits? It's like wearing a box. Is this necessary?"

"The colonel doesn't want us looking like a couple of Badland scouts here," she replied. "It's enough that the Eagle looks like one." She smiled, but the awkwardness she had felt since they had left Delphi two days ago made that smile feel false on her lips.

She had awoken aboard the Eagle with a minor hangover, wondering if that moment near the valley's rim had been a dream. Tychon made no reference to it and seemed oblivious to her discomfort as he readied the ship for take-off. He let her jump the charted reach to Targon by herself and seemed pleased by her performance. In the end, she decided that the thick Feydan wine had led her to imagine things.

They took a shuttle to the arrival gate, their identification as Vanguard passing them swiftly through security checkpoints. She was surprised to see Colonel Carras, their commanding officer, waiting for them.

Tal Carras, a Centauri like most senior Air Command officers, walked with a slight limp when he came up along the ramp to meet them. Heavy jowls and a generous mouth, as well as a sizable girth, did not seem to match his standing as one of the most decorated officers on Union records. Nova had met him only a few times before today and hoped that their previous encounter was not foremost in his memory.

"Major Tychon, Captain Whiteside, welcome to UCB Targon. Just in time for launch."

Tychon saluted and half-turned to Nova. "I've brought you your latest recruit."

Carras shifted his violet eyes, disturbingly luminescent, to Nova for a long and searching look. "Whose record is admirable," he said. "For the most part," he added dryly.

Nova's hand froze in mid-salute, startled when the colonel tipped a wink in Tychon's direction.

Carras turned to lead the way to the elevators. "I've arranged for you to lead Turah squad with the first wave, Major."

"Thank you, sir," Tychon replied. "Always a pleasure to take to a Kite."

Nova walked silently, listening to the men talk like old friends. Carras seemed to have come over to this side of the spaceport for no other reason than to greet them and to hear about Anders' rescue on K'lar. It struck her as strangely casual, and she wondered if the entire Vanguard wing operated like this. Another new thing to get used to, she supposed. The colonel left them at the elevators to the multi-level flight decks.

Nova elbowed Tychon when they reached the concourse two floors below. "Hey, there she is! Cassandra! And I know those two people, too. Maybe we can all get together."

"You are delightful. We are in a war zone and you want to play."

A pilot of Nova's age had turned at her call. She was Centauri, comfortably round and curving where Nova was lithe and long-muscled. Tychon regarded her with some interest.

"Nova! I hadn't dreamed to see you this soon, by the living

ghosts of Djink! I heard about your coup on K'lar. I could never have pulled off something like that. What fucking nerve, walking into a Rhuwac nest! You got cojones, Takhuu." She saluted Tychon. "Major."

"This is Vanguard Seven commander, Major Tychon."

"We have heard about you, too, Major," Cassandra said respectfully before turning back to Nova. "I'll get everyone that isn't on alert together later, once we've hauled Tharron's ass out of here. It'll be fun! But I'll see you at the brief, anyway." She threw Tychon another salute and another curious glance and jumped onto a passing trolley.

"We're on duty," Tychon reminded Nova.

"Just a little party! I haven't seen them—"

"In a few weeks," he said, amused. "It's all right, *Takhuu*. You've been cooped up with me for what probably seems like years."

"That is not at all what I meant," she said at once.

"Yes, you did. Let's find some weather gear. It's going to be a high-altitude scuffle."

* * *

The utter riot of motion and noise that greeted the pilots in the vast caverns below the city belied the efficiency and order for which Targon was noted. Hundreds of Union soldiers milling around their rally points filled the cold air with a thrum of tightly-wound anticipation. Nova gathered from the excited exchanges among them that the enemy carrier had dropped into normal space near Targon and would be here within two hours. There was still time to assign shifts and squadrons before the launch.

They spotted Nova's friend Cassandra waving from across the hall, shouting something that got lost in the din.

"I think I'll catch up with Carras while you do whatever it is that you do with your people," Tychon said. He tugged on a strap sewn to her collar. "That thing pinches if it gets under your helmet. See you on the launch."

Nova was at once surrounded by her friends, all of whom

were eager to hear about her work as Vanguard and the places she had seen. Her sudden, unexplained departure from Myra had been a surprise to them. Some of them watched the major take the steps to the upper gallery a few at time on his way to where Carras and other senior officers were overseeing the preparations. Nova did not miss the furtive exchange of knowing glances among some of them.

"What a nice example of male flesh," a musical voice said behind her.

Nova turned and groaned inwardly. "Clio? I didn't know you were on Targon."

The woman did not seem interested in catching up on news and adventures. She was still watching Tychon move along the concourse. "I always knew you'd go far," she said. "But not that far."

Nova's eyes narrowed. "Yes, thank you. I worked hard to make Vanguard."

"Uh huh. Didn't you have a thing for an alien a while back?"

"Centauri. Long time ago. And we're the aliens around here, I think."

"Well, I guess it gets pretty lonely out there. Any port in a storm, they say."

"Lay off, Clio!" a sharp voice rang past Nova's ear.

Clio blinked at Cassandra, who had threaded her way through the crowd.

"I was only—"

Cassandra smiled sweetly and tapped a finger on the insignia at her shoulder. "Dismissed, Sergeant."

Tight-lipped, the woman saluted without decorum and moved away.

"What a lewd piece of dogdirt."

"Cassy, you didn't have to pull rank," Nova said, amused as always by the Centauri's fondness for expletives. Like most Union soldiers, Cassandra owned few belongings in a system where personnel were moved often to wherever the need was greatest. She collected words like others collected off-world pebbles or currency. She liked to display her collection whenever possible, within or without context.

"Do you have any idea how much I enjoy pulling rank? That Dorftrottel had it coming. Now where is that yummy one of yours? How can you let him out of your sight, Precious?"

"He's not mine!"

Cassandra laughed, and her violet eyes sparkled with the sincerity of her mood. "You get a Delphian to smile in public? He actually touched you! So, out with it. Is it true that they're naked under their clothes?"

"What? Of course they'd... Oh, that. I don't know! I told you."

Her friend laughed. "Oh, fine. Keep us wondering, then. Phril mach doneh!"

"Yes, I had better go."

"Oh, did I say something stupid? I'm just having fun. There's been such furious gossip flying around since you two landed here that I couldn't resist."

"What are they saying?"

"I think you can imagine. Probably jealous. That's got to be the handsomest Blue I have ever seen! But I shouldn't have stuck my flippin' nose where it doesn't belong. I'm sorry if I pissed you off. Gomennasai."

An alert sounded and the pilots now looked up as their assignments scrolled by on an overhead screen. Nova marked her launch chute and joined a group of pilots waiting for a trolley. They were ferried through vast chambers, dodging other trolleys and air cars as the last of the non-combat planes were secured below ground.

At last the connecting storage halls gave way to the launch chutes. Orderly rows of fighter planes faced the tunnel openings. The streamlined Kites easily outclassed the more maneuverable but fragile Shrills used by the Shri-Lan rebel force, but no one yet knew how many of those had been deployed here today. Rebel commanders changed frequently and so did their strategies.

Nova was dropped off near the fighter plane she was to

take into battle. Wherever she looked, people, tows and trolleys scurried in preparation for take-off. Lights flashed to direct the hangar jockeys, and many voices shouted orders, warnings and a joke or two. Tychon's assigned Kite stood nearby and so she readied both planes for take-off after testing the neural link on her fighter. Tychon found her after roll call.

"Going to change your orders, Greenie," he greeted her.

"What? Why? I'm ready to go here."

He shook his head. "You're not flying wing."

She gasped. "Are you serious? I'm not deploying? I'm a fighter pilot, above all. Why would you not want me up there?"

He raised his hand to ward off her outburst. "Remind me to start you on some basic exercises in attaining stillness and balance. It's a valuable skill."

She grimaced.

"Stop being a fighter pilot. Start thinking like Vanguard. Take the Eagle. You'll find it at Gate Nine. Launch at once and power down in the graveyard orbit. Don't get noticed." He looked up when daylight streamed into the tunnel, signaling the imminent launch. "That's me." He pinned his gloves under his arm and raised his hands to touch her face. "Hold still." He tilted her head and placed the tips of his fingers against the neural nodes on her temples.

He closed his eyes.

"Tychon, what..." she began, uneasy now. An eerie, pulsating charge, like an electronic ticking, radiated from his fingertips and met somewhere in her brain. "What are you doing?"

There is more to us Delphians than you know.

"I realize that..." He had not spoken aloud! What was happening?

What's happening, came the reply to her unspoken question, *is that we will be able to stay in touch out there. It's also much faster than talking.* He put on his gloves and helmet and climbed into his plane. She could still understand him even after the Kite's canopy closed over him. *We have to keep com open to talk to the others but this way you and I cannot be overheard.*

This is really weird. Can you read my mind?

No. He seemed amused. *I'm using your neural taps. I can understand only what you intend to communicate. Every bit as precise as the ship's interface.*

Can I still interface with the Eagle?

Yes, plenty of space in your head.

Amazing. What else can you do?

Your head doesn't hurt? You feel euphoric? High?

Nova thought about this for a moment. She felt wonderful. *No.*

He hovered his plane out of the bay to join his squadron at the launch point outside. His attention was on his maneuvers and he sent nothing further, and yet she still perceived the steady contact that his presence, calm and confident, had inside her head.

She flagged a nearby trolley to take her to where the Eagle waited and found that Tychon had already cleared it for take-off. Quickly, she completed her pre-flight and then boarded the ship to prepare for departure.

Tychon's squad was one of many that soared toward a surprised enemy. The Shri-Lan attack force had been approaching in a formation designed to pick off a hastily assembled defense launch. Instead, they met a disciplined offense and were forced to regroup before they entered the planet's thin atmosphere.

Few enemy Shrills even managed to break through the tight net of defenders to reach Targon's above-ground installations. The base received only a few superficial hits. One greenhouse among many was destroyed and a tunnel linking the commercial landing chutes to the distribution center caved in. All visitors and personnel had been herded deep underground, where they waited anxiously, packed into emergency accommodations.

The main battle ensued far above the surface skirmish. Cruising at a distance, Nova listened to Tychon's com link as he relayed his orders, leading his unit competently and with a steady hand. Only she knew his commands before the other team members.

Enough of this furball, Tychon projected his thoughts. Care to join me, Whiteside?

You want me to take the Eagle into a dogfight?

He sent a negative. Go neural.

She settled more comfortably into her couch and engaged the ship's interface, breathing deeply to calm her mind. He acknowledged the connection when he felt her relinquish manual control.

Follow but don't shoot. We're going to pay them a visit.

She frowned. They could be anywhere. That keyhole is long closed. Her eyes widened in disbelief when she guessed his intent. Oh, no, you're not! Are you out of your–

"They're on my tail, they're on my tail," Tychon transmitted to his wing, a peculiar note of panic in his voice. "Bugging out!" Nova, half-amused and half-angry, watched her sensors as his Kite headed farther into space. As he had hoped, several enemy Shrills followed in close pursuit.

Find that com relay, Whiteside!

She focused on the ship's scanners, sweeping wide, ignoring Targon's satellites and the ring of junk floating around the planet, all of it carefully marked by Union beacons. The one she looked for was not Union issue and it was most certainly not among the junk.

Got it! She sent him coordinates and he raced toward it, apparently by coincidence, dodging enemy fire at such close quarters that Nova winced every time she perceived a volley near Tychon.

You've got just a few seconds, Nova. Make it count.

She prepared for the required and not entirely safe acceleration, dismayed when she saw his Kite miscalculate and start to spin out of control. She listened with growing dread to his static reply. "Controls out... no fire power...can't..."

Finally, she saw him gain control of his craft within a cluster of enemy fighters, surrounded and powerless. She chewed her lip, waiting for one of them to decide to take a shot. Seconds passed, too many seconds. What could they possibly be discussing over there? At last, they turned with Tychon in their midst, his surrender accepted.

Are you sure about this? she projected, itching to engage her gun controls.

There it is. Time for you to make an entrance, Captain. She received a very clear impression that any argument would be pointless.

Nova shot toward the point in space to which the enemy relay beacon had led them. Indeed, her systems warned her that the keyhole was about to open - usually a good point in time to move to a safe distance. She felt, through her sensors, the site open to create a transit through subspace to the enemy spanner working on the other side, many light years away.

Incoming!

Nova cursed. Of course they would have used the breach to send more planes to Targon rather than waste energy just to receive a few returning fighters and their captive. She was spotted and targeted even as she saw Tychon and his hosts catapult into the breach. A few hits rattled the Eagle's composure, but the ship held true and followed her mental directive to slip into subspace only seconds behind Tychon and the Shrills.

Silence.

A rapid heartbeat, probably her own.

A moment of panic, definitely hers.

Then substance returned into her life and she looked around, instantly beginning to pick Shrills off Tychon's back. The Eagle's superior armaments took them easily, letting Tychon power up his own systems again and join the battle.

There she blows! Nova exclaimed, caught up in the excitement now.

Who what? Tychon dove under an enemy plane and came up at six.

Enemy carrier ahead.

I see it. Pitiful.

Nova agreed. Not expecting to be found out here, Shri-Lan command had merely sent several squadrons of fighters on a carrier, barely armed and now poorly defended. Yet any carrier in Tharron's employ and the spanners it took to move them through uncharted keyholes was a worthwhile trophy. He was able to replenish his arsenal only at huge expense and great risk.

Both Nova and Tychon dodged volleys emitting from her guns.

How the hell do I blow this up? Got specs you can magically shove into my head?

You're not. Can you see me?

She sent an affirmative. Another Shrill was coming up behind him, targeted and destroyed by the Eagle as soon as Nova perceived its presence.

Thanks. When I take off, head for that long tower over their bridge. Follow that line down to where you see a dark patch near a service bay. See it? Good.

You want me to hit that? From here?

That's the plan. It will disable their power supply systems. And life support, but they'll be fine for a while. Maybe. On your left is a small flap with a hexagon on it. Switch the missile selector to the red line at the end.

Don't tell me...

A minor modification. Let's hope it's enough. Let's do this before they recall the gaggle. You ready?

On your mark.

His Kite swooped past the carrier's array to draw their fire along with the enemy fighters still buzzing around the ship. Nova directed the Eagle into the opposite direction. A few near-hits glanced off her shields. She muttered a few angry expletives, knowing that a more direct strike at this distance would make her first Eagle solo flight her last.

She passed over the ship and aimed her weapon at the point that Tychon had shown her. The missile arrowed toward it, impacted, and pulverized against a shield.

Shielded too hard. Damn. Took out the gate but not much else.

Tychon thought for only a moment before issuing his orders.

Nova felt as if he had punched the air out of her lungs. The audacity of his proposal was too outrageous for her to even begin to protest. She could do little but stare breathlessly at her monitors as he aligned his plane with the damaged gate and programmed a short flight sequence. Then she saw his canopy open and Tychon, complete with pilot couch, catapult into space. Seconds later, his plane collided with the enemy carrier, punched through the weak spot and drove deep into her interior.

Nova immediately dropped the Eagle to hover between the transport and Tychon to shield him as his Kite succeeded in breaking the large ship into several pieces. She winced when debris struck the Eagle's shields.

"Ty!" she shouted and recast her sensors to follow his trajectory away from the blast.

It really, really hurts when you do that, Captain. Don't shout into someone's brain like that. Now if you could come and get me, we could get out of here.

I'm still collecting shrapnel for you.

Kind of you. Let's see if we can fish me out of this pond before I run out of air. Open the cargo bay door.

You'll have to duck. I might have forgotten to secure the galley bins.

Can you see what I'm seeing?

Sort of, she acknowledged. *More like I know what you're seeing. Damn, Shrill coming at us!* She shot away, far enough to flip the Eagle and return, taking the enemy ship head-on. It flung a wide swath of debris past the Eagle's nose. *Please tell me you didn't catch any of that.*

I'm all right, came the unruffled reply. *Focus on what I'm seeing. I'll guide you here. Don't use real-vid or it'll seem like looking in a mirror. Just feel me. Drop the shields and spin down the gravity. Once I get close enough the Eagle should start pulling me. I'd like to end up inside the bay, not stuck to the hull.*

She carefully directed the ship, relying on his infinite patience to help her nudge the Eagle toward where he floated, his inadequate pressure suit the only thing between him and the cold nothing of space. She closed her eyes as she edged closer to him, aware of how small the cargo gate suddenly appeared. It seemed an eternity before he slipped into the bay, using the container rail to pull himself inside. She gasped for breath that she hadn't been aware of holding as she restored gravity and air pressure.

Only moments later, he sauntered into the cabin, grinning triumphantly as he removed his gloves and then stepped out of the pressure suit. *That was some fancy footwork, Captain. Headwork.*

Nova jumped out of her couch, barely taking a moment to disengage her headset. "Are you out of your mind?"

He sent a mental question.

"That was damn risky! What if I hadn't been able to follow through that span? What if they hadn't been interested in captives?"

"They would not turn their noses up at a free Kite, not even a damaged one."

"That is supposing an awful lot! Punching out in the middle of nowhere? You could have been killed!"

"I got that idea from you, actually."

"I bailed with a parachute, not in space! What if you'd been hit by some of that junk? What if we hadn't managed to pick you up? You'd still be floating around out there. We're alone here and no one knows where we are. If you haven't noticed, we don't have a spare spanner on board."

"Welcome to the Vanguard, Captain. This is what we do here. Of course there were risks. But they were a lot lower because I know you can keep it together." He paused a moment. "At least during a scramble, if not after."

Her shoulders slumped. "You're a madman. Sir."

Thank you for worrying about me, he said silently. He stepped closer to her and adjusted his hands around her head.

"What are you doing now?"

Closing the khamal.

"The what?" Nova felt his touch within her mind. As a door closes, so the link between them shut. She could no longer receive his thoughts. She felt a brief sensation of loss, as if he had taken away something that had been an almost physical comfort.

He looked into her eyes for a long moment before he removed his hands from her face. "All right?"

She nodded and stepped away from him, unsettled by his gaze.

"It's called a *khamal*," he said and turned to pick up his discarded suit. "This one is just telepathy of sorts. Not all species are receptive to it. Your interface did most of the work. Khamal is a broad term, really. It just describes any one of many mental states. To us, even sleep is a khamal."

"How many are there?"

"That depends on what training you've had. I can use five or six. Some people can produce more than twenty that I know of. The main purpose of the khamal is to achieve serenity, to help in prayer and meditation. Most of us are usually in one state of khamal or another. It's also used for communication and teaching, even for healing. People sharing a khamal must be touching when it begins and ends."

"Why don't we always talk like this? In our heads."

"It takes a lot of energy and concentration. And it gives me a nasty headache. Probably because you're not Delphian and I have to use your interface nodes to reach you. I'd ask one of our healers about that but I have the feeling they won't like me even telling an off-worlder about this, never mind engaging in it."

"Can I learn this?"

"Not this one, Human. I can teach you some other ones. Like how to stay calm and not shout at your commanding officer."

Not sure if he meant that to remind her of her place in the chain of command, she moved ahead of him into the cockpit. "I'll look forward to that."

"Let's get under way. There's nothing left out there but salvage."

She turned to look back into the ship's cabin. Every loose object had floated free during the rescue and now lay scattered everywhere. "Since it's your fault we had to go zero-G, you get to clean this place up, Major."

He surveyed the mess to see her boots, her helmet, her reader, her gun, her tea bottle, her unfinished charts and several pretty combs that also weren't his. He sighed and dropped heavily onto his pilot bench beside her. "You're going to have to jump, Greenie. My head hurts and I think I got a little buzzed out there." He showed her his fingernails. "Not that you can tell if I turn blue."

"I think you just made a joke."

"It's the hypoxia, I think." He opened an overhead compartment and then fastened an oxygen mask over his mouth and nose.

"Just in case you are seriously impaired, can I remind you, Major, that I've never keyholed on my own before? I'm just a chartjumper, remember? Not a genius."

"It'll be fine," he said, his voice muffled. "The beacon they posted will still be near Targon. So it's sort of like being charted. Just not stable. Let the ship find the keyhole and then look for the beacon. I'll be right here."

"If you're sure..." she said, already engaging her interface, hoping that he would not suddenly come to his senses and remember established operating procedure.

"Ten seconds to the breach, Captain. Punch it."

* * *

Targon was in a state of celebration when the Eagle touched down in the central hangar. A cheer rolled through the crowd when her pilots descended along the lowered rear gate. Overhead, a large screen looped a video that Nova had sent of the enemy carrier falling apart. The exuberant crowd shouted approval each time they saw the major's chair eject from his Kite.

Nova blushed, unaccustomed to so much attention. Tychon winced when he saw the display and hoped to avoid Colonel Carras for a while.

There was a noticeable sobering of spirits when the screens scrolled along the results of the battle. The opponent had been wiped out with unknown casualties on the enemy carrier and sixty-three fighter planes down. Targon had lost six Air Command fighters and sustained some surface damage.

"What did they want?" Tychon wondered aloud. "Hardly any damage to the base. One rebel carrier. Less than a hundred fighters against all of Targon's weaponry? Doesn't add up."

"Probably Tharron flexing his flabby muscles."

"Maybe. Let's see if we can get a break before debrief." He saw Colonel Carras wave to him from the concourse. "Watch me get flak from him, too," he mumbled.

"Tell him you're really sorry about the Kite and that it won't happen again," Nova called after him and then turned her attention to the planes still coming into Targon. She joined the pilots that loitered by the chutes, cheered the new arrivals and waited with dread to find out which of their comrades would not return. She finally saw Cassandra, looking a little peaked but wearing a sassy grin on her face. She held up four fingers, her personal score.

A group of pilots rounded a fueling truck, and before Nova was able to duck out of sight Fynn Bridger spotted her. His initial look of surprise was quickly clouded by a glower. He handed his helmet to one of his squadron mates and let them move along without him.

He glanced up at the overhead screen. "Collecting hero medals, kid?"

Nova smiled, suddenly feeling guilty for having left him on Myra without a farewell. "Hello yourself, Fynn. Glad you made Targon," she said awkwardly. "Sorry I, uh, had to break our date back on Myra. Didn't think I'd be taken out of there so fast. How are you making out?"

"Not as well as you."

"Huh?" The venom in his voice startled her. He had always been easily irked and she had learned to step carefully around his fouler moods. This kind of welcome, however, came unexpected. "Oh, Vanguard. Was quite the surprise, wasn't it?"

"I was talking about the pretty picture you paint with your CO."

"What?"

"The Delphi. Everyone can tell how you made it aboard the Eagle."

Her eyes narrowed in anger. "I was advanced there on my own merits. It had nothing to do with my father!"

"Or who you slept with. Or *what* you slept with."

"You can't be serious! What's gotten into you?"

"Being dumped for one of *them*, for starters. I thought you and I were going places. But you left for brighter skies."

"Fynn," she sighed. "There was never anything there for us. We never even got along all that well. You knew I'd leave Myra at the first chance."

He gripped her wrist. "You really think he's better than the rest of us, don't you? Vanguard. A major. A perfect track record! Probably make lieutenant colonel soon. Well, don't ever forget that he's blue!"

"What?" Nova whispered.

"Why would you want to mess with a Delphian?"

"It is the only model that man comes in. What's got into you?"

"You listen to me, Nova! This type of thing will never be accepted on Delphi or Terra."

"What do I care about Terra!" She pulled her hand out of his grasp.

"Don't you know what those people can do to your head? Have you been brainwashed already? Tell me, Nova, does your father know?"

"Why are you doing this?"

"Hit a nerve there, didn't I?"

"Let me hit one," a low voice rolled out behind them.

Fynn turned and blanched when he saw the Delphian behind him. He stepped away from Nova. "Just congratulating the captain, sir."

Nova's eyes snapped to the pilot. He was afraid! Fynn had his faults, but cowardice was not one of them. He had never shied an insubordination charge and certainly never backed out of a fight. His hand had automatically strayed to his holster. Where did this fear come from?

"Major..." she began.

Tychon gripped the younger man's elbow. Astounded, Nova watched Fynn's expression contort with pain as Tychon's fingers seemed to find some nerve to manipulate there.

"I am Delphi, as you've observed so expertly," Tychon said. "Delphians get very annoyed when you upset their friends. It isn't nice."

Fynn managed a small, unclear sound.

"Perhaps you are tired of your bars, Lieutenant?"

"You can't do that!"

"You have no idea what I can do."

The lieutenant struggled to pull out of Tychon's grasp. "If you think you can try your mind tricks on me you'd better think about your own future!"

Tychon barked a short laugh and released Fynn so suddenly that the younger man stumbled over his own feet.

Nova felt Tychon's rage smoldering, threatening to explode, as they headed for the officers' quarters. He walked in long strides, not looking to see if she kept up. What happened to that renowned Delphian detachment? Soon they entered their assigned suite where he tossed his jacket across the drab room onto a lounge.

"Damn insubordination! What kind of god-cursed army do they run here? You are his superior, damn it. Can you not handle a common soldier?"

"You heard what he said?"

"Enough. It doesn't matter. It shouldn't matter to you if you intend to keep working with me. If you can't handle a jealous boyfriend, I'd like to see how you'd deal with our Delphian bigots." He tugged impatiently on his braid to loosen it. But then he briefly closed his eyes and inhaled deeply. As she had seen him do before Anders' rescue on K'lar, he calmed instantly. His tensed shoulders dropped and his face resumed its usual serene expression as his Delphian mental disciplines did their thing. "I'm sorry," he said. "I should not have let that pilot upset me. And I should not have interfered." He turned toward one of the small bedrooms when he noticed that she still stood by the door, watching him warily. "What's the matter?"

"Why was he scared of you? What was he talking about? Mind tricks? What does that mean?" She touched the small implants at her temples. "What does this khamal-thing do?"

"I told you what it does."

"Tychon, what was he talking about?" Her voice rose even as she sought to control it. "What haven't you told me?"

"He's worried about nothing. He's as ignorant about Delphians as anyone else."

"So am I. Tell me!"

"It's just ancient history. At one point, we used our minds in battle. Long ago when there were still battles to be fought among the clans. If you can reach an enemy's mind, you can cause him pain. You can kill him, even. Or back then, anyway. We do not use that ability anymore."

"It can kill?"

He crossed the room in a few long strides. She shrank back when he grasped her arms. "Don't ever be afraid of me! I could never hurt you. I would have to get unimaginably wound up to even *want* to get into anyone's head like that. Please, Nova. I need you to believe me."

"Why does it matter what I think of you?" She tried to pull away, but he did not release her arms. "You don't care what anyone thinks unless they're Delphian."

"You know that's not true." He moved his hand up to brush his thumb over her temple and the neural node embedded there. "I saw you today, in there. I can't really describe it, but it feels like I know you. Like someone very familiar. And I liked what I saw."

"You told me you can't read my thoughts," she said, not quite trusting her voice.

"Do I have to?"

She searched his face, drawn into the blue depths of his eyes that today did not hide his emotion. To her, the short distance between them suddenly widened into a strange perspective as she battled her own feelings as much as old opinions and trusted beliefs. She held his gaze, unmoving, waiting.

"Gods," he breathed unevenly and bent to kiss her. When she did not object, he parted his lips to kiss her again. She responded fiercely, hungrily, and each second that passed whipped her own need for him to greater heights. When his lips trailed to her throat they could both feel her quiver under his touch.

He picked her up and carried her into one of the suite's bedrooms. Their families and heritages were forgotten when he bent over her to unfasten her flight suit. She, too, tugged at his clothes, discarding the insignia, forgetting what it meant. None of this mattered now, when he kissed her again, wanting to kiss her forever.

Nova was surprised by a peculiar sense of disbelief that this aloof, contained person would come to her with so much passion. The lips that had seemed so cold lit a fire under her skin, trailing the gentle hands that wanted to know every contour of her body. She felt herself respond to his touch until at last she pulled him closer, clawing at the smooth skin, ready for him, wanting him.

He lifted his tousled head to look into her face. His fingers brushed over the interface node at her temple before he moved over her to enter her with a moan of pleasure. She received him eagerly, with a sudden mental clarity and physical awareness she had not experienced before. She saw with his eyes, felt with his body. As he could with hers. This time, the telepathy they shared had no words, but each touch of his skin on her own was answered by a new rush of endorphins.

He moved her slowly, enjoying her reaction, holding them both back until her nails raked the skin of his back and he let himself go, feeling her tension rise to match his own until it surpassed even the dangerous euphoria of an untethered spacewalk. The free fall back to Targon came much too soon.

She let him pull her along when he rolled onto his back, exhausted. She felt his powerful heartbeat under her cheek.

"That was another khamal?" she asked, breaking the silence. Although their startling mental link was rapidly fading, she perceived his fondness for her along with a sated, serene state of mind that closely matched her own. "I could feel you. I mean, I could feel you in my head."

He stroked his hand over her back, and she was suddenly acutely aware that she lacked the ridge of fine hair that females, too, among his people grew along their spines. "It's a sort of mating ritual for us, I suppose," he said. "It is the khamal *shoi*, a mind link like the one earlier today, but mostly physical. I didn't know if you'd like it." He smiled at the memory of her reaction. "I'm glad you did. Joining minds with your mate is the most pleasurable form of the khamal."

Nova nodded, recalling the sensation.

"The khamal in all of its states is a part of what makes us Delphian. We could not live without it. It is what makes our brains different from yours." He paused. "But it is not dangerous, even if rumors of that persist."

She raised her head. "I believe you." She reached out to run her hands through his hair, aware that she had ached to do just that for days.

"I have wanted you," he said. "I might as well admit that."

"So Anders said," she said dryly. She turned her head to let her eyes roam the long-limbed body sprawled beside her.

"What?"

She grinned. "Confirming a rumor."

He rolled his eyes. "Come, let's see if we can find something edible in this place."

They pulled clothes from their kits and dressed carelessly, soon heading for the door of their suite. Nova reached high up under his loose shirt to tug playfully on the strands of hair along his spine. Tychon twisted out of her reach to escape into the hall and nearly collided with someone out there. He stopped so suddenly that she walked up his heels in the doorway.

She peered around him. The visitor's hand was still in the air as if he had been about to knock on the suite's door. The expression on his angular face held no greeting and did not become any warmer when he saw Nova.

Tychon recovered from his surprise. "Velani."

The Delphian was older than Tychon by far; his eyes were almost black under thick blue brows, his hair the color of slate, drawn back in a severe braid that reached to his waist. He wore the blue pantaloons and long vest favored by many of Delphi's elders.

Nova stepped around Tychon. "You know each other?"

Tychon glanced at her. "Nova, this is Shan Velani, my wife's brother." To Velani he said: "Come inside, Elder Brother."

The Delphian followed them into the suite where Nova hastily closed the bedroom door. "Please, sit," she said and was not surprised when he ignored her invitation. He inspected her like an especially nasty species of insect he just discovered crawling across his path.

"I am surprised to see you on Targon," Tychon said, using a Delphian dialect that Nova could follow.

"As am I. However, asking you to see me on Delphi did not achieve the expected result. You can imagine my delight at finding myself in a combat zone, five levels below ground." Velani folded his arms and observed Nova more closely. "I am assuming this is your..." He paused a moment. "Well, I know not what."

"This is Captain Nova Whiteside," Tychon said pointedly. "A Vanguard agent."

The older Delphian nodded. "It is so difficult to tell sometimes," he said, hinting at her lack of uniform.

"I'm not required to display insignia," she said.

"Ah, regulations." Velani strolled about the room, his hands clasped behind his back. "Some of which you follow."

"Get to the point," Tychon snapped. "What are you doing on Targon?"

"The Human doesn't need to be here for this."

"Yes, she does."

Velani observed them a while, his pause artful. At last his

eyes settled on Nova. "This concerns Major Tychon's son, Captain. We believe him to be grossly neglected."

"How is that?" Tychon asked in surprise.

"Why, your very profession! Constantly dashing about to all ends of civilization and beyond, I suppose."

"I was drafted into this."

"You were offered the Vanguard. No one is ordered into that position. You could have had your commission on Delphi. You cannot ensure a safe, comfortable future for Kiran."

"He will always be comfortable. I've seen to that."

"That is my point. You do not even know if you will be alive tomorrow. I have taken the liberty of having the boy assessed on Feyd. The reports show that he is exhibiting signs of anxiety, confusion and stress."

"You are unbalanced, if anyone is. He is happy at that school."

Nova stared from one to the other. Why was Velani so concerned with another man's child?

"I am afraid that our Delphian leaders do not consider you to be a suitable parent," Velani continued, looking at Nova with obvious distaste. "You are not only neglectful by allowing your son to be raised by strangers but, besides breaking Air Command regulations, you are also violating the moral codes of Delphi. Even just cohabitating with this Human is an affront to your people."

"I do not believe this," Nova said.

Tychon smiled mirthlessly. "We are a backward people."

"Do not scoff at your heritage. What you do off planet is your own affair. Your son, on the other hand, has obligations to fulfill. Obligations which, I am sure, you have no intentions of overseeing." Velani shuddered visibly. "We all tried to dissuade my dear sister from choosing you, a commoner, for her mate. A commoner who went on to pursue a career that led to her death. She would be alive if not for you."

"You are going too far," Tychon warned.

"Will someone please..." Nova began, confused.

Velani glanced in her direction for only the briefest

moment before answering. "You did not know that Kiran's name, by birthright, is Phera?"

"It is?"

Velani nodded. "Danaria produced the last heir to Phera's reign. We must see to it that this bloodline continues. He should not be removed from Delphi. He needs proper guidance and tutelage. As it is, he is cast aside in a military school." He glared at Tychon. "He does not even know who he is!"

"He is a little boy."

"That does not exempt him from his duties. Of course, he must be led with caution. I am myself applying for guardianship." Velani headed for the door, perhaps sensing that Tychon was ready to explode. "I am certain that our councils will decide that it is better for Lord Phera's heir to be returned to his clan and the Council than to remain in the custody of a free-living Union agent and his Human consort."

Tychon snarled and stepped closer to Velani.

"I had intended to offer you a choice," Velani said, appearing unruffled. "But after reviewing your public record and hearing about your, ah, adventures, I can see what choice you would prefer."

The door closed silently behind him.

"I can't wait till you translate all of this for me," Nova said.

"We're going to Feyd. Today." Tychon dropped into a chair and reached for a screen on a nearby table. After a few moments, he was cleared to speak to Colonel Carras.

"I need to apply for special leave," he said without preamble.

Nova peered over his shoulder at the colonel's surprised face.

"What the devil is this about? I need you here, Major. You were right, earlier. We found four abandoned Shrills near the east service bays. That means at least four more rebels on the base. This is no time for vacations."

Quickly and with undisguised irritation, Tychon relayed their awkward meeting with Velani.

"Are you sure this is necessary?" Carras said. "Do you really think he'll take the boy from Feyd without your permission?"

"He said as much. He only needs the right governors on Delphi to issue the directives. Look, Tal, he couldn't care less if I was living with six grush cats. The best thing that ever happened to his own ambitions was Dana's death. He will use my son to gain a seat on the Council. That cannot be. I must get to Feyd."

"Phera rules Delphi?" Nova asked. "I thought he was a sort of local leader or an ambassador or something."

Tychon shook his head. "We have a clan system with an appointed council, but Phera has tremendous influence over the people. Danaria was his daughter and Kiran is his official heir. I have every intention of returning him to the clan. But not as Velani's pawn."

"And he's using me? To discredit you?"

"Seems that way." Tychon turned back to the monitor. "Tal, how about that emergency leave? I want Kiran out of there until I can get Phera to step on Velani's plans. He's a reasonable man. I have friends on Magra that will look after the boy."

Carras nodded. "Make it fast. I have the feeling that if I don't let you go, you'll go AWOL. Take the Eagle. I don't have time for you to play civilian. On the way you'll prepare a full report with footage on the incident with the rebel carrier. And, Major," he added, "try not to assault any more of my pilots. At least not in the most heavily surveilled spot on Targon."

Nova grinned at Tychon. She considered for a moment. "So why isn't Velani the heir or whatever you call Kiran on Delphi? He's Phera's son, isn't he?"

"Phera doesn't like him," Tychon said. "Disowned him, in fact. They haven't spoken in probably five years. I don't know what Velani did, but it must have been something terrible. So now he thinks he can use Kiran to get what is owed him."

"At least I now know who's been browsing through your files," Carras said.

"What files?"

"Your family records, mostly. Velani must have been gathering ammo for this meeting. The access logs show that someone looked not just at your files but also the files on Danaria and Kiran."

"Is that legal?" Nova asked. "How would he get clearance?"

"Doesn't need it. Those are public records accessible from anywhere. Because of Phera, the major, Danaria and Kiran are important people. Much has been noted about them and there isn't anything in those files that's not public knowledge. The only reason I was even alerted to that is because of a few attempts to get into your classified files, Tychon. Unsuccessful, of course."

"How would Velani have the means to even try to hack into military information systems?" Nova asked.

"Who else would want to know about me or my clan?" Tychon shrugged and concluded their call to Carras before picking up his flight jacket. "Let's be gone."

She shook her head. "Ty, we can't. You're exhausted and angry. I'm beyond tired. How do you think either one of us is going to jump safely today?"

He frowned, undecided.

She took the jacket from him. "Nothing Velani can hire can travel as fast as the Eagle. We'll get there in one short jump. After we get some food and some sleep."

He continued to scowl at nothing but finally nodded, resigned. "I didn't think he'd go this far, Nova." He glanced at her. "I suppose I've given him plenty of excuse to convince the Council. He won't need much more."

"Because of the Human. Because I'm beneath you. Is that it?"

"That is how they see it."

"Do you?"

He inhaled sharply. "Is that what you think?"

She shook her head and turned away. "I don't know what to think." Tears burned the back of her throat and she fought to keep her voice steady. This day had brought such extraordinary excitement, beginning with the battle above

Targon, the absolute thrill of spanning her very first keyhole, and the wonderful mental connection she had experienced with this man who had then come to her with such passion. And then Velani had taken it all away. Now there was pain and confusion and not a second for her to discover what the moments they had shared meant to Tychon. Had it meant anything at all? "It's been such a bloody long day…"

She felt his hands on her shoulders. "I'm sorry, Nova," he said. "I've dragged you into something you should not have to deal with."

She turned but did not look into his eyes. "Maybe it's best if I asked for a transfer, Ty. There is so much at stake here for you. For Kiran. Don't let this be my fault."

"Out of the question! He'll find another reason to take Kiran. I won't back down because of some outdated principles."

She looked up. "I'm a matter of principle?"

"No!" He took her face into his hands. "Gods, no. I won't use you like that. I won't let *them* use you like that. I…" Unable to find the words, he bent to kiss her. "Just stay with me.Please."

SIX

"Aren't you going to let them know we're coming?" Nova asked when they prepared their approach to Feyd. She had changed into her fatigues, as he had asked, displaying the insignia identifying her as a Union officer.

Tychon climbed out of the pilot's couch to hand the helm over to her while he, too, dressed in uniform. They had flown directly from Targon, taking turns interfacing with the ship to achieve speeds that the autopilot refused to consider. With the single jump required between Feyd and Targon, it had taken less than ten hours to reach the planet.

In the end, they had time to spare before Feyd's terminator turned night into day above the hills that sheltered the school. They had used the time inventively but found that his pilot couch was not the most comfortable place in which to practice Human-Delphian relations. The energy expended by unrestrained physical contact had always been a remedy for Nova when fear or tension threatened to overwhelm. It seemed that Tychon, too, appreciated its value.

"If I know Velani, he's already contacted the school," Tychon said when they prepared to land on the planet. "Who knows what story he'll concoct to stall them. He'll find a way to hold us up until he's got Delphi's governors convinced I beat the boy three times daily. It'll be more awkward if we just land on top of them and look official. I don't want to give them time to think."

She watched him fasten his gun belt. Using the Eagle to transport his son, while not entirely protocol, was acceptable with Carras' permission. But implying their authority in a civilian dispute was quite another matter. It was yet another confirmation that the power of rules, as Anders had told her just days ago, depended on where you break them. She had to admit that, once fully suited up, Tychon did not look like someone who would tolerate an argument. Then he ruined the illusion by straddling her legs.

"Hey, I'm trying to fly this thing," she protested when he leaned down to kiss her. "Get into your chair, we're going in."

She entered Feyd's atmosphere and soon headed toward the city. They bypassed the airfield and flew directly to the school where they descended on an empty playing field. By the time Nova had fastened a respirator over her face and they debarked, two staff members were already hurrying toward their plane.

"Shan Tychon," they were greeted by the breathless administrator. "We don't allow air traffic here at the school. I'm sure you're aware of that."

He had a blue-haired woman in tow, looking less interested in the state of the turf than the strapping Delphian that had landed. Nova's glower went unnoticed as the woman barely spared her a glance. Nova gained a puerile sense of satisfaction when she glanced at Tychon's hands, knowing to what use he had put them only an hour ago.

"I understand," Tychon said. "But we are in a hurry today. I have so little time in my schedule, you see…"

The administrator teacher looked around, smiling. "So where is Kiran? We hadn't expected him back so soon."

Tychon's eyes snapped to him. "What?"

His smile wavered. "Aren't you dropping him off?"

Nova felt her knees weakening. "He's not here?"

"Ah, no," the Delphian woman said. "He's been on Delphi, hasn't he?"

"I think I'd know if he was on Delphi," Tychon said, barely controlling his voice. "Why do you think he's there?"

"Major…" The administrator looked panicked. "I'm sure we will sort all this–"

"Where is my son?"

The man used his com band to call for another supervisor, no doubt afraid that Tychon might dismember him on the spot. Nova thought his fears might be well-founded.

Tychon glanced at her. "Velani."

"Your… your staff came here," the administrator said. "Not Shan Velani. A few days ago. They had your sigil. It all seemed in order. You wanted to meet Kiran for a holiday on Delphi, they said. Winter solstice in the mountains. He was so excited."

"My staff?" Tychon gestured toward Nova. "This is my staff. And no one carries my sigil. Did they say they were on my squad?" He paused for a moment. "Were they even Delphian?"

"Well, no. A Caspian and a… a Human. And a K'lar woman."

Tychon rounded on the Delphian tutor. "You should know better. Phera would never permit him to be taken off planet without a Delphian mentor. Nor would I." He pointed at the building behind her. "Those are children of officers in an active war. What were you thinking?"

Nova stepped closer to him and placed her hand onto his back. The two staff members practically cowered before them now, knowing his anger was justified, afraid of the repercussions to come. Grandson to Phera, Kiran was no ordinary officer's child. "Major," she said softly, "we need to get back in the air."

Tychon stared into the distance for a moment, breathing deeply. "Yes, you're right." He turned back to the staffers. "You two had better get some explanations together. Until then, collect every scrap of video you have of those people and send it to Colonel Carras on Targon."

Nova hurried ahead of him into the ship, already activating her com band to contact Feyd's traffic control. She requested a report on all traffic that passed through the air fields of Talan An and nearby Brishan over the past few days. By the time they had boarded the Eagle and completed pre-flight, she already knew that no delegation from Delphi had used those ports.

Tychon launched the Eagle and headed to the jumpsite to Targon while she ordered a log from both nearby charted jumpsites to be transferred to Targon. Leaps through keyholes, of course, were untraceable, but even Velani would not have easy access to a Level Three spanner.

"We're going to Targon?" she asked when she had closed the com link. "You don't think he's on Delphi?"

"Phera would never stand for this. If there is something legal that Velani can do to get his hands on Kiran, he would not interfere. But kidnapping? Lying to the staff here? That's not something he'd tolerate. See if you can find out where Velani is. If you find him, have him brought back on Targon."

"Can you just arrest him?"

"I can as long as he's not on Delphi."

Nova connected to the relays to send transmissions to Delphi, Magra, Zera and Targon - all likely destinations. Her clearance as Vanguard ensured that her inquiries received priority at every destination. Still, it took a while before they reported back, one by one, during which a tense silence took up all the space in the cockpit. "He's still on Targon," she reported finally. "I guess that's something."

"This is my fault," Tychon said, his eyes on screens that showed nothing of interest. "Why did I ever think he'd be safe on Feyd?"

"Feyd is as safe as any other place."

"Delphi is safer. But I had to show them what I thought of their outdated governance, didn't I? Had to show them that I didn't need them. Had to turn my back on everything after—" He glanced at Nova and fell silent.

"You did what you thought was right for Kiran. There is no point in looking back now. We'll get him back."

"Right."

She regarded him fearfully before daring to give voice to those fears. "Why would he take Kiran and then tell you that he's going to do just that? You are Vanguard. You have hundreds of enemies. You don't really think Velani's got him, do you?"

"Kiran is all I have, Nova. I *have* to think that."

* * *

They arrived on Targon in a state of exhaustion. Neither found any joy in having set a new record for crossing the distance from Feyd to the base. Nova landed the Eagle near maintenance to have the crossdrives checked for damage their abuse may have caused. They stopped for nothing else in their hurry to Carras' suite where Velani awaited them.

"I most certainly hope that you have a very good reason for this," Velani greeted them, his stance conveying irritation that his voice did not. "I should think that you would have enough respect for my position to come to Delphi should you wish to speak to me, rather than hold me here. I am expected there for a meeting. I should have left days ago."

"My son," Tychon snapped. "Where is Kiran?"

Carras, who had risen from his chair when they had entered, collapsed into it with an audible moan. Why were these people making his base their battleground?

Velani blinked. "What?"

"Kiran was taken from Feyd four days ago," Nova said.

Velani stared from one to the other. "By Melyb'ry," he groaned.

Nova studied the man, baffled. She had expected indignation, protest, perhaps even pleas of innocence. But this reaction came unexpected. The haughty exterior had disintegrated, leaving only shock and despair. He made no effort to restore the tranquil facade at which Delphians were so adept.

"Velani?" Tychon said, equally baffled. "What do you know of this?"

"The boy? Gone?"

Carras pushed a chair toward the Delphian elder, certain that he was about to faint.

"Velani..." Tychon pressed.

It seemed a lifetime before Velani recovered enough from Tychon's revelation to speak. "What have we done?"

"Talk," Tychon whispered, barely audible.

"At Kiran's khamal *gzali*..." Velani began. He half-turned to Nova and Carras. "That is a rite for infant Delphians involving what you probably call a mind link. It is performed by elders or a religious leader, believed to impress upon the child a sense of heritage, purpose and loyalty to his past. No one really knows if these embedded memories ever reach the conscious mind. It has become a ritual, even observed symbolically among the low-born."

"Get on with it," Tychon growled. "Must you high-born carry on so?"

Velani's gaze returned to him. "Kiran's khamal, which was performed by none of his true relatives, was attended only by a number of Shantirs."

Tychon's eyes narrowed. "Phera was not there?"

"No. Kiran's grandfather was called away on some Council matter on the day the Shantirs had chosen for the khamal."

"What are Shantirs?" Nova asked.

"Mystics," Tychon said. "Druids, wizards, healers, whatever you wish to call them. They develop their mental acuity to include the kind of non-medical neural and even genetic manipulation that even your people still dream of, Colonel. Then they shroud it all in holy language and convoluted rites so that outsiders think it's all harmless, quaint, like an old religion."

"Tychon!" Velani gasped.

"Broke another one of your moral codes, didn't I? It's time people knew about us."

"Will you go on now!" Nova cried.

Velani turned to the colonel. "When the Union Commonwealth arrived in this sector, what you call Trans-Targon, there was great fear that our world and ways were threatened by the influx of outside evils. We are a peaceful, defenseless planet and our people were afraid of what the Union would bring. Even after your base was built and you pledged to defend us against the rebel threat, the people were still waiting in fear of what would come. They were right, of course. Look at this war you have started."

"Wait a—" Nova began to protest.

"Go on, Velani," Tychon cut the argument short.

"We needed a way to defend ourselves. When Danaria, my sister, chose Tychon for her mate, his genetic material, though far from noble, was deemed suitable."

"Suitable? What does that mean?" Nova asked.

Velani shrugged. "I do not know, but the Shantirs did not object to the match. Not even when Tychon joined the Union's Air Command and became a pilot. Not even when Danaria followed him. She was believed to know her place, to observe tradition, even if her consort turned out to be lacking in loyalties."

"Do not question my affinity to Phera," Tychon warned.

"I question your choice to remove the boy from Delphi, nothing more," Velani replied. He turned to Carras. "Kiran was born a year after the match. There was no reason to think that he would ever leave the influence of the Shantirs." Velani closed his eyes, shaking his head in denial of what he now had to say. "Because of this, more than any other reason, because it was thought that he would never leave Delphi, Kiran was chosen to be the Tughan Wai."

Nova turned at the sound of Tychon slowly sliding down along the wall. He sat on the floor, staring at nothing, as if his knees simply no longer supported him.

"Ty?" Nova was astounded to see him in this attitude of despair. She whirled to Velani, a cat ready to spring. "Translation," she hissed.

"Tughan Wai?" Velani shook his head, trying a hopeless

smile. "The end of all you see here." His gesture included the room, the base, the planet.

"What?" she whispered.

"A mentality capable of such destruction that a single thought can blow this installation to bits."

Nova heard a strangled sound from somewhere within Carras' barrel chest. "How?" she asked. "Why?"

Velani pointed at Nova. "Just like that abomination," he said, pausing when he noted her dumbfounded expression. "I mean your neural interface, Captain Whiteside. That abomination makes it possible for you to find your way through subspace. The Tughan needs neither ships nor machines. His mind alone will let him reach into that subspace while remaining on solid ground here with us, to affect matter itself. He only has to be shown a thing, touch a thing, to change a thing. If he understands the composition of stone and steel, he can take it apart down to the last atom."

"They've been developing this for centuries." Tychon said tonelessly. For the first time Nova was aware that there really was a blue tint in his skin. "Secretly. It was just an experiment to see how we can develop our minds. Some Shantirs dabbling with theories and extrapolation. Resonance, thermal transfer, things like that. But when the Union took hold over the last two hundred years, the experiments were stepped up. Eventually, when it became clear that the Union was a useful alliance, the need for this weapon became less important. The Council at the time ordered the project stopped. It was assumed that the whole idea was abandoned."

"And it wasn't," Nova said.

"Correct," Velani replied.

"This Tughan thing," Carras said. "It isn't a new concept by any means, is it? I am thinking of the Glanep nomads of F'yan Orr. It was nearly limitless what they could do. Then there was the incident on Phi Nine, if I remember correctly."

Velani nodded. "The Glaneps are emotionally incapable of harming anything with it even if they wanted to, and Phi Nine burned."

"What is the extent of the Tughan's ability? What range? Under what conditions? You said he could destroy this base if he wished."

"We do not know," Velani said. "*I* do not know. Perhaps someone on Delphi does."

"If Tharron has Kiran..." Tychon said.

"To be used as this Tughan..." Nova added.

He nodded. "A person like that could walk into any city, base, plant and take it out. No need to carry explosives, no weapons, no ships or bombs. He could be sitting in this room and you'd not know it."

"He is a little boy!" she said.

Velani raised a hand. "That fact may buy us time."

"Time for what?" Nova asked.

"As I understand it, the Tughan can't be put to use at this age." Tychon looked to Velani for confirmation.

Velani nodded. "It could be very dangerous if any attempt was made to use him now. He is too young. Months, years of training are necessary. How else can anyone deal with such power? There are mental exercises of controlling it that must be undertaken before the Shantirs even dare tell him who he is."

"And that means we have some time," Tychon said. He came to his feet and walked to Carras' desk. "I take it that a Shantir is required to release the Tughan. We must restrict all of them to Delphi. Tharron cannot be allowed to recruit one. Kiran will be harmless."

"Enough!" Nova glared at him. "How can you talk like that? He's not a dart gun with a loose trigger. He's your son!" She turned to Velani. "And you knew this, all these years? And you said nothing to Tychon?"

"Shan Velani," Carras said, his authoritative voice demanding, and receiving, their attention. "What if Tharron tries to access Kiran's potential now?"

"Yes, please tell," Tychon said, and Nova thought she had never heard three words sound so much like a threat of violence.

Velani made a helpless gesture. "Overtaxing the young talent could set up a chain reaction that will be impossible to stop. The only way the... the previous candidates had been stopped was by... by termination of the subject."

"They were killed?" Tychon said, raising his voice. "They murdered them?"

Nova stepped in front of Tychon as if to stop him from harming the frail elder. He grasped her arms, perhaps meaning to push her aside, but then just stopped and held her there like a shield against his own fury. His eyes remained fixed on Velani.

"We must assume that Kiran is in rebel hands," Carras said. "If Tharron has somehow discovered the existence and whereabouts of the Tughan, he must also know of its dangers. As a safeguard, I will make sure that he is told. We have ways of reaching his ear."

Tychon nodded. He had recaptured his outward calm, but Nova could feel the tension in his hands and almost hear the pounding of his heart. None of this now showed on his face. He looked down at her and released her arms. Only she noticed his hand brushing across her midriff, a silent apology, when she stepped away from him. "He'll have to wait until Kiran is older," he said. "That will give us time. Years perhaps. We will find him."

Carras ran a not-quite steady hand over his scalp, irrationally thinking that it might be time for a shave. "I know what Tharron will do to gain control. He will find a way to secure the services of a Shantir that will set his ethics aside. Tharron is a very wealthy and powerful man."

"Colonel," Velani protested. "Are you implying that he will be able to buy a member of our most revered sect of—"

"He is not above bribery or blackmail," Tychon said.

"Perhaps when it involves purchasing the services of your Union officers, never a Delphian."

"I don't think I want to hear about Delphian ethics, Elder Brother." There was nothing respectful in the way Tychon used the honorific. He turned to the colonel. "Tal, I want unrestricted access to weapons, ships, personnel and credit. Also Vanguard Nine and One. There are people who owe me a favor or two. Some of them are smugglers and thieves that have been to places we cannot go. We'll start on Magra. V6 is already there. We will find the boy. We will return him to Delphi and the Shantirs." He scowled at Velani. "You have made a monster out of my son! You should have told me about this years ago. I would never have taken Kiran from Delphi."

"I have a responsibility to Delphi's internal matters."

"You have a responsibility to your clan," Tychon replied. His voice was steady. "Hear me, Velani. If harm comes to my son, it will also come to you and every damn Shantir on Delphi."

* * *

The Centauri colonel, alone in his office, stared mournfully at his hand which most persistently refused to have anything to do with the communications console on his desk.

Once Velani had recovered from Tychon's hateful threat and the Vanguard officers had left, Carras had questioned the older Delphian. Velani assured him that a weapon like the Tughan Wai in Tharron's hands would end the wars once and for all, likely not in anyone's favor.

Carras shuddered visibly and moved his finger to activate the intercom. "Soto, prepare a transmission to the Commonwealth Factors. Code One."

He heard a small intake of breath, not quite a gasp. "Code... right away, sir. Which Factor?"

Carras considered. Five Factors were Centauri, as he was. There were two Humans, a Sahani, a Feydan and one, Baroch, was Delphian. Of the Ten, Jacobs, Velu, Chighan and Nor were on Alpha Centauri and two years of travel away.

"I wish to compose a message to Baroch."

The screen on his desktop unit came to life. There would be no open visual or audible communication during a Code One transmission. The recording system was shut down;

unless an enemy intercepted the transmission, there would be no permanent record of this. He typed his message, a bland letter of greeting and news from one official to another.

The message packet arrived at its destination after a trip through subspace to appear on the screen of Baroch's bedside reader on Feyd, where it had awakened him. The Delphian squinted at the screen, reading with growing alarm about a new, possibly profitable import item from Pelion and the ongoing drought on Bellac Tau. When the letter had scrolled from the screen, Baroch was sitting straight up in his bed, feeling his heart pound in his ears. The missive he had gleaned from the letter was coursing through his mind and would not allow him to return to sleep, nor would he do so until he could summon his peers for an emergency council. Carras' message was as clear as his comment about the weather: THARRON OWNS THE TUGHAN!

* * *

A council assembled within days. The Factors stationed in Trans-Targon resided on separate planets and were rarely found in the same room together. Now that one of them deemed it necessary to meet in person rather than take a risk with slow-moving and one-sided communication, an immense security force was put together. It was decided to meet on Coup d'Oeil, a sparsely populated planet beyond Myra and the reach of active rebel movements. A remote airfield was cleared of vehicles and its ground crew replaced by Union personnel. The entire area was swept clean of unidentified machinery, shipping containers and mobile mechanicals. Cordons were erected and local law enforcement instructed to reroute ground traffic. A new ship to surface communications system was brought in and installed.

One at a time, planes from as far away as Pelion arrived on Coup d'Oeil, each delivering one of the Commonwealth leaders. Once dismissed, the planes departed the airfield to hover in orbit among scores of fighter planes, cruisers, one battleship and several Vanguard Eagles.

One of the Eagles was Number Seven, bringing with them Colonel Carras.

"Why can't we be present at this council?" Nova demanded when, after they had idled above the planet for a few days, the Factors were finally assembled and ready to interview the colonel. "This is about Major Tychon's son, after all."

Carras shrugged tiredly and Tychon, at the helm, remained silent, his attention on landing the Eagle. He had no patience for any of this. He had assigned Nova to convey the colonel back to Targon after the meeting while he would go on to Magra Alaric with Vanguard Three. All of them were glad that the waiting had ended when a message arrived, ordering them to bring Carras to the surface.

Once on the ground, the colonel was kept waiting a while longer in one of the appropriated hangars and then searched politely but thoroughly. Only when the security team was satisfied that he would not endanger the lives of the Factors was he allowed to proceed into the council room.

He entered the small chamber, a little uneasy until he had adjusted himself to the deadened atmosphere. No known device could record or transmit the words that would be spoken in this sealed room today. The Factors were seated in a scattering of comfortable chairs. No need for tables, no need for notes.

"Colonel Carras," Baroch said, his voice flat and without echo.

"Sire," Carras replied. The odd condition of the room seemed to snatch the word from his lips as he pronounced it.

"Let's not waste time," Bender, the Feydan Factor said. "I must say I was prepared to hear something extraordinary when summoned here, but this is beyond what I had imagined. Lord Baroch told us of that Tughan Wai creature and what it could mean in Tharron's hands. We will request further information from Delphi's Shantir enclave. Now you will tell us how you have come to know of its existence."

Carras complied, addressing all of them, his voice steady. He had dreaded this meeting; the thought of being confined with the absolute leaders of the Union had threatened to unnerve him. No matter what his rank and experience, he was a soldier, and government dealings had never interested him. It was something ambassadors dealt with, in his opinion.

The Union itself stretched far beyond this small, crowded sector of their galaxy, encompassing not only Terra-Centauri and Trans-Targon but also the lifeless mining planets of Chitta Moor and the newly charted Nenele system. Although several of these men and women had risen from among Air Command ranks, only two of them, both Centauri, were actually charged with military matters. The other eight oversaw commerce, resources and technology, migration and culture. Since Trans-Targon was the sector most populated with habitable, valuable planets and the only one threatened by the rebel enemy, six of the Ten Factors resided here, their presence required to govern the rapid spread of Commonwealth influence. Now that Carras stood before them, he did not feel daunted. He did not feel anything at all.

None of them spoke for what seemed like eons after Carras had told them what he knew. His eyes traveled from one to the next until he could wait no more. "It seems to me, Lords, that our main concern must be to liberate the young Delphian and return him to a safe environment. It means that we must step up our efforts against the rebels. Specifically the Shri-Lan faction. I need resources, ships, more staff."

"Who is aware of this situation?" Factor Coyle asked.

"Factor Baroch issued a gag order. As far as I know, only two Vanguard officers and Shan Velani are aware that the boy is missing. The school isn't about to advertise that they let him disappear, and they have been directed to keep it that way. We don't know if the kidnappers understand the boy's anomalies." He glanced at Baroch. "And we have no way of knowing who on Delphi does."

"Apparently Velani does," Baroch said. "You mentioned that one of the officers is the boy's father?"

"Yes, Factor. Major Tychon."

"Where is his mother in all this?"

"Deceased, sire."

Baroch winced.

"Do you have any leads on who took the child?"

Carras nodded. He stepped out of the way to let them watch excerpts from the school's security video that he now displayed on a nearby screen. A camera had captured the trio of strangers walking down a hallway with a school staff member. Unmistakable among them was a Caspian, his visible skin covered in blond hair as dense and short as that of a horse, striped across the chest and shoulders. When they passed the camera, he lifted his eerily elongated head to smile at them. One of his yellow eyes winked slowly.

"That rogue!" Coyle exclaimed.

Some of the others also grumbled at the affront.

Carras froze the video and pointed at the Caspian. "Pe Khoja, one of Tharron's closest associates. We assume that the K'lar woman is there to look after the boy, which gives me hope that they mean him no harm. She is not known to us. The Human is also one of Tharron's men. As you can see, Pe Khoja does not care if we know of his involvement in this."

"That much is clear," Baroch said. "Please wait outside, Colonel, while we debate this matter."

Carras let himself out of the room and waited impatiently in the stark antechamber, surrounded by stone-faced guards. He had hoped to deliver his report and then be dismissed. Surely, the Ten employed agents who would know how to find a child hostage among the enemy. This would allow him to forbid Tychon and Nova to search for the boy, leaving the matter to those who could remain impartial.

He paced, knowing that his involvement with the Tughan was just beginning. The news of his existence would be classified as secret, not only to avoid panic but also to avoid further strain on the Union's relations with Delphi. And he, Carras, already knew of it. And he, Carras, commanded a squadron of agents that were considered to be the Union's best, the only cohesive group that could be trusted to keep this secret a secret. And two of those already knew of the Tughan.

The same two that could identify the boy at a glance. Vanguard Seven.

Carras mopped his brow, sweating profusely. Had anything in his past career prepared him for a mission such as this? Was his Vanguard prepared? They had studied Tharron until they knew his past and present like their own. They knew where he employed his rag-tag armies and who his associates were. They recognized his voice and could recognize his face in a crowd of K'lars. It was all that his Vanguard were employed to do: Destroy Tharron and, until that was accomplished, discover his bases, towns, advisors and hangers-on. Anticipate his moves and foil his efforts to damage the Union Commonwealth. Major rebel factions like Tharron's Shri-Lan were the only reason that the military was such a vast and expensive organization in Trans-Targon. Anywhere else in the Commonwealth peace prevailed and power struggles were carried out most civilly by huge trade conglomerates and combines, politicians and shipping magnates.

And now, all of this, their entire glorious Union, was threatened by a single madman who would soon control all of it if not stopped. Air Command's vast reserves of men and weapons ceased to matter. They may as well send everyone home.

Carras forced himself to stop pacing and peered intently into the faces of the guards lining the walls of this room. Stalwart. Unmoving. He suspected that they had been genetically engineered, bred and trained for their duty to the Factors. What use was this now? Guards, guns, planes, all toys now. Who would throw pebbles to stop a charging bull?

When Carras heard the knock on the inside door, he knew that the leaders had come to the same conclusion as he had, as Tychon had days ago when they discussed their options aboard the Eagle. There were precious few choices left. They would try to stop the bull or die trying. There was nothing else to do. And he was the boy with the pebbles.

He entered the room and waited while it was resealed, feeling the silence descend over the chamber to drop heavily on his ears.

"Carras," Baroch said as though he had never left the room. "You will employ your agents to locate the boy, but we cannot approve a large-scale operation. If this Tughan works as intended, we no longer out-gun Tharron and so this will remain a covert operation. We will expect progress reports within weeks. We recognize that lives are at stake. Perhaps many lives. Your agents will attempt to liberate the Tughan and return him to Delphi before you try to take him by force. Failing that, you will take immediate action to disable the Tughan in any manner you see fit. Tharron must not be given the opportunity to test its design. Do you understand?"

Carras nodded. Of course he understood. He bared his teeth in a grimace of disgust.

"We would prefer to gain control of the Tughan Wai. The research opportunity would be of value." Baroch's brittle skin wrinkled around blue lips at this understatement. "We trust that you will manage this operation without needing to divulge its nature to anyone but your Vanguard. You are given unlimited clearance. However, anti-Union sentiment is strong on Delphi. We cannot risk our position there by restricting their Shantirs, as you had suggested."

Carras nodded, inwardly wishing the pox on all politicians and their kin.

"I am going to oversee this operation," Baroch continued. "Please report to me as soon as any progress has been made." The Delphian waved a dismissal.

Carras stomped out of the room, a seasoned warrior, nearing his honorable retirement, now officially responsible for the entire sector's military balance. He cursed the day that had made him an officer.

SEVEN

"I would have appreciated a meeting in little more... wholesome surroundings," Velani sniffed disapprovingly. He looked up at the Human who had brought him here, then at the Caspian sitting across the table.

Pe Khoja studied the Delphian through half-closed lids. Pinched, aristocratic face with a beak of a nose. A voice that grated. Not so young anymore; Pe Khoja judged him to be third, maybe even fourth quarter. Skin of the left forefinger worn-looking as if from the chafe of a heavy ring worn for years. Maybe the sapphire ring worn by Shantirs. Just as interesting, the Delphian was barely able to maintain the arrogant indifference so carefully practiced by his people.

He slumped deep into his seat and drew a knee up against the edge of the table. His eyes searched through the noisy, surging crowd around them, seeing no one loiter, no one watching. If there were Union agents here, they were well concealed. The nervous Delphian before him sat erect in a crowd of slouchers, eyeing a brawlsome group of travelers at a nearby table as if he expected an imminent assault. He looked out of place here in Feron's only public airport and interstellar launch.

It took hard-earned experience to distinguish ticket-holding commuters from the riffraff of thieves, panhandlers and whores. Moneyed people used Feron's Union-owned airdrome on the other side of the glaring, blaring city. No one ever came here to stay. It was a stopover at best. A fortunate few used the launch to leave this place forever. For Pe Khoja, the mining planet was a place to meet pirates and renegades, his most valuable contacts. When possible, he avoided it altogether.

He glanced up at the pilot that had delivered Velani. "Get lost."

Fynn Bridger looked from him to the Delphian and then moved away, his eyes on the surging crowd around them.

"This will do for our first date," Pe Khoja said to Velani. "Now tell me why a Delphian is looking for the likes of me."

"That man is paid to guard me," Velani objected. "Who knows what felons frequent this place." Velani did not bother to explain that Fynn Bridger had sought him out after Velani had spent three days in awkward attempts to find someone in the lower holds of Targon with some sort of connection to the Shri-Lan. He had practically dragged Velani out of the crew quarters before someone could wonder why, of all people, a Delphian elder was haunting those crude halls. Velani suspected that the pilot had his own reasons for wanting to leave Targon. Now AWOL and flying a hired ship, returning there was not an option.

Pe Khoja observed the Delphian curiously. Clearly, the man had no idea who was hosting this particular interview. "You get to keep him, no worries," he said. "What do you want?"

"You know what I want."

"Entertain me."

"I have something that Tharron needs," Velani said. "I know you have the boy. I have the means to make him useful to you."

"And what would that be?"

"Look," Velani said. He shrank back when a trio of Genen bipeds lurched past their table, shrieking something akin to laughter. Malodorous fumes wafted into his nostrils, and he suddenly felt the need for a bath. He closed his eyes, meditating, shutting out his noxious surroundings. He drifted into a state of mind that let him block out everything except the rebel in front of him. "I may not be the sort of person you are used to dealing with, but you should not underestimate me. You want the Tughan, and I can give him to you. You'll not get such an offer from anyone else."

Pe Khoja leaned forward and rested his elbows on the table. "That is the part that confuses me, Shantir. Share with me the reasons why you, a Delphian, would take up with yonder deserter," —he gestured toward Fynn— "and travel all the way out here to offer us your services."

"My reasons are my own," Velani said. "You can take my offer or not. If not, I'll thank you for your time and be on my way."

The Caspian regarded him for several moments before barking laughter that had nearby travelers turning their heads. He sobered, still chuckling in amusement, when one of his men approached him. "Delphi, you are so very much past that option already." He waved Velani's panicked reply aside to study a small screen that was being shown to him.

The data concerned the Air Command pilot that had brought the Shantir here to Feron. He had been imaged and identified, and Pe Khoja read the information with growing interest. Undistinguished record, long list of transgressions and misdemeanors, questionable associations, frequent transfers from one command to the next. Hunter Class pilot and exceptional marksman. Perfect, Pe Khoja thought. Then another item caught his eye. He glanced up at his aide. "Really?" The information listed among the pilot's past and close associates one Captain Nova Whiteside.

"Confirmed."

Pe Khoja grinned, showing sharp teeth. Tharron had not been pleased to learn that Whiteside, long a thorn in his side, had been assigned to the boy's father. No doubt she was using her considerable tenacity at this very moment to track them down. She had become a symbol of Union presence to their

K'lar leader and he blamed her even for events in which she had had no part at all. It seemed that whenever one of their schemes failed or was foiled by the Union, Whiteside was sure to be listed among the reasons. And now her old boyfriend was applying for a job. This might be fun.

He turned his attention back to the Delphian. "Tharron will want some proof that you're sincere, wizard. For all we know, the Union sent you to spy on us and play your mental tricks with us all." Pe Khoja groaned inwardly for having voiced such nonsense.

Velani bristled. "I assure you I am sincere. I care nothing about Union dealings."

The Caspian pretended to ponder a while. "We'll make this simple. You tell me where we can find Nova Whiteside, and I'll take that as proof we can trust you."

Velani gasped. "Nova... What does this have to do with the captain?"

"Nothing. We'd just like to know where she is."

"So you can murder her."

"It's what we do."

Velani shifted in his chair and cast his eyes around the concourse for some way of starting this whole sorry day over again. This had all gone too fast! He had meant to make inquiries, perhaps get information from one of the rebels embedded among the Union pilots on Targon. Maybe convey hints that he was interested in taking a closer look at the Tughan-to-be. Instead, Fynn Bridger had bundled him onto a cramped and filth-encrusted cruiser and shipped him all the way out to Feron, barely speaking throughout the two-jump journey it took to get here. And here he was. With this Caspian who was surely no minor follower among Tharron's men. It had not taken Pe Khoja's threat to make clear that there was no turning back from here.

He squared his shoulders. It mattered not. There was no price too high to pay for finding Kiran before the others did.

"The captain is irrelevant to me," he said. "They left days ago with the colonel on some errand. I know not what. After that, they will be on Magra until a transport from the Badlands comes in."

"Tychon is with her?"

"You asked about the captain!"

Pe Khoja stood up and waved to his men to keep an eye on the Delphian while he sauntered over to where Fynn Bridger loitered. He leaned against a pillar and regarded the Human silently. Brawn, enough scars to evidence hands-on experience, probably not a lot of scruples, if judged by his records. His visible weapons were excellent and well cared-for.

Fynn returned his stare. "See something?"

"Not so far," Pe Khoja said. "Quinlan vouched for you. What do you want from us?"

"Not a damn thing. I want out of Targon. Out of Air Command. You need pilots."

"We do."

"So am I in?"

Pe Khoja put his hand on the man's shoulder and steered him back toward Velani. "I have a job for you," he said. "Then we'll see."

EIGHT

Five days after the council on Coup d'Oeil, the Eagle brought Nova down onto the airfields of Deen. By unspoken agreement, this Magran city was frequented by Union personnel just as another, distant town received Tharron's planes. Parts of the planet were eternally at war and not at all opposed to using the larger conflict between Union and rebel to their advantage. Corruption ruled the distribution of smuggled weapons on both sides and few of the main continents were unaffected by the ravages these battles wrought.

Nova arranged for the servicing of the ship by a trusted outfit that called itself Extra Spatial and borrowed a skimmer from the owner, soon on her way along the coast to where Tychon and his group waited.

She had hoped that the drive along the pretty countryside would ease her apprehension and the suffocating feeling that something dark and ominous hovered just over her shoulder. The lonely trip back from Targon had offered few distractions from the nagging sense of doom that had come aboard as soon as Colonel Carras had disembarked.

Although she had dreaded a two-day confinement aboard

the small ship with the colonel on the way back from Coup d'Oeil, it had been interesting. He used the time working on whatever it was that didn't concern junior officers, but they had also spent hours poring over intelligence reports, contacting remote outposts, reviewing files about the more important rebel leaders and trading bits of non-restricted information with Tychon for as long as he was in communication range. Systematically, they eliminated many locations for being too remote or too inhospitable, sympathizers with too much at stake, governments too beholden to the Union to want to harbor a stolen Delphian child, for whatever reason.

Carras arranged to have Anders Devaughn placed under his command. Given Anders' position on Delphi, he would be able to monitor the movements of the Shantirs who had no means of leaving the planet without using the Union base. For his part, Velani readily agreed that none of the Shantirs that knew of Kiran's design must know of his disappearance. If asked, he would maintain the fiction that Tychon still kept the boy hidden and refused to return him to Phera's family.

Carras had emerged from Tychon's cabin as they neared Targon, carrying his travel kit. He dropped it near the cargo bay door and came into the main room.

"Captain," he said. "Please join me up here."

She left the cockpit. "There's not even time for tea. We're on approach."

He shook his head and sat on one of the map table chairs. "I have to thank you for an enjoyable few days, Captain. Major Tychon is correct in his assessment of you and I'm glad to have you on my Vanguard."

"Thank you, sir. I've learned a lot from both of you."

He took his wrist array and sidearm from where he had left them on the map table and fussed with their adjustment. "I've studied you, too, over these past few days," he said finally. "Well, I've studied you since you joined my Vanguard."

"Yes..." she began, mystified and a little disturbed by his solemn demeanor.

"Your loyalty to the Union is absolute; you follow orders even if they don't reflect your own views. You have no trouble expressing those, as I've experienced myself, but you don't deviate from a directive."

"No, of course not, sir."

"You have also shown that you perform well under duress and in isolation. The Naiya incident was a tough test of your loyalties. I'm familiar with some of the... the actions you've taken part of on Bellac and Ud Mrak."

She said nothing. There was nothing to say. What was he getting at? Whatever it was, he spoke to her as a superior officer, not the man looking for a cup of tea before landing. She realized that, as he had talked, she had squared her shoulders, feet firmly planted, her hands clasped behind her back.

"I am going to give you an order, Captain."

"Yessir."

"It could take weeks or months before we can get even a hunch about where the boy is being held. But I believe that we will find him. We have as many spies and scouts in Tharron's camp as he does in ours."

She waited.

"Your orders are to retrieve the child and return him to Delphi by whatever means necessary."

"I'm aware, sir."

He paused. "If there comes a moment, Captain, that this mission is in danger of failing. If the boy proves to be irretrievable. If you find that any... damage has been done to him already. If there is any chance that they will escape with him again..."

Nova's breath caught in her throat.

"You will terminate him."

"Sir, I..." she began. "Kiran? You want me to kill Tychon's son?"

"I do." He stood up and paced as much as the small space allowed. "I cannot order Major Tychon to do this. There are limits to what even he is willing and able to do. And certainly to what I am willing to ask of him."

"Sir, I don't know if I can do this. Don't ask this of me, either!"

He ground his teeth. "I am not asking, Captain. There is no one else as close to Tychon as you are. If I replace you now with another agent, he will know. He cannot know."

"He will kill me," she said, but that fact was not foremost on her mind. He would not just kill her. This would kill him as well. Losing Kiran, too, in this war would hurt him in ways that the colonel likely understood. But losing him at Nova's hands would destroy him utterly. She had seen the unspeakable fury he unleashed upon his Rhuwac victims; how much more hatred would he feel for her and her kind if she took his son?

"Yes, he may. I will arrange an immediate transfer to a safe location for you."

She closed her eyes. Did he really not know? Had he not seen the way Tychon looked at her when he thought no one else was watching? Had he not noticed their stolen kisses and furtive touches over these past few days? Could he not tell that just seeing Tychon walk into the room lit a delicious spark of pleasure deep inside her body? They had kept Vanguard Three waiting on the airfield after Carras left for his meeting, barely shutting the gate before tearing out of their clothes to make up for four days of pretense and unrelenting craving. Was it really not obvious?

She looked into his face, and the answer was clearly written there. He did not want to know. He had allowed himself to become too close to his subordinates and now the order handed to him by their governors was sure to devastate them all. There was no truth about Tychon and her that he wanted to hear at this moment.

"It may not come to that. I have faith in your abilities. But your lives cannot come before the safety of thousands of others. We cannot take chances. Do your job."

Remembering this painful conversation, Nova looked out over the pink-tinted dunes that drifted past the dome of her air car as she sped along the deserted coast. There was no more clarity for her than when she had left Carras on Targon. It was too large a concept to grapple, slipping out of her reach as soon as she tried to get a firm grip on it. Could she do what Carras had ordered? Was the threat of this Tughan really so great?

"Whoa!" She pulled up on the skimmer's controls when she nearly collided with the remains of a shuttle that had crashed into the shoreline rocks.

Tychon had warned her during her approach to Magra that they had suffered a rebel attack on the previous evening, but the destruction she saw here was far more extensive than he reported.

She slowed her skimmer, hovering close to the ground, when she approached the remains of a town. She retracted the car's canopy and attached an interface link to tap into the skimmer's sensors to enhance her own.

The settlement was ruined. Besides the scorch marks of laser fire, she saw evidence of explosives as well as percussion charges. Roofs were caved in; many houses had been reduced to mere outlines in stone. Dead animals lay scattered here and there but the casualties had been removed. Why would anyone destroy a fishing village?

Her scanner showed a cluster of people nearby, thankfully standing upright. She settled the skimmer noiselessly onto the ground and moved along the silent street until she heard voices coming from one of the larger buildings still more or less erect. Her weapon drawn, she entered, stepping around a door that had been blown from its hinges. "Major?" she called when she recognized one of the voices.

"In here," came the reply.

Tychon was standing amid the rubble caved in from above. A few Vanguard officers were with him; one of them held a map, another was poking at a computer screen. She felt a quick stab of excitement when she saw Tychon and then once again the weight of that ugly *something* descended over her, reminding her that things just weren't as alright as they had been just a few days ago. He glanced up when she entered and then returned his gaze to the map. When she joined them he touched her arm in greeting.

"Shri-Lan?" she asked. She nodded to Vanguard One's Major Adachi and smiled when she saw Dylan perched on a blasted window sill. He waved and smiled back and she thought how much more tired he looked since she last saw him on Myra. They all looked tired. Their fatigues were dust-covered and stained and even Tychon looked disheveled.

"Yes. Retaliation for the ship from Nebdan we took," he said.

"Why this place?"

"These people were Centauri, not Magran. There'll be less of an uproar over this among the locals, but it'll send a clear message to Targon."

"Casualties?"

"Nearly half. It was a complete surprise. There were almost a hundred and fifty settlers here this time of year." He cursed, a rare occurrence. "We didn't get here fast enough. Cubber, any news from Stormer and Haddad?"

The man whose neural interface was plugged into the computer in front of him nodded. "Coming in from the city. Should be here shortly."

Nova strolled over to Dylan. "Been fun?" She hopped onto the sill beside him.

"Not the way I'd put it," he replied, making room for her. "Last night was bad. Just one air assault after another. We didn't get here until most of the damage was done. Then just hours of endless sniping for no damn reason. Now we're just waiting for the clean-up crew to finish so we can get out of this hole." He shrugged tiredly. "But, overall, not a bad assignment. Adachi is a solid CO, if you can deal with his snoring. How are things with the..." he coughed, catching himself. "Major."

Nova looked over to Tychon and Adachi engrossed in conversation over their map. "Best spanner I've ever watched," she said, looking for a new subject. "Were you guys on Aram when that went down?"

He nodded. "Never been so damn cold in my life! Took a

blast in the leg, but we had a good medic. Awful lot of casualties."

"You kids! Get away from the damn window!"

Both Dylan and Nova obeyed the command before realizing that it had issued from outside the building, delivered by a bellicose voice that could only have originated in Bowie Haddad's barrel chest. She heard Cubber's mocking laugh when he saw them leap from the sill.

Haddad was a legend among the younger officers. His experience as the longest-lived Vanguard member and his vast inventory of tales made him a frequent lecturer at the academies and training upgrades. Nova thought that, if they weren't on alert and likely to fire back at once, he would have aimed a shot at the window to teach them a lesson.

He marched into the room, his large frame nearly filling the doorway. His co-pilot, half his size, followed in his wake along with their spanner. The frail Centauri was burdened with several bags and parcels, and Dylan moved to help her with the load.

"Thought you folks might want some real food," Haddad boomed. He gestured to Dylan. "Step lively, boy. Let's have a bite before your bosses perish for lack of edibles."

Dylan grinned and started to unpack the parcels. The very presence of this animated individual was enough to lighten the somber mood permeating this room. The others rearranged themselves around the scatter of broken furniture and masonry and began to pass around boxes and bowls of food that looked and smelled like it had originated in a real kitchen. Haddad himself set up a portable unit to brew cups of steaming and fragrant tea.

Nova perched close to Tychon on an upended storage box before she caught a few amused glances from her squadron mates. Too late to shift to a more respectful distance now, she turned her attention to unwrapping a foil parcel.

Tychon looked up. "Try this rice thing." He passed his bowl to her. "Wonderful, whatever it is."

Nova blushed for no particular reason and then cursed

herself for it.

Bowie Haddad cleared his throat, which, like most of the noises that emitted from him, was thunderous. "So, now that we're all tucked in, how about we find out what we're doing out here, other than count bodies."

"The last evac is headed back to Deen," Cubber reported. "We're clear."

Tychon nodded to him and sipped his tea. "I've already briefed V6 and Nine," he said. "They've left for some leads on Pelion and Targon." Briefly, and without delving into any of the details that made this matter so very personal to him, he outlined the problem of the Tughan Wai. Nova watched the faces of those around her. Dylan stared open-mouthed, Adachi's lips had formed a thin, hard line. Haddad had stopped chewing. Cubber's attention was on his sensors, but both of Haddad's officers looked every bit as alarmed as Dylan by the time Tychon had finished.

"Forgive me for saying so, Ty," Bowie Haddad said after a pause, "but your Delphi wizards are tragically disturbed individuals."

Tychon shrugged. "I am in agreement there," he said, reaching for more tea. Nova recognized the tilt of his body and realized that his composure was largely false. Not because of Haddad's opinion of Shantirs but because he had taken great pains to play down the fact that the Tughan Wai was his only son, likely the only child he would ever have. She glanced at Haddad's female navigator and saw that realization there, too.

"We've got orders from Carras," Tychon continued. "Covert operation, as per the Ten. No real support till we find something."

Nova heard Haddad curse.

"Adachi is going to head out to Aram."

This time Dylan swore.

"Whiteside and I are going to see what's to be found on Delphi. Captain Devaughn has also been briefed and will work with the Council and the Shantirate. That leaves Magra Torley to you, Bowie. I thought you'd enjoy turning a few rebel dives upside down."

Haddad laughed, startling Cubber from his work with the scanners. "Got that right! I'm also interested in whoever decided to remove this place from the map."

"Did they say why we can't get more support?" Dylan asked. "With a hundred scouts on the ground, we could shake down a lot more places than we can with a dozen."

"Because it's Delphi," Nova said.

Tychon turned his head, curious.

"Union governors don't want this getting out," she continued. "What Delphi did once they can do again. We here are just doing damage control, but you can be sure that the Union and the Clan Council are huddling right now. Imagine if this sort of mental ability becomes more commonplace. We don't guard Delphi so tightly just because of their resources, the crystal or the water, or because the rebels might want to recruit pilots from there." She shook her head. "Delphi isn't even officially a Commonwealth member. It's their other talents that have everyone worried. So the last thing anyone wants is for outsiders to know what these folks can really do with their heads."

"Thanks, Whiteside," Tychon said drily. "Don't all look at me like I've got three noses. She's talking about a future generation. And mostly politics. I don't know what the Shantirs are up to, and I don't care. This is now. And speaking of now, Carras wants a debrief while we're all here."

The others got busy with their data systems, not without another speculative glance at the Delphian among them. Cubber recorded their reports as each downloaded information about their work on various assignments into the message going back to Targon.

There had been the surprise rebel attack on the peaceful colony of Nebdan. Settlers murdered, whole families taken to slave camps on Drar Drogh, livestock and machinery destroyed. Not just by Shri-Lan, but the Arawaj faction, increasingly willing to cooperate with Tharron, was also implicated.

There had been the evacuation of Pelion's third moon, Bria. Vanguard Nine and One had made countless trips to protect the refugee ships as they ran before Tharron's guerrillas. Bria was laid to waste.

There had been the loss of one of the super stations, Skyranch Eight. Haddad's team had arrived in time to watch it fragment. Two thousand dead.

And there had been the rebel takeover of Zera, dangerously close to Targon and Delphi. A costly counter offensive won the planet back only after heavy losses.

Adachi reported on yet another lab suspected on Bellac where Tharron's people dabbled with defoliants, viruses and nerve gasses. Doctor Comori was becoming more inventive. And cheaper than the hardware required to destroy towns like this one.

Nova listened silently, more distraught with each account. Was there nothing Tharron considered out of bounds? Nothing sacred? Hiding his outposts among civilian populations, he carried out his operations in plain sight, safe in the knowledge that the Union's dealings were ruled by public opinion. Instead of conducting all-out warfare against the scattered rebel armies, much of the Union's methods were preventative. Using special ops teams like the Vanguard remained the most effective method against places like Tamotsu Comori's laboratories, but for every scheme they uncovered, his people devised three more.

She looked around the demolished room, saw her squadron mates, heavily armed, dirty, combat-ready but exhausted, perched on broken bits of other people's lives. Eagle Eight had been destroyed with all hands two weeks ago. Eagle Twelve was gone, too. How would any of them stop Tharron if the rebel leader was handed a weapon that needed nothing more than a cheap ticket on a commuter transport to wreak destruction that would otherwise require ships, explosives, manpower and currency? What more would the K'lar leader be willing to do? How many more civilians would get in his way?

Her eyes lit on Tychon, who had also fallen into a dismal

mood as the reports continued. Perhaps Colonel Carras was right. How could the sacrifice he demanded of Tychon possibly measure up against the horror of these events? Even Tychon would not put Kiran's life ahead of so many others. But would he pull that trigger? Nova looked into her bowl of rice as if to find the answers there. But like her tea cup it was empty, and no leaves at the bottom revealed what lay ahead.

"Boys," Cubber said, looking up from his screen. "And assorted not-boys. Time to do the dishes. Bogeys coming in fast."

All of them came to their feet. "Let's bug out, then," Haddad said. "I'll rush into their waiting arms while you get skyward. It's Shrill-hunting time!"

"We'll come along," Adachi said. "Whiteside left her Eagle in Deen for some light housekeeping. Let's give them a head start."

Haddad laughed raucously. "What's a little flak compared to clean sheets, I always say."

She wrinkled her nose at him. "Eagle was out of air. And coolant."

The group filed out of the building. Vanguard Two and One were airborne and heading toward the rebel recon group before Tychon and Nova had even reached her skimmer.

"How did it go with Carras?" Tychon asked.

"Fine. I didn't stay long on Targon."

"Because you missed me?" He placed a hand on her rump. "So much so that you couldn't wait to get back here and forgot to load up some air?"

Nova frowned, irritated by his mild censure. She gestured back toward the ruined building. "I suppose those boys all think I'm sleeping with you."

"You *are* sleeping with me." He peered into her face. "What's wrong?"

She shrugged. "They don't need to know, that's all."

"Nova, they don't care! They know you didn't sleep your way into Vanguard, if that's what you're worried about. Bowie had you vetted for the team months ago when he was lecturing on Myra. In fact, he wanted you for V2, but he needed a spanner so he drew the little Centauri, whatever her name is." He grinned. "I'm convinced I got the better deal." He climbed into the skimmer. "It gets lonely out here, Nova. Don't think that Dylan and Cubber aren't sharing a bunk, and Adachi couldn't care less as long as they do that quietly. Frankly, Dylan would look good to me, too, after a few weeks on Aram. You drive."

Nova was silent on their flight back to Deen. They hurried over an inland road through tall vegetation to hide them from distant eyes. Haddad and Adachi were doing their job. No Shrill found its way out to the coast to harass them on their way back to the airfield.

She stole glances at Tychon's sharp profile as they drove. He was lost in some khamal that allowed him to recharge without needing sleep and she read nothing but tranquility there. She recalled her brief conversation with Anders Devaughn on their way back from K'lar. Had he been right when he told her about the distance between a Delphian's body and his soul? Was Tychon's affection for her little more than simply gratitude for sharing his bed? Having given his heart once, would he really never do so again? Perhaps that was all there was 'out here'. Sex for convenience on a lonely and dangerous mission.

* * *

"You are beyond the definition of utterly awe-inspiring," Tychon opined when he saw the connectors leading to the Eagle at the service station on the outskirts of Deen. One of them was a water hookup. "I am going to stand in the shower for about an hour, I think."

They passed through the cargo space and into the interior of the ship.

"No, you're not," she said. She unbuckled his weapons belt and let it drop to the floor.

"I'm a filthy mess, Nova," he protested, not especially forcefully when she stepped into his embrace.

She kissed him. It was not a tender kiss.

"My boots. Can I–"

"No. Leave them." She loosened her waistband and let her pants slip to the floor. Once he pulled her shirt over her head she pressed her body against his and he grunted in surprise when she ground her hip against him.

He nudged her backward until she dropped onto the cabin lounger. She pulled him down with her and flipped him onto his back as he fell. Astride him now, she kissed him and when his fingers brushed over the interface nodes at her temples, she felt his gentle touch inside her mind just as she felt it on her skin. Too gentle.

"You're a live wire," he murmured, perceiving the tension that occupied her conscious mind. "What's got you so–"

She gripped the collar of his fatigues and stopped his words with another kiss, demanding from him the thoughtless oblivion that their mental and physical coupling brought. She wanted to stop thinking, to feel him inside her head and her body and let his powerful presence erase the orders she had been given and the doubts in her mind.

He needed no further persuasion, and within moments he grasped her hips to pull her over himself. She groaned and began to move, slowly, until his patience broke and he pulled her down to turn her onto her back, his movements as rough as she needed him to be. Nova clutched his clothes, feeling the rasp of the coarse fabric and the hard edges of fasteners and buckles digging into her skin as he moved, lost in the ancient rhythms that their mental connection churned into a tempest of physical ecstasy. Both of them held back for as long as they could until, finally, Nova cried out and he pulled her close, finding his own release in almost painful bolts of pleasure.

He collapsed drunkenly, struggling to catch his breath.

Nova squirmed out from under him. "All right," she said, equally breathless. "You can go have your bath now."

"Thank you, Captain," he gasped and flopped onto his back. "I had no idea you were that fond of uniforms." He watched his hand move through a long strand of her hair.

"Feel better now?" he said.

"Hmm? Oh yes, don't you?"

"I was just fine." He stroked a finger along an angry red mark left behind by his collar clasp. "What is bothering you?"

"Not a thing. Go get cleaned up."

"Don't go anywhere. We're not done here."

"Yessir!"

He struggled across her and off the lounger, dropping pieces of his clothing as he headed for the tiny bath stall that connected the two sleeping cabins.

Nova stretched and purred, feeling tired and content but not enough of either to fall asleep before he returned from his shower. She made an attempt at straightening the rumpled blankets when something near the cockpit caught her eye.

Not long later, Tychon re-entered the cabin wearing a long robe, apparently not ready to make good on his promise to spend an hour in the bath. He found her by the communications station. "I appreciate that you're naked, but can you be that in bed?" He stood behind her and nuzzled her neck. "This control board is a bit too fragile for what I have in mind."

"Aaag, your hair is wet!" she protested. "Look."

"Hmm?"

"Message. From K'lar."

He lifted his head. "K'lar? What does it say?"

"You won't believe it. Someone has information about Kiran."

He nudged her aside and bent to the screen to read the written message. It was barely literate and sprinkled with words from several languages, but the message was clear. The sender promised information about Kiran's location if they met him or her on Tor Ag, a distant, relatively neutral planet that Nova had not visited before.

"What do you think?" she said.

He ran his hands through his hair. "Seems a little fortuitous, doesn't it? Rebels selling each other out already?"

"Rebels are rebels," she said. "But how did they find us

here? I didn't file a flight plan. Someone must have tracked me from Targon to see what jumpsite I'd be using. The Eagle should have noticed that, even if I didn't."

He nodded thoughtfully and then gestured at the screen. "We should check this out."

"We should look for the rest of the message," she said. "Must have gotten lost."

"What rest?"

"The bit that says 'It's a trap'."

"Oh, that." He shrugged. "We can't *not* check it out. I'll send a report to Carras. We'll leave in the morning." He spent a few moments in silent contemplation of her and then steered her back to the lounger. "I need you to do something for me."

She reclined enticingly. "What did you have in mind?"

He snatched something from a compartment by the map table and joined her on the bed. "We may have to deal with some government bodies to get to Kiran. If he's being held on a planet where we have some influence, we can get by with Vanguard clearance, but you may need more identification if we split up."

"No splitting up," she pouted. She put her hand on his thigh. "I work better in a team."

"Sure you do. Anyway, hang on to this. If you need proof that you're acting on my behalf, it will give you that authority." He opened a small leather pouch and upended it into his palm. What tumbled out was an octagonal plate of metal with deeply etched engravings she recognized as Delphian lettering. Hesitantly, Nova ran a finger over the glyphs and then turned the plate over in his palm. Two metal bands held a large, flat sapphire onto the back. The jewel had the look and feel of something old and very sacred.

"Ty," she said, awed. "That... that's your sigil, isn't it?" She looked up, stunned.

"Yes. Although it escapes me how those idiots at the school could have mistaken a forgery for it. There is a lot of information in there that you can scan, but not record on it." He pointed out a thin layer running through the disk itself.

"The stone is just pretty."

Nova bit her lip. "This is... I mean... this is your sigil!" She looked into his face, again feeling the dark weight that Carras had placed on her shoulders pressing down on them. This jewel was more than just identification. It had to do with clans and affinities and so many other things that she still didn't understand about Delphi. She did know it was not traded casually. "Thank you. For... for trusting me with this."

He placed it into her hand. "Just keep it safe."

NINE

Tor Ag proved to be dreary. The most interesting color here was gray in various shades of boring. Gray mist hung in the air and gray ooze covered the ground. Nova shook her feet with every step. Although the surface appeared solid, she sunk ankle-deep into a powdery mass before finding a firm foothold. The dry substance seeped back into place where they had walked, leaving no tracks.

"You come here often?" Nova peered at Tychon over her respirator, still able to smell ammonia. She kicked at the dust around her feet, sending up a billowing cloud of grayness. Her eyes were watering and felt raw.

He scanned the empty, blurred street over his own mask. Few of Tor Ag's inhabitants walked, preferring the safety of covered sleds that moved noiselessly over the surface dust. "I think that's the place over there."

"This is disgusting."

The moistureless clouds were less dense here than they had been on the airfield and she could spot gnarled shapes of gray vegetation between shuttered buildings. She, who was well used to the dead emptiness of space, suddenly wished for even the slightest fragment of color. A single green leaf would have been a relief. Those withered bits of shrubbery seemed to exist without the chlorophyll so vitally needed in most of the places she had visited. How could anything grow in this world?

Walking closer to Tychon, she looked up at the sun she knew to be there and saw only a milky brightness, exactly where it had been when they had landed here a few hours ago. She shivered. When he stopped to consult the screen on his forearm her eyes adhered to the patch of bright red shirt by his collar. She wished he hadn't worn his gray duster over it.

Tychon led them into another, equally deserted street. They moved slowly, alert to what may come to meet them, but their guns remained holstered. She touched his elbow when she spotted the open bay door of the repair station they had been instructed to find. Both of them stopped at a distance from the building, raising their hands slightly to show they were empty. Just inside the storage area, four hulking figures waited in the drifts of fog settling among crates and barrels.

The one in front, a stooped and thickly-robed K'lar, gestured to them.

"Out here is fine," Nova said. "We prefer the fresh air."

The K'lar stepped out of the shelter, his guards close behind. Nova saw scaled, tufted skin and recognized the shambling creatures as Rhuwacs. Her skin crawled and she fought the impulse to take a few steps back. She glanced at Tychon but, except for a fleeting twitch of his upper lip, his expression remained carefully neutral.

"You." The K'lar pointed at Nova. "Whiteside?"

She nodded.

He held up two thick fingers. "Two hundred."

She gasped, surprised by the amount.

Tychon reached into a pocket and withdrew a clear plastic case of triangular tokens. He shook it. "Proof?"

"Have tape," the K'lar said, using an awkward mix of Union mainvoice and bits of his own language. "Picture tape. Delphi boy good. Not problem."

"How did you get that?" Nova asked.

"No askings. Boy not far."

"Where? Here on Tor Ag?"

"No. Give that." He raised his hand toward Tychon and the box of coins. But then he groaned, and his eyes widened to show more of the yellows. He stumbled back a few steps, and none of his Rhuwacs caught him when he crumpled to the ground. A new hole in his dirty robe quickly stained with blood. No one had heard the shot that had taken the rebel down.

Tychon's weapon was in his hand and one of the Rhuwacs fell even before any of the others had comprehended what had happened. "Come on!"

"Wait!" Nova squatted beside the writhing K'lar and held her breath as she searched his pockets.

The other two Rhuwacs now roared something unintelligible and one lunged at her even as her fingers closed over a small, round object. She whirled to run after Tychon, back to the main street and the airfield, leaving the slow-moving Rhuwacs behind.

"Told you there was another part to that message, didn't I?" Nova panted when she had caught up with Tychon.

He dodged into an alley when a large shape loomed out of the mist. "Rhuwacs up ahead."

They raced through a maze of alleys and narrow streets to reach the safety of the Eagle. A look over her shoulder confirmed that more Rhuwacs followed. Nova stumbled over something hidden in the layer of surface dust and barely caught herself. An icy pain shot through her foot. Tychon had sprinted ahead, far ahead, before he turned to see her no longer following.

"Nova!"

Three Rhuwacs were only steps behind her. Without time to turn and aim her own weapon, she limped onward, pain flaring up from her foot in measurable bolts of agony. She could almost feel the Rhuwacs behind her and heard their strained gasps for air. She was losing ground now, her strength ebbing. Her respirator had come loose and her throat was on fire.

Two of her pursuers galloped past her, toward Tychon, their guns forcing him to duck into a doorway.

Then she felt a rough, scaled hand grab a fistful of her hair and jerk her off her feet. She sprawled into the dust, desperately twisting around to get her gun between herself and the beast looming over her. He wrenched the weapon from her grip and tossed it aside.

She looked up into the brutal face of her captor. Two rows of teeth angled like ancient tombstones and cold, thoughtless eyes stared at her above a splayed, scarred nose. His carrion stench blasted her face. She noted all this with interest, observing her terror as part of this nightmare. He was leaning on her with one hand in the pit of her stomach and she realized dimly that she could not breathe. A knife was pressed under her chin, its tip already piercing the skin.

The Rhuwac mumbled something and an idiotic grin pulled his heavy features into a carnival mask that Nova had seen, long ago, when she had been a child growing up on Skyranch Four. She hadn't understood the mask until now.

Then he was not there anymore.

Tychon was there instead, staring down at the fallen Rhuwac, his gun still in his hand. The loose strands of hair and the thick billows of dust did not obscure the boundless hate and rage burning in his eyes. In one quick motion, he twisted the knife from the Rhuwac's grip and slashed at the large body.

Nova rolled away, frightened by the sounds now bursting from the beast. The sour taste of bile rose in her throat when she saw where Tychon was inflicting horrible wounds. Blood spurted from a severed femoral artery.

"Gods, Ty! Kill him! Finish it!"

Tychon looked from the blade in his hand to Nova as if surprised by their presence. He flung the knife aside and killed the Rhuwac with his gun. His arms were drenched in blood to the elbows.

"We're even," he said.

Nova blacked out, almost gratefully.

She was vaguely aware of being picked up and carried back

to the airfield. No one stopped them, no one came to help. Like on other worlds she had seen, rebel matters were left to rebels and the locals had learned to stay out of their way.

When he put her down, she could see the Eagle's scuffed hull crouching in the rolling mist, uninviting and unfamiliar. She longed to be within its clean, comfortable interior and gone, long gone.

"Are you all right?" he said. "Let's get you some air before you pass out again. You hurt your foot?"

She leaned heavily on his arm, willing herself not to throw up. "Ty, you cut his... You didn't have to..."

"Shouldn't attack Union officers." Tychon's voice was roughened by more than the ammonia in the air. He wiped at the blood that trickled along her neck. He was gentler when he helped her into the ship.

They launched and left orbit, more to quit this dismal planet than any real need to hurry. The autopilot took them away from Tor Ag and Nova felt better with every minute that passed.

Tychon winced as much as she did when he removed her boots to reveal a bruised ankle. He helped her pull off her torn and blood-stained clothes and then removed his also, stuffing all of it into a bag which he then tossed into the cargo hold where the smell of ammonia could not reach them. They cleaned up the blood, dust and gore and slipped into clean clothes before he examined her foot. Neither the cut on her neck nor the bruised ankle was especially worrisome.

"I wonder who shot that K'lar," she said.

He placed a cold pack on her ankle. "Wish I knew. The lizards must have thought it was me. Too stupid to see I was carrying a laser."

Nova was uneager to discuss the Rhuwacs. "Probably another rebel, shooting the K'lar for being a traitor. Oh, the tape!"

"Huh?"

"I got a disk from that man."

He went back into the cargo bay to dig through her clothes.

"Found it," she heard him call. He re-entered the cabin, thoughtfully examining the small spool in his hand. "Centauri markings."

"Do we have something to play it on?"

"I think so. The main screen, maybe."

He helped her hobble to the cockpit where she waited until he had inserted the spool into an adapter. When he settled into his bench she climbed into his lap. He smiled and wrapped his arms around her after making sure that her cold pack was back in place on her foot.

The tape threaded slow. Tychon adjusted the unit until most of the static cleared. They saw an image of a two-storied building. The picture shook as the viewer moved closer. A high wire fence surrounded the house. Dense forest formed a background.

"Look!" Nova exclaimed.

Two children crouched within the small yard, intent on a game. They wore only short pants, their feet bare. Tychon swallowed hard when one of them flung a mass of blue curls back over his shoulder. The other was no larger than a toddler, with startling blond hair and very dark skin.

The door to the house opened and a K'lar woman appeared, speaking to the children. They seemed to understand a command and rose to pick up a few toys. The smaller child shouted something and tried to wrestle Kiran to the ground.

The woman grabbed each boy by an arm to pull them apart, but when she half-turned to the camera an indulgent smile was clear on her face. She ruffled Kiran's hair and the three walked into the house, Kiran's arm wrapped loosely around the woman's thick waist.

The image dissolved into static. Nova felt Tychon breathing evenly in the dark of the cockpit, but she knew by now that this would be no barometer of the turmoil he felt.

"He's fine, Ty," she said.

He absently stroked her hair. "Yes."

She looked up at him. "Are you?"

He kissed her before rising from the couch, taking her

along with him. He crossed the cabin and placed her onto the lounger. "I am. You should get some sleep. Do you need something for the pain in your foot?"

"No. Are you coming to bed?"

"In a while. I want to study the tape for a bit."

TEN

Velani leaned heavily against the wooden frame of the door to the boy's room. His heart beat high in his throat when he saw Kiran on the floor, his blue-topped head bent over a captured rodent in a jar. Velani clasped his nervous hands and sought to control his emotions.

He had arrived!

After their meeting in that cesspit on Feron, Pe Khoja had spirited Velani away on his ship while sending the Delphian's hired pilot on another errand. The trip had taken forever, spanning several breaches, including one so deep that Velani had spent most of the time in fearful prayer. For the long intervals between jumps, he had remained in a soothing khamal that allowed him to avoid any thought but that which concerned the Tughan Wai.

Velani shuddered when he recalled his meeting with Pe Khoja. He hadn't needed to touch the Caspian's mind to perceive the sociopathic void that passed for his soul and the terrible intelligence that guided his spirit. No wonder the Union sought so desperately to rid themselves of men like him. Velani suspected that Delphi's relative isolation had so far sheltered him from a great many things he preferred not to even think about.

Too bad about Nova. Although merely Human, he had sensed a great strength there and he had not missed Tychon's attachment to her. Briefly, he wondered if the rebels, in their quest to rid themselves of her, would also harm Tychon, his kinsman. He pushed that thought aside, too. The high price paid seemed insignificant to the prize that was soon to be his.

Upon Velani's arrival on Shaddallam, Tharron had brought Velani before him and, lavishly, offered him control of Delphi once the Tughan had driven the Union out of Trans-Targon.

Velani had not even expected this boon, so focused was he on the opportunity to meet the Tughan Wai. But Delphi was his birthright! A birthright stolen from him when Phera disowned him for offering Kiran to the Shantirate almost six years ago. Then, rubbing salt into Velani's wounds, Phera had made Kiran his heir, binding him to Delphi's court lest he be tempted to leave the necessary protection of the Shantirate. It had been Phera's mistake to allow Tychon to take the child from Delphi.

Velani took a few steps into the room. "Kiran?"

"Shan Velani!" The child jumped up and raced toward his uncle. "Have you come to take me back to Feyd? Can we leave now?"

His uncle awkwardly patted the boy's curls. "Not yet, Kiran. I don't have a plane to go that far, you see? Your father will come for you soon."

"Yes, Shanee, Ema said you need an Eagle to come all that way. Only Dadda has an Eagle."

How easy this deception was! Too young to understand space travel and well used to his father's frequent absences, none of this seemed troublesome to the child. He had simply gotten lost and Tychon would soon come to take him home.

"Indeed he does," Velani said. He pulled up a chair. "Tychon asked me to check up on you once in a while until he can get here." He held out a hand. "May I?"

In answer, the boy stepped closer and Velani touched his forehead.

Tell me how you like it here. Are the people nice? he asked conversationally. *Is that a midgie in that bottle?*

Kiran began to relate his feelings about Shaddallam, mentally prattling about his day, which revolved mostly around his nurse, Ema, and a few of the diminutive Shaddallama children still living in this town. Barely listening, Velani closed his eyes and began to pry into Kiran's complex levels of consciousness.

It was there!

It was all there, as planned. Lying dormant within Kiran was the knowledge and the power to give life to the Tughan Wai. Lesser beings would grant him the title of God when his ability to manipulate the secret harmonics of subspace would make him appear to change matter and energy. Entire sections of the boy's cortex seemed re-wired yet still asleep, offering infinite possibility, waiting only for the key to put it all together. Velani sighed, tempted to search further.

No! The khamal slammed shut, expelling Velani with enough force to cause physical pain. His hands flew to his temples.

"I'm sorry, Shanee!" Kiran cried. "I don't know why I did that. Did I hurt you?" The boy's lower lip trembled.

Velani blinked at him, dazed. "No, of course not." He forced a wan smile. "You can go back to your midgie now. I will see you at breakfast." He rose abruptly and staggered into the corridor, blindly feeling his way along the hall while a murderous pain in his head nearly brought him to his knees.

Of course! Certain safeguards had been installed to protect the sleeping Tughan from hapless intruders. There was so much to learn! He found his way into the room where the K'lar giant awaited his analysis.

"Well?" Tharron growled. He had been in an expansive, easy mood upon Velani's arrival. Now his sour expression warned of barely restrained fury. His fist, as usual, gripped a bottle of vile-smelling liquid.

In his excitement, the Shantir took no notice of his host's foul temper and did not notice that those who constantly

Chris Reher

hovered around the leader were now doing so at a safe distance. "It is he," Velani proclaimed. "You have the Tughan Wai!"

"Good," Tharron said. "Get to work, Shantir. I want the Union destroyed! You hear me, Shantir? Their very bones I want pulverized and scattered from one cursed end of this galaxy to another!" He took a deep draft from his flask.

Velani noticed the uncertain glances from Comori and the carefully subdued, amused expression on Pe Khoja's streamlined face. "Tharron…"

"You will address me as 'Lord Tharron' or you will see your precious Delphi burn!"

Velani looked for help to Comori, who merely shrugged. "My Lord," he began again. "I must return to Delphi for more information. A little more study. I know where to find it."

"Delays! You told me you can do what must be done to release this Tughan. Are you saying you're incapable of it?"

"No, Lord, not at all. It is only a small matter without which I cannot proceed. I will be gone no more than a few days, if I can prevail upon one of your pilots once again. Then the training may begin." Velani did not dare tell Tharron that, although he would indeed return to Shaddallam within days, Kiran's conversion from child to Tughan could take months, perhaps years. He would find out soon enough. Velani looked forward to the creation. Kiran would become his pupil, growing toward his future under the Shantir's careful supervision. Many Shantirs had been trained for this; only he, Velani, would actually see the wonder unfold!

Tharron regarded him with red-rimmed eyes. "Whatever. Be gone. But be certain, Shantir, that if you cross me, Delphi will burn. And it will not take the Tughan to destroy your pitiful cities!"

"I guarantee that I will return quickly," Velani said, surprised that anyone would doubt his word. "Then we can go to work."

Tharron grunted, staring out of a window overlooking the courtyard as if to find something out there in the dark. "First among the dead," he said, "will be that woman. I will tear her limb from limb with my own hands!"

"Nova?" Velani said. "But she is dead!"

The horrible noise issuing from their leader might have been laughter. "Through my fingers, once again! How many times has she escaped? How many of my best men has she destroyed?" Tharron shook his large head. "No more, Shantir, no more. No more sniping from the shadows. Next time she will be brought to me alive. It will be Tharron who will terminate her personally." He waved an arm in a broad gesture. "Comori! Comori will see to it that she does not die quickly."

ELEVEN

Dawn on Delphi was, at worst, inspirational. Each of the short seasons here, north of the richly forested equator, greeted the morning sun in a different, yet equally breathtaking way. Just now, Delphi's star began to tint the Chaliss'Ya mountain range pink, revealing the distant snow-covered peaks against a pale blue sky. Soon life-giving light descended onto the valley floor to blot out the morning mist with its warmth and energy. The brief dawn passed in minutes, turning night into day, illuminating the cool, moist richness of Delphi's Chaliss valley.

On one of many balconies, Cylas stood motionless in the face of such beauty, all that made up his mind and body open to the sun, reaching out across the breathtaking vista. He wore only loose-fitting blue trousers to feel the delicious chill of the fresh new day. His heart was one with the flow of life. His mind was one with the tides of the universe. His body was one with the power of nature. He was happy.

When the sun had climbed above Chaliss'Ya's peaks and begun its journey to the opposite range, Cylas returned indoors, this morning's exercise complete, already anticipating tomorrow's. He slipped a tunic over his slight body, twisted his hair into a neat blue braid and left his rooms to begin his day's duties. The corridor was abuzz with blue-robed men and women, equally pleased by the blessing of the dawn. Their sun had been their first god; all of the Shantirs' bed chambers faced toward morning.

There were forty Shantirs currently living in the sect's main enclave within the city of Chaib Psa. Here they taught promising acolytes and dispensed the mind-healing to a people that would never know a doctor or need a hospital. This house was neither church nor monastery. Religion had very little to do with the daily activities of the Shantirs. No prayers ever rang through these halls and abstinence among the Shantirs was rare and purely by choice. The sect had learned to conduct their public business amidst rites and mysterious symbolism simply because outsiders preferred to believe in a superior being than in a superior mind.

He climbed a staircase to what was truly the think-tank of all of Delphi. A broad corridor led to Chaib Psa's wealthiest library. It contained ancient scrolls, skins and musty tomes doused liberally in preservatives, and archives dating back thousands of years. It was Cylas' duty to preserve and maintain this collection, making some of the priceless items available as needed and to assemble lectures for the sect's teachers. But this was also the site of an electronic information storage system that contained more knowledge than could ever be shelved in a thousand of these rooms. Some of the secrets stored here were of such importance that they were shielded from any outside transmission.

He opened the door to the library, ready to sift through the day's requests from teachers and scholars.

"What is this?" he exclaimed.

Someone hunched over one of the access ports. He spun around when Cylas' words cut through the silent chamber.

The librarian stepped into the room. "Shan Velani, is it not? I had not expected anyone here so early." He smiled and touched two fingers to his forehead in a respectful greeting. This elder Delphian was not only a seasoned Shantir but also of the house of Phera.

"It is," Velani replied crisply.

Cylas saw another man to his right, bent over a display case. He was dressed in the long robe of an acolyte and had not even turned to see who had entered. A deep hood covered his face completely.

The young Shantir approached Velani. He had heard of this Shantir prince who traveled freely among Union stations on diplomatic missions. Could he be engaged in a conversation? Cylas yearned to learn about his work among the off-worlders. It was some moments before he saw where Velani was standing.

"Shan Velani, that port is restricted! How did you obtain the access code? Have you made recordings? Who authorized this?" He stared in disbelief at the data on the screen. No one was permitted to access that information. The consent of three Shantirs and the Council was required before the file could be opened. It was quite possibly the most dangerous information stored in this room and no one, including Cylas, its keeper, had ever accessed it.

It described the mental block that held back the Tughan Wai.

Cylas staggered backward, his eyes full of fear and understanding. He groped for the door behind him, unable to force his voice to call out for help.

Then a strong hand gripped his thin scholar's shoulder. A lightning bolt of pain shot into his back and found his heart. He stared at the still immobile Shantir before him, knowing that he, Cylas, would be spared from ever knowing the ungodly terror that was Delphi's most ambitious creation. He died quickly.

Velani broke out of his trance and rushed to the lifeless librarian.

"He won't need your help, Shantir," Pe Khoja said and threw his hood back. He inspected the long needle in his hand, still dripping a clear poison. He retracted it into the sheath lashed to his forearm after dabbing the liquid away. "Did you get what you came for?"

"You killed him!" Velani accused.

"I noticed." Pe Khoja stepped over the body to return to the display case. His expression had not changed. The yellow eyes remained flat and lifeless as he mused over a work of intricate poetry, his command of Delphi mainvoice flawless.

"You're a monster!"

Pe Khoja shifted to another scroll. "And you are a monster maker. Mind if I keep this?" The butt of his sidearm shattered the glass case. He brushed a few shards from the vellum and rolled it carefully. "Finish what you were doing."

Velani took a few minutes to bring himself under control, whispering his invocations to calm his racing mind. "Monster maker?"

Pe Khoja regarded him coldly. "Isn't that what you're doing? Do you think Lord Tharron is going to play Points with him? Discuss the meaning of life, maybe?"

Velani turned away to shut the access port down. "Meaning of life," he said bitterly. "What meaning does life hold for you?"

The Caspian strode to a small door set unobtrusively between two of the far wall shelves. *About as much it does Tharron,* he thought, impatient to be gone from this sleepy little planet.

Pe Khoja was a ruthless, cruel being with few emotions. His intelligence made him valuable, his absence of conscience or pity made him even more so. He knew that he was incapable of joy or pleasure, and he struggled daily to keep his baser instincts in check. As a result, all he ever felt was a complete lack of satisfaction. Forever the outsider, he looked at this universe with detached interest, hoping for a glimpse at something larger.

There had to be something larger. Pe Khoja needed more than this. Things might have been different for him had the Union discovered him before Tharron. But it had not, and Pe Khoja had become a rebel, first rising to the top of the small Caspian Arawaj faction and then offering his services to the

Shri-Lan, where he was now indispensably installed in Tharron's inner circle. Neither side of this war interested him. He cared nothing for the Union's civilian activities or their control over most of Trans-Targon. Tharron had quickly ceased to awe him and the K'lar's cowardly rebellion against the Union was becoming tiresome.

But he had his principles. As a rebel, he had funds and planes to travel where others could not go, see what others could not see. He would remain a rebel because he would not, could not switch sides.

The one thing he truly hated was a traitor. A traitor like Velani. A quick stab in the back with a poison needle was too good for that one.

TWELVE

Besides the battlefield on Bellac, this was likely the vilest-smelling place Nova had ever encountered. The stench permeated every part of the town they had so far explored. Shad-Lengh carved out a meager existence for itself in the tanning of hides into fine leathers that were then traded into parts of the planet that could afford to live without the stink of the factories. Nova herself owned a fine pair of trousers that originated in this vile pit. The thin veil now obscuring her face did nothing to keep the smell out of her nose.

Nova threaded her way past long, low-roofed buildings that seemed to be heaps of stones held together by mud or dung. Here and there stood a tent made of hides and, rarely, a wooden shack or two. Well trodden, winding pathways connected the buildings. Although she had seen a skimmer in the distance, there was no room between the buildings for driving such a vehicle unless one parked on a roof and slid from there to the ground.

She had tried to converse with some of the natives she encountered, but it seemed that only children were about and every time she hailed one, it quickly disappeared among the buildings. Eventually the pathways widened and she emerged into an open area. In the center stood yet another stone building, this one at least four times as large, if not as high, as the others.

Nova turned toward it, recognizing it as some sort of communal hall, perhaps even as whatever passed as the local seat of government. There was no door. She paced around the heap of stone twice before she realized that she was walking in circles. Confounded, she looked around the deserted square, wondering if she should find Tychon to help solve this mystery.

Then she saw a sign attached to one of the ramshackle wooden buildings on the north side of the plaza. Then another, further down. There were large windows and merchandise set out for sale. Happily, she realized that she was able to read the signs. Strangers were not that uncommon here, after all.

She entered a shop, pleased to note that here a more appetizing odor prevailed. She walked past rows of bins containing dried herbs, spices and roots, often needing to duck under items hanging from the low ceiling. A very short storekeeper resembled the ropes of shriveled fruit hung from the rafters.

"Man," she addressed him, hoping that he was, indeed, a male of the species. "You own shop?"

He studied her with eyes sunk deep in furrowed skin. "Yes, do you wish to make a purchase?" His command of the trade language she had chosen was by far better than hers.

"Maybe." She held up a picture that expert technicians on Targon had isolated from the tape found on Tor Ag, showing a tree with fronds growing all along its long trunk. She and Tychon had spent hours studying every second of the precious video fragment and had sent frames of it to various labs, careful to include no information that would alert an eavesdropping enemy. Planets whose climate matched the images were shortlisted. So were atmospheric conditions that allowed Kiran to move about without protective gear. Finally, the toddler in the image was identified as a Shaddallam native, close to Kiran's own age. An analysis of the vegetation in the image narrowed things down to Shaddallam's temperate northern hemisphere. Four of the Vanguard teams were immediately dispatched to begin the search. "I is botanist. Look for healing tree like so. Is here on Shaddallam. Where?"

The proprietor reached for the picture with a multi-jointed arm. He chuckled. "Healing tree? I'd say you have strange ailments. There is nothing medicinal about that tree."

"Not for you," Nova said. "Where tree?"

He returned the image to her. "You won't find that around here. Go north. They grow in the region of Shad-Laika."

"Are cities there? Towns?"

"Certainly they don't grow in towns!" He laughed. "But, yes, there are a few towns up there."

She nodded and turned away.

"I would not go there," he called after her. "They don't like Humans unless you're one of *them*. Won't care about the difference between a botanist and a soldier."

She stopped at the door. This ancient had a good eye. "There no Humans here?"

"Not often in Shad-Laika." He snatched a small bag from a shelf. From a bin on her left he took a handful of herbs and, after shredding them, added them to the bag. "Take this."

She regarded him suspiciously. His leathery hand took hers to place the parcel on it. "Mix it with water and drink it fast. It will turn your skin very red. The people of Bellac Tau are a more common sight in the north."

"Many rebels here on Shaddallam?"

He nodded. "We have no numbers for them, but they are gathering in the north."

She tucked the bag into a pocket. "Why you help me?"

He stepped back. "Your reasons for seeking our oppressors are your own. But I shall hate to see your quest untimely ended because of your inept ploy to disguise yourself as a botanist." His cackle was old-womanish as he retreated to the back of the store.

"Man," Nova called after him.

He poked his head around a stack of crates.

"Why no door on that building? Why all people hide?"

"Oh, there is a door. But it isn't on the building. And why do we hide?" He came forward again. "Strangers come here. Not the odd trader that passes by here from your world beyond the sun, but strangers who take all and give nothing. They come here sometimes from Shad-Laika. So we hide."

Nova left the shop and hurried across the square, the smell of rotted meat, sewage and the tanneries again assaulting her senses. Tychon would be waiting for her at the path leading into the dusty plains that surrounded Shad-Lengh. She walked faster, eager to share her find with him.

* * *

Tychon leaned against the wall of a stable, morosely watching the little people scurry about that maze which they called a town. No one had wanted to speak to him. It didn't seem to be shyness that kept them at a distance but a rather profound loathing for strangers.

When he had finally caught a child by the cowl of its robe, he had succeeded only at being soundly cursed; one did not need to be a linguist to know when one was insulted. The child had not been a child, but an adult female. He thought it rather admirable that she had neither cowered in fear nor tried to stab him with some hidden weapon. Tychon berated himself for not having taken the time to learn something about the natives of Shaddallam and a few words of their incomprehensible language.

He loosened his stifling burnoose to spit into the sand. This place lived with the fear of the rebels, he could taste it, smell it.

He let his attention wander, observing a group of hunters returning with the day's catch of large desert birds destined for the tannery. He recognized the creatures as sandrunners, Shaddallam's main source of clothing, food, transportation and income. At least that much he knew of this place.

"Tychon," a low voice sounding like thunder at the end of a storm made the hair along his spine bristle. He turned, coming to face the most dreaded of Tharron's officers.

Tychon's initial impulse was to run; the Caspian before him bore an overwhelming presence that made his three companions seem like an army. All of them were Caspian, wearing only knee-length kilts to display the intricate markings of their hides. Although descended from simians, like all Prime Species of Trans-Targon, their taut, angular bodies in addition to those whorls and stripes made them seem like a pack of cats about to pounce upon their prey. Four guns sighted on him.

He tried an easy smile. "Pe Khoja, as I'm still standing! I haven't seen you since you got thrown out of Aram."

Pe Khoja ignored the barb. "Didn't think you'd track us down quite this quickly."

"I'm honored that you would welcome me personally." Tychon moved away from the wall, cursing their luck. They had traded planes with Vanguard Five before taking the last jump to Shaddallam, exchanging one nondescript vessel for another. Five had recently been refitted - surely rebel spies had not yet identified it. Shaddallam received enough off-world traffic that they would not have raised suspicion by landing here. Yet it seemed that all traffic arriving on Shaddallam was met with great scrutiny. Tychon wondered if this was more than just a place to hide Kiran. Could this be Tharron's main base? His home? "Running short on minions already?"

"You taking out a few Rhuwacs isn't exactly leaving us short-handed."

Tychon glanced along the now empty path behind him. Miraculously, everyone seemed to have found some urgent business to keep them indoors. By now the Eagle would be surrounded by Rhuwacs.

He watched Pe Khoja's fingers play over the firing mechanism of his gun. The rebel would not even call this an execution. But what was he waiting for? Everything Tychon knew about this Caspian would have him on the ground already, of no more significance than any of the hundreds of other dead Union members that didn't bother Pe Khoja's conscience. Yet he hesitated, his hooded eyes studying Tychon as if some scheme was forming, not quite decided upon, but possibly useful.

"Ty!"

The five men turned at the sound of Nova's voice. Tychon groaned.

"Ty! There you are. I found—" Nova stepped from among the houses and froze when the rebel detail came into her line of sight. Her eyes lit on Pe Khoja's smooth features. Although she had never met him, she had seen his picture often enough to have it etched into her mind.

"Captain Whiteside," Pe Khoja breathed, a slow grin touching his lips. He, too, had seen her likeness many times. He had always envisioned a formidable she-warrior of size and strength to match her Delphian mate and the stories that were told of them. Tharron would not be pleased that his hated adversary had turned out to be no more than a slip of a girl, tall, slender and, he had to admit, quite beautiful for a Human.

Tychon thought that he had caught an expression of hatred for her, and all that she stood for, pass over the rebel's face.

Nova's hand flashed to her gun. Before her weapon was drawn, a single beam of light cut across the space between her and one of Pe Khoja's men. Her body shook in a brief spasm and then crumpled into the dust.

"Nova!" Tychon rushed to her.

Pe Khoja whirled and struck the marksman hard enough to throw him off his feet. "Idiot!"

The rebel raised his hands to ward off further blows. His visions of reward and praise faded at the sight of Pe Khoja's angry visage.

The leader watched Tychon crouch beside the still figure. "Take her along," Pe Khoja snapped. "She'll come around."

Tychon looked back over his shoulder, his hand still touching her neck. "She's dead."

Pe Khoja motioned to another of his guards to confirm Tychon's words. The rebel dropped to one knee beside her, feeling for signs of life. Tychon closed his eyes.

"So she is." The soldier used his clawed foot to turn Nova over. "Looks like we finally got her."

Pe Khoja studied Tychon's pale and stunned expression. "I think Tharron might have a few questions for you, Delphi. Let's take your plane. Eagle Class, isn't it? I've admired them for some time now." He looked back to Nova's inert figure, then at Tychon. "Leave her here," he said to his men. "Perhaps they'll make use of her in the tanneries."

One of the rebels unclipped Nova's weapons belt and pulled it roughly from under her, then took the data sleeve from her forearm. He studied it appreciatively. "This set is worth more than what I paid for your sister, Jhos."

The Caspians' rough laughter accompanied them as Tychon was led away, disarmed, a gun stabbing his ribs on either side. He did not look back at Nova. His head ached.

* * *

Since the invitation to take a seat among the ten leaders of the Union, Baroch had had to resign himself to the constant and watchful presence of others at closer quarters, even as he slept. Even during precious time spent with his wife and their two children, even in his quiet moments lost in study or absorbed in khamal, Union agents maintained a vigil over him. As one of the Ten Factors, he had grown accustomed to the intrusion but would never come to like it.

To remain impartial, Baroch had made his home on Feyd rather than on his native Delphi. In spite of the relentless heat, it was a good place to build a home, not as harsh and fast-paced as Targon and not as remote and dull as Pelion or Myra.

The house itself was large, rambling into several directions with deep, open verandas designed to catch every breeze. It did not have an office. On this one thing Baroch had insisted. Any business conducted on Feyd was handled in one of several comfortable sitting rooms, more often than not in the presence of his wife and over a tray of Feydan delicacies. If formality was required, the dining room converted into a soundproof, bugproof meeting room.

He was not certain of the formality called for when his ever-present guards announced the arrival of four Shantirs on

Feyd. The audience had been requested politely but the purpose for it had not been disclosed. That it was urgent was evident; Shantirs did not travel this far to visit a Factor for social reasons.

Baroch decided to receive them in the ornately paneled, secure dining room. Knowing what he did of members of the sect, he was certain that they would prefer to sit in formal austerity rather than lounge casually around a pitcher of tea. As an afterthought, his aide replaced the humorous Nebdanese tapestry with a likeness of Phera.

The Shantirs were ushered in and guards posted themselves outside. Normally, two or three would remain with Baroch as standard security protocol. But to a Shantir, even an honor guard would mean immeasurable insult.

Introductions were made. Baroch knew one of them, Shan Moghen. All three were Shantirs of the highest order and the Factor made no attempt at small talk.

"Your presence here is welcome, Elder Brothers and Sister," he said. "How can I be of service?"

Moghen was their spokesman. Baroch understood that his guests were telepathically linked and required only one voice. "Lord Baroch," he began. "We are here to represent the Shantir community, not the Clan Council of Delphi. An unfortunate incident has occurred within our enclave in Chaib Psa. It was decided to report this incident to you. We have also come to you to confirm a suspicion which we have harbored for some weeks now."

"Tell me of the incident," Baroch replied guardedly.

"One of our number has been murdered. We discovered his body in our library."

Baroch sighed inwardly. A dead librarian. Were these people suspecting rebels inside their monastery?

"He died while defending our stores of most valuable archives. A so-far tamperproof access system was bypassed and copies were taken."

"Copies of what?"

Moghen hesitated only briefly. "The accessed file pertains

to the removal of an artificially induced mental block. One specific mental block. It is the one given to Kiran Tar Phera."

"By the Gods!" Baroch breathed.

Moghen regarded him shrewdly. Baroch knew what he was talking about. Baroch had not asked why the child carried a mental block. He had not asked why anyone would want this file badly enough to murder a Shantir. "Lord, since you appear to be aware of the reality of the Tughan Wai, our suspicion is confirmed. People outside the Shantirate know that he exists and they know who he is. Most likely, he is at large and no longer on Feyd, or with Shan Tychon and his consort. Quite possibly, he is in the hands of your enemy! Is that not so, Lord Baroch?"

Baroch glared at Moghen, furious for having been put on the defensive. The man sounded accusing. A number of retorts ached to be flung back at the Shantir. You created this abomination! You let him leave Delphi! You relied on a mindless machine to guard your secrets! You made this mistake, Shantir!

The Factor said none of these things. Mentally, he was already composing a few urgent messages. "Who was it that broke into your information system?"

Moghen seemed uncomfortable now. "A traitor, no doubt. Someone who has fallen under Tharron's manic influence."

Baroch's blue eyebrows knitted into one thick line. "Who would know where to find the file? Who can possibly train the child? It was a Shantir, was it not? It had to be! One of your very own."

Moghen cleared his throat. "Velani Tar Phera."

"Impossible!" Baroch said. "Are you saying that the boy's own uncle is a rebel?"

"He may be under Tharron's influence," Moghen allowed. "When Shan Tychon removed his son from Delphi, Velani offered to find and return him, using his position in Phera's clan. Since Tychon continued to refuse to return his son to the Court, Shan Velani spent many months in places where rebels come and go freely. He was tempted, no doubt. The advent of the Tughan Wai is a challenge of phenomenal magnitude." The Shantir paused, appearing to listen to some unspoken comment. "He arrived on Delphi past midnight," he continued. "A private liftplane brought him to your Union base near Chaib Psa. It was shown that he left Delphi again by mid-morning. The declared flight plan was false. It listed an intention to span to Targon but the ship was traced as far as the jumpsite to K'lar."

"Shaddallam." Baroch nodded to himself but then gasped as he calculated. "K'lar? Did you say K'lar? Even an Air Command cruiser would take at least fourteen hours to get to that site from Delphi. Are you telling me that you have waited that long before coming here?" He calculated rapidly. "Given the time it took for you to travel here, your 'incident' took place three days ago!"

"Four," Moghen said. "Please understand that this matter involves one of Delphi's most secret sciences. We had to deliberate carefully over all possible consequences."

Baroch closed his eyes. Consequences! How about tens of thousands of lives at stake? "What do you suggest?" he asked with forced politeness. He had to send a message to Targon at once. Did Carras know about the mental block? If Tharron now had a Shantir with the secret to reach the Tughan, time was no longer on their side.

Moghen glanced at his silent companions. "Of course, we would like to have the opportunity to study the Tughan and its effects on the boy. When Kiran had reached an age of reason, we had intended to take him into the Shantirate. It would mean much to Delphi to know how our experiment fared. But, after much discussion and many reviews of all information available, we now feel that the experiment should be aborted."

"Aborted?"

Moghen nodded. "Kiran is only six years of age, by Targon standard time. The Delphian brain develops at a tremendous rate at that age. We cannot know what will happen. He has not been under our supervision, he has had no training. We do not know how the Tughan may be controlled once awakened."

"We know where he is," Baroch said. "Our agents are even now infiltrating the planet on which the boy has been detained. Our intention is to extract him quietly and return him to you."

The Shantir eyed him coldly. "Lord, that is a risk that must not be taken. We have brought information that illustrates the possible consequences should Velani complete the creation." He reached into his belt pocket for a few data slips and placed them before the Factor. "Kiran is too young. Of course, he could die, but we cannot hope for that. You must move at once to end it. Order your agents to destroy the boy on sight."

"That is extreme!"

Moghen nodded to the Shantir seated on his left.

"Lord," Shan Yriam said, gesturing toward the slips. "These will explain the extremes we consider necessary. If you care to study them, you will come to agree with us."

Baroch sighed and tapped the table top to engage a display system. He went through the motions of loading the first of the Shantirs' slips, his mind already dealing with his message to Carras.

Yriam began to explain the data, her voice monotonous. Baroch watched, wanting to get this over with. Then a few phrases caught his attention. He leaned forward, now absorbed by what the Shantir had to tell him. Soon he was listening raptly, his eyes widening at what he was shown. Barely aware of it, he continuously folded and unfolded his hands to keep them from shaking. The Shantirs were merciless, going on and on with their dreadful tale, oblivious of the terror that was growing within the Factor.

He was not aware that the display had ended, nor did he rise to usher the Shantirs from the room. When his aide cautiously approached him, he looked into the face of a man who had aged ten years in one afternoon.

* * *

Nova jarred into consciousness as though catapulted out of a nightmare of vast proportions. She recognized the foreign sun above and then the ground below her as something having

183

to do with her personally. She blinked, becoming aware of the pain that engulfed her entire body. That, too, was to be taken personally. She crawled into a covered doorway and waited for her head to clear. A sharp wind blowing from the plains had turned the day very cold and she shivered as she tried to understand what had happened.

"Ty?" She looked around, half expecting to see his body in the dust of the road. It took her a moment of staring at her forearm to understand that her com system had been taken. Wonderful. Vanguard One was searching for the same tree only a continent away and now she had no way of reaching them.

Nova? came a faint reply.

Ty! Nova projected. *Where are you?*

Tychon nearly severed his link to her when she groped for his mental contact. *Easy!* he warned. *That hurts. Pe Khoja is taking me and the Eagle north. Kiran is there and I'm beginning to think that Tharron is, too. I can't keep talking to you like this. But through this khamal you should be able to follow.*

You're going north?

He sent an affirmative. *Looks like mostly flatlands. See if you can get a skimmer or something.* He paused, his signal fading. *Hurry. I don't know how long I can tolerate an open khamal with you.* Tychon retreated, but his presence stayed with her like a distant white noise in her mind.

Nova took a moment to focus her thoughts, using her mind the way Tychon had begun to show her to attain the sort of tranquility that seemed to come so easily to him. It took a long time before she felt well enough to even stand up and look around. She staggered back through the village, grumbling and groaning and wishing for nothing so much as a warm bed to fall into. Few people had dared to move outdoors again and even fewer noted her distress. None offered help. She was barely able to reach the herb grocer's shop.

"Hey now, the Human!" he exclaimed when she stumbled into the room.

Seeing nothing resembling a chair, Nova collapsed onto the

floor. "Got shot."

He shook his head. "I knew you'd be trouble. Didn't even make it to Shad-Laika to find it."

She groaned. "Need air car. Transmitter."

"Do you really? Well, I have neither of these things." He began to move about the room, looking through jars and bins. "Air car, dear me. Can hardly walk and wants to fly!"

Nova barely listened to his mutterings, feeling herself pass out again. Her vision was edged in red.

"Here, Human."

She blinked. "What?"

"Drink this."

She shook her head. Her test kit, along with her guns, communicator and other tools was in the belt that now likely graced the waist of a Caspian.

He laughed. "I'm not about to poison you. I assure you that our foodstuff is quite safe for Humans. I've not seen one fall dead because of it. This remedy will do much to restore you."

She reached for the vessel and drained it, not without much gagging. "It smell bad."

He helped her to her feet, for which she was grateful even though she was a full head taller than he. "Our she-warrior is rude. Maybe I won't help, then."

Nova smiled weakly, sorry for her behavior and beginning to feel better. "You already have, old man."

He led her into a back room that was just as filled with vials and jars and the tools of his trade as the rest of the store. He walked her toward a cot on which several stacks of books and scrolls competed for space with some sort of furry pet, possibly a rodent.

"You can sleep here in safety for a while." He pushed the clutter off the bed.

She sat down. "You find air car?"

He shook his head. "You are still going north?"

"Yes. Must. Enemy have..." She cleared her throat. "Enemy have my mate."

The much-wrinkled brow furrowed even more. "I cannot

get a skimmer here. But I can try to find something to help you get there. It will be expensive."

"No matter." She reached into her jacket and removed a long necklace. "Need supplies, too. Food, guns. This pays." She looked around the jumbled room and picked up a long metal prong, possibly some type of eating utensil. Carefully, she used the tool to pry the Delphi sapphire from the back of Tychon's sigil. She bit her lip when she handed the crystal to the shop keeper.

The merchant held it to the light of the only lamp in the room. "This is the best I have seen in a long time."

Nova did not look at it again. "Take it," she grumbled. "Get guns, too." She closed her eyes. By the time the little man had locked his doors and gone on his errands she was already immersed in a deep, healing sleep. It was a dreamless rest, made possible by the grocer's potion.

She awoke just as abruptly. The darkness seemed to bring the walls around her closer with every breath. Adjusting her eyes to the gloom, Nova studied the many strange objects piled on shelves or hung from pegs in the walls and ceiling. A small movement in the bend of her knees startled her. It was the rodent, curled in a small fur ball, sharing her warmth.

Nova sat up slowly, remembering her predicament. How long had she been asleep? Where was that old man? She looked to the door. Was he even now leading a rebel detail to her hiding place?

"You are such an idiot," she whispered to herself. What part of her training had allowed her to trust a stranger on a rebel planet? Not only had she practically told him who she was but she had also given him the Delphi sapphire that had adorned Tychon's sigil. No doubt he was long gone to savor his newfound wealth in another part of Shaddallam.

She crept to the door to listen for sounds within the dark shop. She made out the hunched shapes of his display bins in the gloom. Beyond those the main door led to the street. There were voices outside; someone was singing hoarsely. She sensed a passage to her left and carefully picked her way through piles of stacked boxes and baskets to what she hoped was a rear exit.

A series of muffled sounds caused her to flatten herself against the wall. She detected more than one set of footsteps outside, along with the creak of leather and a muffled clanking of chain. The door before her opened without a sound.

She darted forward and grasped the intruder to pin him against the wall.

"Human! It is I, Ishet, the shopkeeper here. You guard my home well."

Nova looked over his head into the alley. "You alone?"

He pushed her hands aside. "I have your supplies." He bustled into the shop, drawing curtains and shutters before lighting a lamp. Nova looked through the bundle he had dropped.

"Put these clothes on. They are native to Bellac Tau but not so uncommon here. The food and guns are outside."

She nodded, examining the robe. "Smells funny."

"You might be grateful for once!"

Nova looked up, startled. After a moment, she shrugged. "Forgive. I worried. And not understanding why you help."

He pushed her into the back room to change her clothes. "Why should I not help? This planet has not seen peace since Tharron landed here. Not all of us believe in his cause. Hurry up now."

Nova soon found herself dressed in a voluminous, coarse robe, her hair covered by a dirty burnoose. Strangely, her legs remained bare. Her host snickered when he bent to adjust her foot coverings that were little more than leather rags lashed clumsily up to her shins.

"How can I walk so?" she complained, although, once he had retied the thongs, she found that the skins felt lighter and allowed for more movement than her own boots.

Ishet led her into the alley behind his shop.

"What the hell is that?"

"Eh?" He turned at the sound of the strange language she had used.

187

"That!" She gestured.

"Fastest sandrunner my brother would sell."

Disbelieving, Nova walked around the ungainly animal. Its two ostrich legs were longer than she was tall, each of its four knees as large as her head. The gray-feathered body, plumeless, sported two short wings that would never carry it in flight. Its bare neck was short. Large, intelligent eyes observed her over a rounded beak.

She turned to Ishet. "I am taking this?"

He chuckled. "It is taking you. I have also found a guide to accompany you." Ishet looked about the darkness of the alley. "Greah? Now where has that fellow gone to?" Ishet turned back to Nova. "There are no skimmers or shuttles here that do not belong to the Shri-Lan. This sandrunner is fast. It will bring you to Shad-Laika within two or three days."

One could be halfway to Targon in three days, Nova thought but did not say aloud. "How long your days?"

Ishet seemed confused. "Why, as long as a day takes."

"About half of yours," a light, musical voice interjected.

"Whoa!" Nova sprang back from the bird. "What the..?"

"There you are, Greah. Sometimes I swear you're invisible." Ishet smiled at the small person that had appeared at the bird's feet.

"I've sat here all along," Greah replied, his laugh like the chime of a bell.

"Who this child?" Nova said.

Greah's head barely reached to her elbow and his body was as slender and unformed as that of a boy. Each arm and leg, like Ishet's and the bird's, had two joints. And, like them, he had no ears. The large head and smooth skin made him seem more juvenile than Ishet.

"Child?" Ishet said. "Hardly. Greah has traveled farther on this planet than anyone I know. You will be safer riding in his company than alone."

"He look like our children at home."

Greah laughed, a pleasing sound that seemed to come easily to this creature. "We should go now. It will be light soon and we must have left town by then." He turned to the towering bird that had stood silently, unmoving. It took only a tap on the muscled legs to command the sandrunner to lower itself. A deep saddle, laden with packages, was strapped to its back. He took her bundle of clothes and added it to the baggage.

"I don't believe this." Nova climbed aboard, understanding now why her thick robe had seemed too short. In the simple stirrups, her legs were tucked comfortably into its folds. Greah turned to Ishet and they conversed a while in their native tongue. Nova saw that the belt that crossed his bare chest secured a projectile rifle on his back. Other than that, he wore only a brief kilt and, like Nova, clumsy footwear.

At last, Greah climbed onto the runner in front of her saddle and bade the bird to rise.

Nova looked down onto her new friend. "Thank you, Ishet. I not forget your help."

"I wish you luck, Human." Ishet waved a farewell. "Perhaps you will come back to tell me your name."

"Perhaps," she said, a little sad at the parting. "But I will tell my people of kindness you give. You not be forgotten."

* * *

The sandrunner moved at a terrific speed. Once they had cleared the outskirts of Shad-Lengh, it ceased its uncomfortable, jouncing trot and reached with long legs into a full run to finally escape the cloying stench of the tanneries. Nova could hardly feel any motion as they seemed to glide over the uneven ground as steady as any air car. She suspected that the twice-jointed legs were the cause of the sandrunner's smooth gait.

The sun moved over the horizon to turn dawn into day. Featureless flatlands stretched ahead, broken only by a low ridge in the far distance. The runner now seemed to be heading straight for that line of rocks. Nova hoped it would mark the end of this desert. She saw a few caravans in the distance; no one else seemed willing to wander through these flatlands alone. She felt exposed.

Now that it was light, Nova was able to study the small being slumped in front of her. His smooth skin was deeply tanned and he seemed to blend well into the dun tones of their barren surroundings. Startling yellow hair ringed the back of his head from temple to temple, leaving most of his skull bare. The fine strands curled where they met his shoulders. Looking closely, Nova discovered a pink, elongated aperture at the base of his skull. She thought it a strange place to develop an ear.

"How can I sleep when you stare at me?"

Nova flinched. "Huh? I wasn't... How can you sleep? You are supposed to steer this thing!"

Owl like, his head turned around on his scrawny shoulders. "He knows where he goes." He gave her an impish grin.

Nova was a little unsettled by the sight of his face where the back of his head should be. Understanding her discomfort, he swung a leg over the gently nodding head of the bird and sat sideways to face her. "I told him where we're going, you know," he explained earnestly.

"How come you know our language?"

"I learn fast!" he said nasally. "Actually, I had to work for your rebel friends for a while."

She regarded him curiously. "You're not from Shad-Lengh, are you?"

"No. I been everywhere on Shaddallam and stay where I like. My home was Shad-Laika before Tharron come. When Ishet told me of you, I wanted to meet you, Star Traveler."

"One does not travel to stars. I am an Eagle pilot, though."

"What's an Eagle?" He savored the unfamiliar word.

"It's a ship. A small cruiser with a small crew. But powerful."

"I seen them land at the rebel base."

"Those could not have been Eagles. What do you know of the rebels here?"

"They want to destroy the Union. There are a few bases on Shadallam. They have not been here for long. I been to them all, to see and to learn. Why d'you wanna see the one in Shad-Laika? Nothing there of value."

Nova felt a silent presence in the back of her mind, like a hand touching her shoulder to get her attention. She concentrated on its source.

Ty?

He replied wordlessly. She could almost feel the pain he endured in maintaining their khamal. She sent him a mental image of their surroundings.

That's a sandrunner, no? Who's the kid?

Cute, isn't he? No kid, either. He's got information on the rebels here. Where are you?

Don't know. Did you contact the others?

Haven't been able to find a transmitter. Will you be all right?

They're avoiding any real damage for some reason. Want to leave before they get serious.

Are you in a lot of pain?

Yes. This khamal is keeping my mind off the beatings, or the beatings are keeping my mind off this pain in my head.

Nova sent him a gentle, reassuring touch that surprised her as much as it did him.

Do that when I'm around. He began to fade. *Hurry up! Get me out of here!*

Nova sighed, opening her eyes that she hadn't been aware of closing. Greah was staring at her intently, his pug nose nearly touching hers. She jerked back in surprise.

"Something wrong?"

She shook her head, then nodded. "I'll tell you later."

"I got time now," Greah said, moving his head to indicate the distance still before them.

Nova glanced into his serious little face, somehow reminded of storybook elves. Nothing hinted at his age which, she was certain, by far exceeded her own. Only the deadly weapon slung over his shoulder would seem out of place in a fairy tale.

Slowly, she began to speak, initially outlining her current situation. As the hours passed, her life unfolded before him: The strife of the Union against the rebels, strange worlds that she had seen, people that she had met and never known long enough. She spoke of Tychon and his son and why they were here, staying just within the limit of their mission's classification. The words continued to come and she left little out of the narration.

They had reached the long ridge of monolithic outcroppings when she at last fell silent. Greah had not spoken at all. His eyes had rarely left hers as he listened and learned, remembering all, judging nothing.

He was wordless even now when the sandrunner picked its way to a grove of low trees that more or less prospered in the lee of the rocks. The bird lowered itself to the ground and Nova groaned when her stiff legs refused to unbend after all these hours. She watched as Greah heat-blasted a large stone and unburdened the runner. Efficiently, he started to prepare a meal from the dried fruit and boiled dough Ishet had sent.

At last he handed her a portion of food and leaned comfortably against the sandrunner. "Tell me more," he said.

"I've told you my story." Nova nibbled her food and found it tasteless.

Perhaps Greah read her expression; perhaps she was too tired to hide it. He rose and hunted around their campsite for a while. When he returned he showed her his find of velvety, succulent leaves. Nova imitated him when he showed her how to wrap the leaves around a morsel of dough, giving moisture to their preserved food. She succeeded making a bite-sized wad and tasted it.

"Ugh!" She unwrapped her food and gave the herbs back to him, preferring the dry dough to the bitter taste imparted by the greenery.

Greah laughed, accepting her strangeness. "Tell me about those planets." His thin arm stretched to the sky. "How long does it take to get to them?"

She looked up at the stars. "There are a lot of them, aren't there? We haven't even begun to travel to even a small number them. We're stuck in this little part of our galaxy for now. Less than one planet in many thousands can be visited by people like you and me. Sometimes a few habitable planets are close enough together for trade and commercial traffic, like in Trans-Targon and Terra-Centauri. That is what the Commonwealth tries to encourage. It profits through investment. Someday, your people can sell your leathers to any planet that wants them and ship them there with your own freighters. Until then, outside traders or Union shipping companies do that for you. We sometimes call that Single Reach Commerce. Shipping costs increase with every jump you make." Her eyes continued to search the overhead patterns. "It takes three jumps to get here from Targon if you use the charted jumpsites. You can make it in one, but that takes a huge amount of energy and a very good spanner. And a keyhole, of course. Without gates like that, you couldn't get to a place even if it was the system next door."

"Is that how you got here? Through a keyhole?"

"No, there isn't one that leads here. At least not one we've been able to find. We had to come the long way, through the charted jumpsites like everybody else."

"A long time ago, my people thought that your people came from the gods. But you didn't look like our gods."

"Well, we're supposed to leave planets like yours alone and let them evolve for a few more generations. 'Course, Tharron isn't up to date on our policies. Then you've got private traders that think nothing of going wherever they want to make profit. With all our good intentions, the Union is the last outsider to get here." She looked up again. "So you see, there aren't many *stars* for us to travel to."

He snickered. "And meanwhile you fight over those that you can reach."

"Yeah, we do. We're a vicious breed." She picked at the dry lumps of food in her hand.

"I suppose wars are bound to happen when everyone's so different."

"Wars happen because we are the same."

"The same!"

She nodded. "Sure, we breathe the same air, eat the same food, mostly, and water is water. Of course, some of us have adapted to our native planets. Your four knees or my ears don't make for much variety. Your blood is so much like mine that it's assumed we all started in the same place. No one knows where that was or why and how we ended up scattered so far, but wanting to find that out is what brought the Centauri out here to Trans-Targon in the first place."

Greah looked from his hands to Nova's. "You're saying we're not different species at all?"

"Yeah, I am. You just ended up shorter than my people. I don't lose any sleep over any of this. I call us humanoids, but here we're all lumped under 'Prime Species'. A designation mostly having to do with DNA."

"Are there no exceptions?"

"Yes, there are sentient species that have nothing in common with us. There are, well, squid-things living out by the Pelion system. The natives on PT-30 look like no person or animal I've ever seen. More like acidic blobs of skin that roll around and don't do much at all. But they can communicate and they are self-aware."

"What adventure, to see such things!"

She smiled. "Yes, it is."

"Can I leave here with you'n Ty?" Greah asked suddenly, as if that thought had not been foremost on his mind since meeting Nova.

"With us?" Nova shook her head. "No, we can't take civilians aboard unless it's Union business."

"Like planning to take Kiran to the Badlands?"

She grimaced.

"There are exceptions." He smiled, satisfied.

"Go to sleep," Nova curled up close to the heated stone between them.

Greah watched her for a moment. His eyes traveled to the night sky and his narrow chest rose with a wistful sigh. Then he got up and wandered around their camp, searching the horizon. All was quiet; no one there.

THIRTEEN

Brightness. Sudden, brilliant brightness drove through his eyes and into his brain like a red hot skewer. It was not the light of day that poured through the opened door but the harsh glare of a diffused laser. The light dimmed when someone moved between it and the prisoner.

"Get up!" A booted foot crashed against ribs, not hard enough to fracture them. Tychon groaned and squeezed swollen lids shut against the light of their lamp. He had heard that voice before, somewhere. On Targon? He combed his memory for the owner of the voice, concentrating on that until the pain in his side ebbed a little. Yes, Targon. The pilot who'd known Nova. The other guard was Centauri. He drew a shaky breath, mildly pleased with the success of his exercise.

Rough hands pulled him up and forced him from his cell across the dark compound, once a small market square. He could make out walls and corners of stone buildings where lamps stabbed into the dark with cold beams of light. Rhuwac guards passed from flood-lit areas into night without hesitation, their sense of smell keener than their eyes.

Tychon craned his neck, knowing that the town's fortification wall lay just behind these buildings. He was probably looking at it right now. He turned to walk backward for a few steps, disheartened by the number of Rhuwacs patrolling the grounds.

"Get along, Delphi," the Centauri snarled, gripping his elbow to turn him around. Tychon raised his arm to shrug the hand away. A moment later he was on the ground, a new pain blossoming in the back of his head.

"Son of a motherless Rhuwac," Fynn Bridger guffawed. "I thought the Delphi was gonna make a run for it, Akela." His boot connected sharply with Tychon's thigh. "That is for getting me stuck shipping a bunch of stinking Rhuwacs to Tor Ag and then wasting most of them. And don't think I've forgotten about you putting your hands on Nova Whiteside. You can thank your stars that Pe Furface wants you kept alive."

Tychon was picked up again and manhandled into a large residential building where he soon stood before Tharron, his hands bound together in front of him as if he had the strength to raise them against the Shri-Lan leader.

Tharron was enthroned upon the raised floor of what used to be an eating alcove. It made a fine dais. His Chayko-skin covered chair was flanked by two Rhuwac guards and a brazier beside him was brewing some evil-smelling drink. Tharron himself was dressed in loose leather trousers, his massive chest bare except for a diagonal leather belt studded with the teeth of his enemies, according to rumors. The whole arrangement was obviously meant to inspire fear and awe. Tychon thought it was ridiculous. He was faintly nauseated by the chair coverings. The shy, mute Chaykos had recently been declared sentient by the Union.

"Delphi," Tharron snarled. "I am in the mood to continue our conversation now that you've had time to reconsider your manners. Why are you on Shaddallam?"

Tychon considered the reply he had given to that question earlier. It had been the one that had earned him one of several beatings. He decided on a variation of it, as so often lately borrowing from Nova's more colorful vocabulary. "Why the hell do you think we're here?"

The butt of a long gun slammed into his gut, dropping him to his knees. He wanted to vomit but, since he hadn't been fed, did not. He allowed himself to descend deeper into the khamal that kept his pain and dread from distracting him.

Tharron laughed and took up the goblet from the brazier. "Looking for your firstborn, are you? Well, you found him. I finally have something that will free us all of the great oppression brought down on us by those vile Centauri and their Human pets!" He glared blearily around the room at his guards and officers, speaking to them. "We will be free to tend our fields and children without paying tribute to these interlopers. We shall throw off the yoke of their tyranny and break the chains that keep us in slavery. We shall be free!" Grandly, he drank from his cup.

Tychon looked around the room at those hovering nearby. Their expressions were carefully guarded, but he saw disgusted fascination on some of the faces, especially on Pe Khoja's and those of the two Centauri beside him. "You people believe that lunacy?" he asked conversationally. "He's read that somewhere, you know."

Tharron roared something that none here understood and heaved his cup at Tychon. It glanced sharply along his cheek and opened a deep cut below his eye. Blood poured over his face.

"How do you like that, pretty boy?" Tharron growled. "Ah, but scars can be erased. Perhaps we should take off your hair. Huh?" He looked around for approval from his men. "Huh? And the scalp with it!"

Tychon ground his teeth.

"How did you know where to find me?" Tharron asked, furious over Comori's failure in coming up with a truth serum that worked properly on a Delphian.

Tychon shook his head; it neither lessened nor increased his headache.

"Who else knows?"

"No one," Tychon said. "This is just one place among

dozens we're checking out."

"You lie." Tharron half-turned toward Pe Khoja. "We move in the morning."

"Running away again, Tharron?" Tychon said. Surely Nova would find the means to contact the other Vanguard teams that had come along to Shaddallam to help with the search. It would not be long before they'd discover this place and the presence of the rebels in the valley. "You're hidden quite well in this hole. I never would have expected your quarters down here if your goons hadn't made such a fuss."

"Does Carras know where you are? Is Targon mobilizing? Talk!"

Tychon squinted at the giant. "Targon who?"

A boot caught him in the small of his back, sprawling at Tharron's feet.

"Enough!" Tharron shouted.

Tychon turned his head and saw that Bridger had been about to brain him with the stock of his gun. The Human reluctantly lowered his weapon and retreated.

"It does not matter," Tharron declared. "I am tired of this. We move back to the city in the morning and then get off this rock." He motioned for someone to lift Tychon to his feet. "Some of my men are eager to dispose of you, Delphi. But there is something you can do for me."

"Your wish is my command," Tychon hissed, sounding not quite as sarcastic as he had intended.

"Whiteside," Tharron said. "She is not really dead, is she? Some of your Delphi wizardry back there, wasn't it? She'll probably try to find you."

Tychon did not reply.

Tharron's lips twisted into something like a smile. "I think I'll leave you here for her to find. You can give her a message from me. Actually, Pe Khoja thought of it, and I agree it's going to be fun for everyone. Wouldn't you like that? Comori!"

Tychon turned his head to see a figure separate from the shadows in the back of the room. The small man was neatly dressed and unarmed. He pushed his sleeve back to show

Tychon the object on the palm of his hand.

Tychon's eyes widened. "No!"

"Do it fast before he drops dead like the other one," Tharron advised.

Two of Tharron's guards seized Tychon and led him from the room, struggling with a man who was fighting for his life and sanity. Comori had to sedate him before he could begin his work.

* * *

The sun of Shaddallam had risen as quickly as it had set. Its red orb glared over the horizon, reaching across the flatlands in still weak beams of light broken only occasionally by the clumps of stunted trees that still held pockets of early morning fog.

The two travelers had broken their fast and their camp quickly, spurred by the cold as much as the desire to reach the edge of this desert. Nova moved sluggishly, bothered by a terrible nightmare that had tortured her for most of the night without ever presenting clear images.

They raced atop the sandrunner, aware that the land around them was changing. Nova was startled to find a deep valley in their path. The ground simply dropped, offering a view of moisture laden clouds below them. She saw forests and meadows, birds in the air and the silver ribbons of rivers. She looked back over her shoulder. The flatlands had not been the main feature of Shaddallam after all. Instead of reaching the end of a desert, they had come to the edge of a plateau.

"Who would have thought that a place like this exists on Shaddallam," she said. "It's beautiful!"

Greah's gaze took in the rich lowlands. "This is where I used to live," he said wistfully. "Before your enemy drove us away. They took our towns but left us to our plantations. I lived in the city of Shad Areen at the time. My house is now theirs." His voice broke on the last word.

Nova patted his thin shoulder, feeling awkward. She shielded her eyes with her hand to scan the far horizon. "Over there," she said. "Air traffic. Mostly just skimmers, though, and some Shrills."

"Yes, that's Shad- Laika. Shad-Areen is a ways back, by the lakes."

They began their descent into the valley. Soon Greah slid off the bird's back to jog ahead, finding pathways that the animal could negotiate. The small creature seemed tireless. Nova spotted his slight form now and again among the dense foliage. He paused at times and listened, then whistled softly. Twice he climbed a tree as nimbly as the monkey-like animals she saw more frequently now. Then he startled her by overtaking them when she had been certain she had just seen his multi-jointed body slip through a stand of broadleaf ferns in front of her.

Nova closed her eyes and concentrated on Tychon's signal, ready to pull back should she touch him too firmly. The already tenuous contact of their khamal had faded to nearly nothing. When she prodded, he responded with a startled flinch, then puzzlement. He would not answer.

Ty?

There was no reply.

"Greah!"

He appeared at once, making a running jump at the bird. "We almost reached the edge of this forest," he reported, smiling at the trees above. "Then we cross the meadows and ford a river. We make our camp on the northern bank."

"Ty's not answering," Nova interrupted.

"Is he dead?"

"No! Don't say that. I can still feel him." Her voice shook. "I know they've beaten him to make him talk. Now he's too hurt to even talk to me."

"Could he be sleeping?"

"I'd know that. No, Greah, he's sick or something."

Greah spurred the sandrunner on. "But not dead," he said.

As he had promised, they reached a treeless, marshy area where the runner gained speed in great, splashing strides. Without hesitation, it followed Greah's command to wade into the river. Once across, they continued on foot through the low marsh that ran along the river and then onto higher ground where they stopped to rest.

The dry morsels of food from their baggage almost made Nova wish for a hot tray of 'space slop'. Their meager supplies were nearly gone. Ishet had not taken her size into account when he had packed their provisions. Soon Nova would have to get used to eating the bitter succulents that supplemented Greah's diet.

"We're now in Shad-Laika." Greah scratched a crude map into the dark soil near a tree. "The rebel base is not far." He pointed past her shoulder. "It was a town at one point, though much of it is now ruined. Their planes are kept on the western side."

"We'll need one of those. How well is the town guarded?"

"Very."

"Then we should go in the dark, my vague little friend. Now."

"Now?"

She nodded. "It will be dark by the time we get there. If your picture there is to scale."

"What is your plan?"

"I have no plan. A plan is good only if you have an army to lead and no time to change plans if necessary. With luck I'll come up with something when I see the place."

"That's as good a plan as any. Perhaps Ty's been able to think of something."

"Right now he's not even thinking," Nova mumbled.

They mounted the runner that now headed west at Greah's urging. Nova huddled in her short robe, swathed against the growing chill of the evening as well as Shaddallam's annoying, innumerable insects. They followed the calm waterway in silence. Nova had almost begun to doze when the bird halted. Greah dropped to the ground and led it into a thicket of low bushes.

"Should be all right here," he announced, commanding the runner to settle. Nova climbed off and relieved the bird of their small store of supplies.

They set out at once in the direction of the ruined town, taking only their guns. Shaddallam's sun had gone down, leaving them to find their way in the moonless dark. A crude road, no more than an overgrown path, signaled nearby settlement. They kept to the underbrush, remaining hidden. Nova was startled when a high wall suddenly barred her way. She had been intent on the uneven ground before them.

They crept closer to the road where the gate loomed open and forbidding. She scanned the wall, looking for surveillance cameras, and saw only clumps of grass and moss growing between the rough stones.

She peered around the gate. Dimly, she made out the hulking shapes of houses and the winding streets between them. "You see anything?"

Greah shook his head. "Looks deserted. Maybe they're all in another part of the town."

"No. I can feel Ty close by. This seems a little odd, doesn't it? No lights, no sound." She looked up. "No planes! Greah, this is a rebel base. Why is no one coming or going?" She stepped over a few stone slabs partially buried where they had fallen from the wall. "This can't be a trap. They think I'm dead. Unless Ty told them differently."

Greah shook his head. "Such a trap for just one person? If they knew you were coming, they'd just send some of their creatures to get you. Maybe they all left."

"Don't say that! I don't even have the means to get off this planet." She crept along the wall. "I'm afraid you're right, though. This place is dead. But they've left Ty. He must be awfully hurt. Maybe he's dying!"

He patted her arm. "Nova..."

She shook her head impatiently. "Come on, Greenie, hold it together." She turned back to Greah. "I'll go for Ty. You check out if they've left anything flyable behind. A ground vehicle will do, too, for now. Try to find some food and clean water. We'll meet back here."

Greah nodded and disappeared at once. Nova was not sure

if she had actually seen him move from the spot. He had simply faded into the darkness.

Feeling her way along the deserted town was a matter of stubbed toes and scraped hands in the deep Shaddallam night. Her brightest beacon was Tychon's mute signal. She searched for a cell or other enclosure that could be used as a prison. Many of the structures here lay in ruin, helped along by the carelessness of the looters that had taken the town from its rightful owners. The streets were littered with furnishings and building materials, garbage and excrement. Many of the small buildings' doorways had been smashed by those tired of stooping to gain access.

The source of the mental contact emitted from a low building, its door wide open, at the edge of a plaza. She crept closer, listening for sounds in the dark. Hiding in the cover of a central fountain, she thought she heard a voice, but whatever it was fell silent again. She dashed across the open space and peered into the building. A lamp shone within, allowing her to see inside. The long hall housed two rows of rough-hewn bunks and little else. She guessed it to have been a temporary shelter for Tharron's Rhuwacs. The stench gave that away.

"Ty!" Nova's relief was boundless. She holstered her gun and entered the building.

Tychon, without shirt or jacket, faced away from her, sitting on a bunk, and did not flinch when her call broke the silence of the dead town.

Nova hesitated. The skin of his back and arms was bruised in many places. His long hair hung unheeded over oozing wounds and, like much of him, was matted with dirt. Or blood.

"Tychon?" Nova called again, coming closer to him.

He turned to watch her approach.

"What did they do to you?" she cried, seeing deep scratches across his chest. His lip was cut and one eye was nearly closed by a blood-encrusted bruise.

He smiled, and perhaps that was the worst sight of all. He raised both hands which, trembling, held a pistol clearly adjusted to emit a wide flash. Aimed at her now, it would kill him just as quickly.

* * *

"Why was I not informed, Soto?" Colonel Tal Carras stormed along the halls of Targon's Air Command headquarters, buttoning the collar of his uniform. His aide hurried after him with his gun belt, as necessary as the polished insignia on the colonel's sleeve.

"*Erato* only dropped into normal space a few minutes ago, sir. We were not advised of her arrival. Security measures, I was told."

"Doesn't anyone use charts anymore?" Carras barely waited for him to clear the doors into the lift shaft. "Who's *Erato*'s commander now?"

"Lieutenant Colonel McDougall, sir. He has requested a clear flight path."

"At least someone's thinking!"

"Yessir," Soto said. *Erato* had come in without a whisper. When the reasons for the battleship's sudden appearance were questioned, a coded message arrived that Baroch, one of the Ten Factors, was aboard. Baroch on a battleship! On Targon! Soto barely contained his curiosity. "Shall I order a security detachment?"

"Negative," Carras said. "Business as usual."

They arrived in the hangars in time to catch their breath before two of *Erato*'s Kites dove out of the sky and into the landing bays. Two pilots eventually emerged from the small ships and walked toward a ready room without removing their helmets.

"Fetch my flight suit, Soto. Baroch has sent his own honor guard." Carras, too, moved toward the lounge. His aide disappeared.

Carras entered the room. "This is a surprise," he said. "Perhaps we may be warned before you drop such exalted company onto our heads." His hand reached for a flight helmet before he realized that one of the pilots had remained standing at attention, unusual on the flight decks, even in the presence of a colonel. The other was only now removing his helmet. Carras' hand snapped back from the shelf and joined the other behind his back. "Factor!"

Baroch untangled his long braid from the helmet visor. "At ease, Carras. And yes, I do feel exalted whenever I have the privilege of flying a fine ship such as the Kite."

Carras did not relax his formal stance. "Forgive me, sir, I had expected to meet with you aboard the *Erato*."

The Delphian smiled. "Ah, never assume, never expect. Had you known me, you would have expected me to enjoy the Kite. Had you expected me, you would have insisted on boarding *Erato*. Am I assuming too much?"

"No, sir, your safety on Targon is questionable. Aboard the *Erato*—"

"Aboard the *Erato*, I would not have had the opportunity to reacquaint myself with the Kite. Allow me my pleasures, these days they are few."

Baroch loosened his uniform to let his braid slip beneath his suit. Then he unfolded a hood from his rolled collar and draped it over his head. "To a safe room, then, so that we may talk."

The other pilot stepped close to his side, now carrying Baroch's helmet. Carras realized that he had seen him before, back on Coup d'Oeil. Not just a bodyguard, this man was a Prime Staff agent, one of the Ten's separate security force that answered to no one else. When Soto rejoined him, Carras motioned to him with a private signal. Soto fell into step with them, his hand near his pistol, his eyes alert to danger.

The four men walked only a few steps and ascended a staircase that led to a long, narrow room overlooking the landing area. It was empty at this time of day. No visitors toured here to observe the activities below, no tired pilots rested here between shifts. Carras knew this to be so. Long ago, he had begun to discourage the use of this room. It was a convenient place to detain suspect visitors for questioning before they saw more of the base than the bays. A small, steadily glowing indicator by the food service area assured that the room was free of listening devices.

Baroch looked about and nodded, satisfied. "You may leave us," he said to both Soto and his own guard.

When they were alone, he turned to Carras. "I assume," he smiled, "that you would appreciate an explanation."

Carras nodded. "It is not often that one of the Elected Ten Factors will commandeer one of our battleships for a personal conveyance. Especially not the *Erato*."

Baroch stood by the one-way glass wall, unseen by those below. "This is a military matter, I assure you. Not only did I summon *Erato*, but battleship *Teti* will also arrive within a few hours."

"*Teti?*"

"Your old command, correct? Well, you will once again take her, if only for a few days." The Delphian turned to Carras, his expression grave. "We will take them both to Shaddallam."

"I believe we have that situation under control," Carras objected. "V7 and One are on the ground and actively engaged in the investigation. Three and Nine are in the sector. All outgoing traffic from any part of Shaddallam is monitored. It may take a while before our agents can locate the boy's exact position. Shaddallam is a large planet. I've had no indication that further support is required. Mobilizing two battleships is a provocation we don't need at this point."

"A delegation from Delphi met with me on Feyd," Baroch said as if he had heard none of Carras' assurances. "Shantirs."

"Oh?"

Baroch held his gaze.

"How bad is it?" Carras said finally, his voice hoarse.

"Bad," Baroch said. "Worse. I have files with me that explain what Delphi hoped to gain from this creature Tughan Wai. It is beyond what we imagined."

"I can imagine a few things."

"If you could, you would not be sitting complacently in your offices, shuffling duty rosters and requisitions!" Baroch snapped, startling the colonel with his vehemence. "I am sure that you have heard those grand, overblown legends about the Tughan Wai. Heroic stories of a superbeing that will protect the people of Delphi. They tell of some savior figure that will blow up battleships and collapse jumpsites. The truth is much simpler, Carras. The Tughan kills. It wants to kill. Once released, it cannot be stopped. Mentally, it feeds on what it kills and grows to include what it has killed. Kill a thousand men, and it becomes those thousand men, weak or strong, within one body. The Tughan will gain complete understanding of all of them. And what will he do with this knowledge? He sure as you're standing there will not be blowing up enemy ships for Delphi or anyone else for that matter!"

Baroch closed his eyes to allow himself a moment to regain his usual equilibrium. Calmer, he went on to explain. "The concept for the Tughan Wai is based on the khamal, which is initiated by touch. Except that this creature does not just share its partner's thought and mind, it absorbs it entirely. It copies and understands every connection and every synapse ever made by that mind. Unfortunately, the victim's brain is destroyed by this. That is the design flaw that the Shantirs fear. And none of them know just how much touch is required to do this. Perhaps none at all. Perhaps it can simply *think* itself into a khamal with any one of us. With any thousand of us. Who knows? Perhaps tens of thousands."

Carras swallowed hard, understanding. "Unless..."

"Unless the body now occupied by the Tughan Wai dies. He is as mortal as you and I. For now. But who can really know what he will become?"

"My agents have orders to return the child to Delphi at once. We all understand the research opportunities."

"Can you not understand the threat of this thing? It can never be contained. Delphi does not want him. Their studies over the past few years dug up some interesting conclusions. The boy was already marked for termination. Had Tharron not taken him, he would have been destroyed by the Shantirate before the Tughan emerges on its own at the end of his puberty, around the age of twenty-five."

"I have confidence in my people. They will be able to retrieve the boy."

"Colonel," Baroch said. "Suppose that he does not wish to be retrieved."

Carras paled.

Baroch folded his arms and leaned against the window, his eyes on the shift change below. Patrol planes landed, their crews deplaned, waving tiredly to their replacements before heading toward the dressing rooms and on to fourteen hours of downtime before their next shift. "You are concerned about a living, walking bomb. You think Tharron has a gun bigger than ours. So it may be. And so what? Time will pass. People live, they die, whether led by us or by him. It does not matter." Baroch turned back to face him. "Our worry has gone beyond this. This living, walking bomb has a living, working mind. Probably the finest mind ever conceived, once the creation is complete. Once the Tughan awakes, he will understand Tharron. He will touch Tharron and he will know more about Tharron than Tharron does."

"He will not remain as a tool in rebel hands."

"Nor ours. He is a greater force than the Shri-Lan and the Union Commonwealth combined. He will be beyond anything we can ever hope to understand." Baroch leaned closer to Carras. "He will hate us for what we have done to him. He may destroy all of us in the rage he will feel over his creation. And he won't stop then because he needs to kill in order to grow. And he will live to god-like proportions."

"But he is Delphian! His nature–"

"His nature will change with every single thing he touches. There is no such thing as a benevolent god! We have made it so with every religion we invented."

Carras' mind was churning madly, groping for reason among the dreadful visions his brain even now tried to digest.

Baroch gave him no time for contemplation. "We were beyond lucky to have found them on Shaddallam as quickly as we did. Our luck won't hold forever. You and I both know that the odds are great that Tharron himself is also on

Shaddallam. We cannot take the chance that he will hide the boy elsewhere if he is unable to use him now. We have intercepted a message that one of Tharron's carriers has left for Shaddallam. What can your agents there possibly accomplish against a battleship? We will go to Shaddallam as soon as the *Teti* arrives. He will not get away. No one must leave that planet until the Tughan is eliminated."

* * *

Nova wasted no time in assessing her situation. She launched herself forward to use her momentum and this instance of surprise to ram her shoulder into Tychon's midriff, throwing both of them over the cot and onto the floor. His gun spun into the shadows.

He pushed her away and struggled to his feet. His knees buckled drunkenly and he swayed to keep his balance. But he circled her, ready to pounce.

"Ty, it's me! Don't you recognize me?"

"You're one of them. Don't come any closer."

Desperately, Nova tried to remember what she had learned of the mind altering methods used by their enemies. She groped for long-forgotten classroom sessions dealing with Tharron's ways and searched her memory for cases of mental domination. If Tychon had fallen victim to Tharron's drugs they would surely have been administered in a quantity to kill him eventually.

She moved toward him, sure that he was about to collapse. But he surprised her. When she reached for him, he lunged and his fist caught her shoulder, throwing her back to collide with the wall behind her. Something was lending him strength, perhaps pumping adrenalin where nothing else was keeping him upright.

She whipped around him, measuring how fast he followed, and moved toward the door. "Ty, come on. It's me, Nova. Look at me!"

"Nova is dead. Your people killed her!"

"No, please listen. Hear my voice. I'm right here."

He shook his head, seeing nothing before him but an enemy. "You killed her," he said, his face a mask of anguish. "You killed my wife. Then you took my son. And now you took her, too." His words faded to barely a whisper. "Should have killed me."

Nova's tears doubled and trebled his image before her. Her tears were for the bruises on his body and the blood that smeared his skin and clothes. He trembled from head to foot as he fought to remain standing. Tharron's torturers had managed to bury the man he was and left him blank, a mere shell in which to place their murderous assignment. "Please wake up!" she pleaded.

He lurched toward her as if massive weights were tied to his feet.

"Think, you stupid greenie," Nova berated herself. "Think like a Delphian." She backed away from Tychon, moving slowly. His voice sounded hollow and coarse, she suspected dehydration. But his words were not slurred by drugs and his pale eyes were focused. What else would work quickly enough to make him susceptible to their tampering? It had to be something mechanical, something that could be turned off.

Then it came to her. Somewhere on his back would be a small metal plug. A crude device that was one of Tharron's favorites. Once embedded in the skin, it would send disturbing messages to its carrier's brain along the nerves in the spine. It would then only take a few hours of constantly repeated suggestions to plant a belief or an attitude into the subject's mind. And Tychon's mind was already taxed to exhaustion by their khamal.

The khamal! Nova focused on their mental link and screamed her fear into his wide open mind.

He lurched away from her, clutching his head. His legs gave out and he crashed to the floor.

She scrambled to where he had fallen, distraught by the pain she had caused him. "Ty? Ty, talk to me!" She shook his shoulder. "Please, Ty!"

He lowered his arms from his head, breathing heavily.

"You okay? I'm sorry." She helped him to sit up.

Nova did not struggle when his long fingers closed around her neck. She conserved her air, beating down the waves of panic, knowing that if she gave in to her fear now, she would be dead in minutes. Her hand reached around his back and slipped under his hair. She touched a hard, metallic protrusion close to his spine. The flesh around it was hot and swollen. Perhaps it would still be safe to remove it. She felt herself weakening, sure that her head was about to explode, followed closely by her lungs. Her nails dug into his skin, tearing at the hard edges of the control unit. It wrenched from his back with a small, insignificant sound that she would never forget.

She stifled his roar of pain with her bloodied hand and held him down with her body while she coughed, gasping for air. He was writhing. Beads of sweat appeared on his face as he fought the agony she had inflicted, his eyes bulging, not leaving hers until he was able to breathe again.

"Ty?" she whispered, taking her weight off him. She crushed the disk under her heel and kicked it away. "Can you hear me? I'm sorry. You'll be fine now, really. It's over." She grasped the hands that were clenched in pain. She hoped that what she said was true.

Nova felt nothing but absolute hatred for Tharron at this moment. He could have simply left a detail of his men waiting in ambush for her, knowing that she was coming. Snipers could have taken her and Greah out from a safe distance. But he had taken the time needed to bend Tychon to his will, ordering her execution by one of her own people!

A noise behind her startled her into a dive for Tychon's gun. She rolled and brought the gun up to point at the door.

"Hey!" Greah yelled. "It's me!"

"You scared the stuffing out of me!" Nova reset the gun safety. Her hands were still shaking.

Greah approached Tychon who was now barely conscious, trembling with pain and exhaustion. "That the major? They made him over, didn't they? What a mess. Is he dying?"

"No. I did this to him. I'm sure he can handle the scratches they gave him. He's gone into shock or something."

"How'd you do that?" Greah opened a satchel. It contained medication, bandages, water. "Lots of things lying around here. They left in a big hurry."

She waved a hand at the broken control on the floor. "They made him think I'm one of them. He probably told them I was alive and what we were doing here. Then they left him to take care of me."

Greah nudged the device with his furred boot. Long metal teeth edged the disk to which bits of Tychon's skin and hair still clung. "That thing can do that?"

She nodded, searching through the kit for items meant for Centauri physiology, close enough to Tychon's to be useful. "Let's get him on his feet and back down to the river. This town feels like a graveyard."

She applied painkillers and packed the fresh wound on Tychon's back. He was more alert now, but still shivering. The deep blue was returning to his eyes.

"This is some kind of pain," he groaned.

"Probably because there is a big hole in your back." She leaned down to him. "Shut the khamal."

He lifted his hands with effort and touched her face. Once the mental link between them had come apart, the ache in his head began to subside.

It was a slow, tedious process to help Tychon back to where the sandrunner waited by the river. By the time the sun began to make the day's short journey across the sky, Nova had cleaned his wounds and sponged his body. She winced each time she found a new cut beneath the layers of dried blood and dirt on his skin. Most of his pain had receded, now consolidated into a dull headache.

"Sleep now," she decided while she braided his hair to keep it from his lacerations. "We can't go on today."

He nodded and wrapped his arms around a blanket that served as a pillow. They watched Greah play by the river with the sandrunner and listed to his musical laughter. She ran her fingers along his spine as he drifted off, pleased to hear something between a purr and a contented groan when she touched him.

"I'm sorry you had to go through this," he said. "I still can't believe it happened."

"You didn't know it was me."

"I meant what I said," he said after a moment. "Back there. You mean that much to me. I can't lose you." He smiled crookedly. "I haven't known you all that long, Greenie, but I've been in your head. I like it in there. And I don't want anyone else in mine."

She stretched out beside him and kissed the part of his mouth that wasn't bruised. "I'm not going anywhere."

* * *

Nova kept Tychon sedated throughout the short day and the following night, working with the meager supply of medication to ease his injuries and reduce the swelling of his bruises. He woke only to receive more painkillers and, once, a bowl of soup. His normally silent rest was disturbed by nightmares, and he mumbled and moaned as he dreamed.

She dozed fitfully, unaccustomed to Shaddallam's swift rotation. She woke whenever he did, maintaining her watch over him, anxiously checking his temperature. During a lucid moment, he told her that Kiran was close by, still on the planet. But it was clear that until he was well enough, there could be no thought of going on.

Greah, perpetually restless, returned to the empty town, successfully breaking into a few more of the buildings, enjoying his role as thief and provider. He liberated a further supply of medication and food, as well as blankets and a few decent bottles of berry wine from the abandoned stores of loot. Unlike Tychon, Nova welcomed a few good swigs of the delicious liquid.

Nova awoke upon the next daybreak, not at all sure of where she was but finally feeling rested. She stretched, looking for Greah. It seemed that he had gone on another raid. The bird squatted nearby, observing her silently. She moved around

Tychon and carefully started to re-bandage his wounds.

He hissed softly.

"Sorry. You awake?"

"Hmm. How does it look?"

"Good! Well, at least not awful. It's healing. You'll have a mess of scars, though. I don't think we can get you blasted in time." She reapplied fine strip of tape that sealed a deep cut under his eye.

He sat up to stretch his limbs. "But I'm alive, thanks to you. That thing on my back would have killed me, too, if the gun hadn't. Remind me to get you promoted if we ever get back to Targon. I'll overlook the fact that you assaulted a superior officer."

Nova grinned. "Can you travel today?"

He nodded, touching his lips. "I've got a loose tooth."

She reached for the medi-kit. "You want another shot?"

He pulled her arm back. "No! I've been out of my head long enough. It's not something my people appreciate."

"Awake, are you?" Greah appeared, as usual out of nowhere. "Is it time to decide how we're gonna go on from here?"

Nova turned away from Greah. "What... is... that?" She pointed over her shoulder into his direction.

He held aloft two small carcasses. "Real food! I thought you wanted some."

"Get it away! I have seen enough blood." She helped Tychon to his feet.

"Looks good to me," Tychon said, dropping his blanket. Nova winced at the sight of his injuries. "I'll just go and powder my nose."

"Powder his nose? Why?" Greah asked.

Nova smiled, watching Tychon walk into the river. She began to dig through a heap of clothes that Greah had found and judged to be roughly of their size. Most of it was various men's bits and pieces, mainly Centauri or Bellac and little of it very clean. Still, it looked less likely to have originated in Union territory than her own clothes. She decided to keep her

Shaddallam boots, having grown rather fond of their fit and style.

By the time Tychon returned and had dressed, Greah had prepared their food and was roasting it over a smokeless fire. Even Nova's untrained sense of smell was enticed by the aroma. Tychon bit into his share, hesitated, and shot her a warning glance. She tried hers and found it generously seasoned with the bitter herb that Greah seemed to favor. She sighed and ate, too ravenous to really care anymore.

"They're still on Shaddallam but getting ready to move," Tychon said between bites. "There are a few more bases here, not as well hidden but heavily guarded. Tharron keeps himself well protected. He's crazy, by the way."

"I know that. The man's a maniac," Nova said.

"No, I mean he's really crazy. Insane. I know enough K'lars to know when one of them is missing a few chips. He really believes he's saving his people from persecution by trying to ram his head against the Union. Ideologically, he's more like the Arawaj."

"But not his people."

"Not a bit. I saw their faces when he was speechifying. They're quite happy to use his rants to rally the troops. While he is attacking Union settlements and blowing up churches, they set up their drug labs and smuggling operations and organize raids just for the loot. I think Tharron doesn't even know they're doing all that and setting him up to take the blame. He's little more than a figurehead."

Greah sighed. "I almost feel sorry for him. To be so insane and used and shunned."

Nova frowned. "He is still a murderer. We have to stop him."

"He should have been stopped years ago," Tychon said. "Now he's got himself a new pistol. I'm sure even his own people are worried. He's gotten too powerful. I'll bet they're wishing he'd just kept on being a nuisance. He is much more than that now. I think they're ready to make a move."

"What move?"

"Velani is here. He arrived a few days ago."

"Velani! Here?"

He winced, already anticipating her reaction. "Velani is a Shantir."

She gaped at him, taken aback by this revelation. "You knew that? And you didn't think that might be a problem?"

Tychon shrugged. "The idea that any Shantir would go to Tharron is an absurdity. Unthinkable. And to even consider that Kiran's own uncle would do that just didn't occur to me."

"Did you see Kiran?"

"While I was being beaten into a bloody mess? I can only be glad that he didn't see me."

"That's true. So what happened with Velani?"

"He met with Tharron for quite a while. They must have reached a decision. They said something about Shad-Arion."

"Shad-Areen," Greah said. "A rebel stronghold not far down the river. The city still functions, no one's been expelled. But he keeps hordes of rebels there."

"That's why so many of them left on foot. I figured it was close by. I guess then that Shad-Areen is our next stop." Tychon grimaced when he unfolded his long limbs and paced around their camp to test his legs. He began to load packs and parcels onto the sandrunner.

Nova turned to Greah. "You know it wouldn't be fair to ask you to go further with us. You were hired to lead me to Shad-Laika, not get killed for us."

"You're not asking. I am offering! Do you really think I'm gonna go home now?"

Tychon laughed. "No, we can use every fighting body we have."

"You used to live in Shad-Areen, didn't you?" Nova asked Greah.

"Yes. It's a big town, lots of people. I know folks there that can help us." He wrinkled his forehead into a thoughtful expression. "You know, I've wondered why your Union doesn't just blast in here. You must have more firepower'n Tharron. Why don't they send your armies?"

"Why would they? They don't even know for sure that Kiran is here. And until we can reach one of the other Eagles, we have no way of telling them. But even then, it's not that easy. No other sector is crawling with rebels as much as this one. We couldn't get a fleet as far as K'lar without Tharron knowing about it. Besides, we can't just march in here and risk your people in some big battle. That's not what the Union is about. So we're on our own for now." She began to scatter their fire, damping it with loose soil. "And we've got their hostage to worry about. When Tharron sees me, he'll wish that our regular army *had* landed on him. Let's move. We'll want to get to Shad-Areen by mid-morning."

FOURTEEN

The dense, moist forest of the Shad-Laika basin eventually gave way to lower, less concentrated vegetation that made their going easier. They moved as quickly as possible at a forced pace between rest stops. Frequently, the travelers came upon narrow paths leading to the river or spotted signs of now deserted campsites. Greah, in his role as native scout, examined each one and explained how many had slept at each fire, what they had eaten and how many guards they had posted.

Nova grew more irritable with each stop. The nomads of Shad-Laika were of no interest to her; Greah would find a more receptive audience for his findings in the bird trailing behind them.

She tapped her foot impatiently when Tychon bent to listen to yet another of Greah's long-winded reports.

"Strange," Tychon said when they at last continued on their way.

"What?" Nova ducked under the branches of a tree, turning to lead the bird through. "Shouldn't we try to hurry?"

"Greah said that there was a road, sort of a highway leading into the town, half a kil north of here. Yet these people keep to the side and don't even follow the same trail. It's like they don't want to be seen."

"So? I wouldn't, either."

"Yes, but these camps were made by Greah's people. They have no reason to hide from the rebels. Tharron doesn't take them half-seriously. They post guards like they were on the run or had something to hide."

"Maybe they do." Nova tugged on the runner's leash. "Come on, you!"

Greah appeared beside them and tapped the bird's legs. It seemed to understand this and moved faster. "That's because they're afraid of the beasts Tharron keeps around himself. When they have nothing to do, Tharron lets them run around out here to keep things in order. He doesn't care what they do when they find people they don't like."

"Rhuwacs," Nova said. "They don't like most people."

"That's them. If they catch us out here..." His young-old face contorted into an expression of terror, and he gripped his gun to his chest as though to ward off the evil spirits Tharron had brought into this world.

Nova resisted an impulse to crouch down to hug the small man. Instead, she gripped his shoulder, reminding herself that he was not a child in need of comforting. But the look on his face was one she had seen on an infinite number of people left to the devices of Tharron's dogs. "Even Rhuwacs know what your gun is for," she assured him. "Don't be afraid."

He shook his head. "I met them and I'm still alive. But my people... you don't understand. We do not kill other... other sentients. Not even our worst enemy. We kill only for food and to make leather. That's the way it was written when Sen Lienn made this world for us. No killing, she said. That's why we build walls around our cities. To keep, uh, strangers out. The people from the south." He pointed skyward. "They don't keep out strangers that come from above."

"But you carry a gun! You have killed," Nova exclaimed. Seeing Greah in such despair worried her.

"Against his nature," Tychon said. "Greah's people aren't

the only race that doesn't kill their own. They found other means to settle things. It just wasn't necessary before our glorious Union showed us all how to live. And die. And now Greah will fight for his people, as do Delphians that now fight for the Union. It has to start somewhere."

Nova took her eyes off Greah's unhappy face to glower at Tychon. "You're saying that this is the Union's fault? All of this?"

"Are we not teaching these people how to kill? Tharron is just an inevitable by-product. You put someone in power and someone else rebels against it. Now we're involving people that should be left alone to worship their harvest gods. The Clan Council of Delphi saw all that long ago. Maybe they are not so wrong in opposing what you call progress. Without the Union, Tharron would never have left K'lar."

"You are part of this Union!"

He nodded. "So I am. That doesn't make this right." He nudged the gun strapped to her thigh. "You don't even think about killing anymore. How do you know that you've got the right to kill anyone? Because they're rebels? You are of a warrior breed developed by the Centauri. You are no more Human than I am Delphian."

"Why are you talking like this?"

Tychon glanced at Greah, not entirely sure why he was talking like this. "Maybe this is getting to me, finally. If it weren't for us, people like Greah wouldn't have to worry about people like Tharron."

"Of course not! If it wasn't for us, Tharron would be in control and being eaten alive by Rhuwacs would be a way of life and nothing to fuss about!"

"Tharron wouldn't be here. He wouldn't have Rhuwacs. You're not listening..."

"Come, you two!" Greah stepped between them. "Don't carry on so. Let's get on. Maybe if we manage to find the boy, both your Union and the Shri-Lan will leave this planet and save me the trouble of having to show my kinsmen how to kill. I will only need to invent a harvest god." He turned to walk ahead again, soon swallowed up by the undergrowth.

Nova followed him, a little annoyed with Tychon. More than that, she worried over Greah's revelation concerning his people. She had begun to count on them for help against Tharron and his army. In her mind, she had seen a battlefield of nimble-footed, heavily-armed Greahs pitted against the slow Rhuwac soldiers. They would not fight? Was that not an instinct to most things that crawled, swam and walked? She recalled Tychon's words. Of course she had been trained for this! Killing one's enemy was what war was all about, was it not?

"Can you believe it?" she grumbled, more to herself than to Tychon. "They won't fight! We're going up against Tharron, just the three of us. The only chance we'll have is that he'll laugh himself to death. We'll–" She nearly fell over Greah, who had come to an abrupt halt in the middle of the path, straining forward, listening.

She crouched at once, her gun in her hand before her thoughts had caught up with the reflex. Something about Greah's stance called for absolute caution. Nova looked behind her to see the bird standing still, Tychon's hand clamped around its beak.

She squinted to see through the thicket in front of them, soon making out five Rhuwacs, broad backs turned toward them.

Nova shifted her weight left to show Tychon the direction she would take. They were too close now. The bird could never be moved quietly. She prayed that none of the Rhuwacs would sense them, smell them perhaps.

Something in their midst seemed to occupy them. Nova winced when she discovered a Shaddallama lying motionless on the ground while another one, this one female, cowered at his side, fearfully staring at the Rhuwacs.

Nova turned to Greah, about to send him back to calm the sandrunner. But he had already discovered the object of the Rhuwacs' interest. Before she could restrain him he had launched himself at the beasts with the fiercest of battle cries.

* * *

Velani reclined comfortably on Tharron's open courtyard, enjoying the fragrant air that wafted over the garden. Again, Tharron had confiscated the most palatial house of the beleaguered city for himself. Complete with little native servants, Velani remarked to himself, nothing too good for our leader.

He mused over this. He was calling Tharron 'our leader' now. Did that make him a rebel? He doubted this. He was a Shantir. Neutral. Totally neutral. And about to be part of the most wonderful miracle the galaxy had ever seen!

He watched the K'lar giant stomp along the archway to the gardens. Oh, he was in a state again! Just look at his underlings cringe and cower as he rages. And had he just kicked that little servant? Such a vulgar, crude man. A voice loud enough to shake the walls.

Velani fanned himself, wondering if he should call for one of the refreshing berry drinks he enjoyed so much. He was no longer afraid of Tharron. The man needed him; there was no one else who could give him the Tughan Wai. So why whine and quake at Tharron's feet?

Of course, Tharron was one thing. Pe Khoja was quite another. Velani's face clouded. Pe Khoja, Taelros and others like them despised Velani, that much was clear. The reason for their loathing was less definite. It worried the Shantir, and he stepped with caution around them.

Tharron strode to Velani's lounge."Get up, wizard! You have work to do."

"I studied with the boy this morning and then sent him to play. He is such an exceptional child! But we must be careful. I suggest two hours in the morning and two in the afternoon."

"Forget your study. We've been discovered. It wasn't enough to move to Shad-Areen. We must leave this planet."

Velani rose. "Where are we going?"

"As far as orbit. It is time to fight. Give me the Tughan."

"That is impossible! It should take months to prepare him.

The child is not ready."

Tharron regarded the Shantir with the same amused curiosity that showed when he tried to converse with Kiran. "There are two Union battleships on a direct course for Shaddallam. They will be here by tomorrow. They'll have enough of your Delphi wizards on board to turn your brains into gruel. My people estimate over four hundred combat fighters. A couple of Eagles are already buzzing around this planet, just hoping to intercept our escape."

"What about your men? You have ships. You have guns."

"I have nothing! We were able to reach only one of my battleships before both of my com relays were destroyed. One! That will give me less than two hundred fighters besides what I have down here. We're surrounded and outnumbered. The only way we'll get out is by demonstrating my new weapon."

"But there is still time! If we leave at once, we only need to worry about the Eagles. Surely you have enough firepower to overcome them. We can run before Air Command arrives."

"Tharron does not run!" the leader roared. "We will make our stand here over Shaddallam, tomorrow!"

"They would not dare risk the life of this child. I know what you did on Tannaday. They will let us go, knowing that we have the boy."

Tharron's expression shifted. Even Velani could not suppress a shudder when he looked into the cold eyes within the fleshy folds of the K'lar's face. "This is not Tannaday. This is not about children. They would not hesitate to blow us out of the skies."

"Then let us stay here. We are safe on the ground. This city is filled to bursting with people. As the Union's armies would not oppose the children of Tannaday, so they would not risk the people of Shaddallam. They can't touch us here."

"These people will not be here for much longer," Tharron said. "I know what the Tughan needs. I've seen the files you found on Delphi. He will feed, wizard. But not on Rhuwacs. I've brought something tastier for him."

Velani only stared, utterly dumbfounded.

"Of course," Tharron continued. "Thanks to your Union friends, we now have a real banquet arriving. Air Command is delivering warriors, engineers, Shantirs, pilots! What a feast for the Tughan Wai!"

"You... you can't mean this!"

"Make sure the boy is ready. You will destroy the Union fleet and then we will strike Feyd. Or Targon itself."

Velani coughed to conceal what would have been a whimper. "Targon? Those are high stakes, Lord! I thought you had considered Aram or Myra."

"Delphi, perhaps?"

"Delphi is mine!"

Tharron laughed, a sound like breaking glass. "So it will be. When the Ten Factors are ten dead bodies. We will leave here as soon as you've prepared the boy. He will destroy the Union fleet and then we leave for Targon."

"He is young. I have only now been able to reach his mental block. It could kill him."

The K'lar turned to leave. "I only need to use him once. No one will call my bluff twice. If I can take Targon intact, by threat alone, I will have gained much. When the Union fleet arrives, we will take the boy into orbit and you will let him take those ships out of the sky. See that you are ready."

Velani stared after Tharron, speechless. Tomorrow! He thought of the Union's ships steadily advancing, preparing for battle. The Tughan would deal with them easily. Child's play! Perhaps he could... yes, it was possible! Velani hurried into the house, calling for Kiran. There was so much to do!

* * *

Greah blurred past Nova, his outraged cry ringing in her ears. His gun shattered the head of the closest Rhuwac with enough power to leave the decapitated, spurting body standing upright beside his astounded compatriots before it crumpled to the ground.

Surprise was all that was left to them. Nova flung herself into the clearing, firing. Another Rhuwac fell.

The beasts moved in a daze, slow to reach for their own guns. When Tychon felled one of the giants to the left, the remaining two realized that they were surrounded. One lurched toward the two Shaddallam natives and grasped Greah by the neck, lifting him to cover himself.

"Greah!" Nova shouted. The Rhuwac roared in fear and triumph.

He had never met a Shaddallama capable of self defense. Gurgling, Greah twisted his multi-jointed arms and aimed his gun. The force of the charge tore through his foe and exploded out of his back. Tychon had to leap out of the way to avoid being crushed beneath the massive body. Greah was flung in the opposite direction.

Nova disposed of the last of the Rhuwacs as he turned to make his escape. "There's one I don't mind shooting in the back," she said, watching him fall. She looked around. The unscheduled attack had lasted no more than a few seconds. "Everyone all right? Ty?"

"Fine." He took his shirt off and threw it away. "I seem to be splattered with Rhuwac innards, but I don't think they had the time to shoot anything else."

Greah crouched beside the frightened woman and helped her to her feet. She stared round-eyed at Tychon and Nova, then at Greah and finally at her dead mate. She wailed and flung herself over the body, shaking the lifeless arm, sobbing incoherently.

Tychon holstered his gun and dug another shirt from their diminishing stores. "Calm her down, Greah. We'll take her to the city with us. The body, too. But shut her up."

Greah did his best, and soon she tramped along with them, shell-shocked and silent.

It was not long now before their path met the main road. They halted when they saw a steady stream of people moving toward Shad-Areen. In the distance, a stone bridge spanned the river. A small group of natives was making the cross, leading furred animals. Now that the highway had broadened, they were no longer making an effort at concealing themselves.

"We're not far now," Greah said. "We'll keep meeting other people. Cover yourselves up a little. You look much too Human."

"I am not Human," Tychon grumbled. He tied his hair back and threw a blanket over his head as a sort of cowl.

"You're not Shaddallama, either!"

Nova went back to the sandrunner and searched through her parcels. "Give me your water bottle." The others watched in silence as she poured a powder into the leather flask and then shook it carefully.

"What is that?" Tychon asked.

"Ishet gave me this. Turns your skin red. Apparently there are lots of Bellac Tau traders in this area. That right, Greah?"

He nodded. "Skin traders, leather merchants. Rebels, too." He giggled when Tychon sniffed the bottle and made a face.

"Drink it fast," Nova advised.

Tychon squeezed his eyes shut when he did so. "That stuff is ugly!" he gasped.

Nova drained the rest of the concoction, nearly retching. They looked at each other. "So?"

Tychon dropped into the high grass. "I guess we'll wait and see what happens." He beckoned the bird to settle.

They waited in silence. Nova's stomach ceased its protest over the unfamiliar substance. Her skin tingled. She looked at her hands. "I'll be grounded! Look at this!" She turned to Tychon. "Look at you!"

"Not if I look like you."

Their skin had turned an agitated, sickly red in place of the rich and velvety hue she had expected from the grocer's concoction. Still, at a distance it would pass as Bellac skin. "This had better wear off," she said. "Greah, do you know anything about this stuff?"

"Never heard of it."

"I guess I should have asked Ishet." Nova covered her hair, thankful that the potion had not turned it white.

None of the people they now met along their trail took notice of the two tall Bellacs walking their way with the

Shaddallamas and their runner. As in Shad-Lengh, they seemed to avoid strangers. True to Greah's word, not one of the natives carried so much as a stick for a weapon.

More and more of the paths emerged from the undergrowth until the trails had formed a busy road where everyone seemed to travel in just one direction. Nova felt like a giant walking among the Shaddallamas, most of whom traveled in groups and journeyed with livestock and carts.

At last the dense vegetation parted to reveal the city before them. Surrounded by a sloping stone wall, it resembled a fortress into which their road led without bypass. Armed guards paced atop the wall at even intervals. Packs of Rhuwacs patrolled the road below, harassing people at random.

Planes came and went, indicating an airfield within. Nova scrutinized each one, seeing mostly the unmarked ships likely belonging to Tharron's fleet. Only one or two were designed for long distance travel. She wondered if he kept deep space ships in other parts of Shaddallam, perhaps cruisers in orbit.

"Not a lot of useful planes," she said to Tychon, speaking Bellac. Her accent was imperfect and she kept her voice low. "I'm guessing the Eagle is here, since we didn't find it in Shad-Laika. Adachi and his crew should be able to track it here."

"Yes, except they don't know we've misplaced it," Tychon said. "For all they know we're still looking for that tree."

She sighed. Standard procedure on a rebel-held planet would prevent Vanguard Three and One from communicating with the others unless their objective had been reached. Although it had been days since their arrival on Shaddallam, their silence would not yet be cause for alarm.

"Besides," Tychon said, peering at the Rhuwacs from beneath his hood, "Pe Khoja surely knows to remove the ship's squawker. He seemed familiar with the Eagle's specs. I'm guessing it's powered down and dead silent by now."

The steady pedestrian traffic slowed as each caravan was questioned at the city gate. While awaiting their turn, Tychon peered up to study Shad-Areen's outer defenses. "I think the guards up there are for show," he said. "Look at those cameras by each buttress."

"What's your business here?" A Centauri guard held his gun to Tychon's chest. Meta, their new acquaintance, squealed fearfully.

"Eh? What does it say?" Tychon inquired.

"We are not on Bellac, you," the leather-garbed soldier growled. He looked to Greah. "Do you speak D'gabi?"

Tychon gambled. "Tell this foul-smelling pig dog to remove its weapon from my person."

Nova tensed, but the guard had not understood the insult.

"What did he say?" he asked her.

She smiled prettily. "He begs you to lift your gun, sir."

The rebel studied Nova. He did not look at her face. "What's your business here?"

"We are only looking for a place to rest for the night," Greah said quickly. "His lungs, you see. They are weak. Another cold night outside would worsen him."

Nova winced at this. Bellacs had only one rather complicated lung; a fact of which she hoped the guard was as ignorant as Greah.

The soldier eyed them suspiciously. At last, after another long look at Nova's legs, he waved them through. "You can find the other Bellacs in the south quarter. See to it that you stay there."

Tychon shambled his way past him, smiling idiotically. "May a makal monkey visit your sister and may the meeting be fruitful."

Nova shoved him through the gate. "Cut it out!" she snapped when they had passed.

"Couldn't help myself. At least we know that a lot of the rebels here don't speak Bellac. That's something. If they did, they'd have an interpreter at the gate."

Greah tugged on his arm. "We better find a place to stay."

Tychon agreed. A wound on his leg had begun to throb steadily. "Where is that Bellac quarter?"

Greah shook his head. "We may have squeezed past the Centauri, but you won't fool a real Bellac. Meta said we can go to the house of her people. I'll send for my friends from there."

Greah seemed to find his way through the winding streets without error. Why, thought Nova, did it seem that every beggar and merchant had converged here, in Shad-Areen? She caught the impression of carefully manufactured squalor. The houses and shops that lined the road were simple constructions, as on so many planets of Trans-Targon, but they were large and well kept. Yet beggars huddled in doorways and transients slept in the streets. Overcrowded, noisy, the city was awash with people of a half dozen different points of origin. What were they all doing here?

"Crowds," Tychon mumbled. "So many people."

"That's what I was just—"

He grasped her wrist. "That's it! Tharron is bringing all of these people here from other parts of Shaddallam. Think of how this would look on scanners in orbit. This would appear like a vast army. Without uniforms, it'll be hard to tell rebels from locals. At least the taller ones."

"Sly," she commented. "Although it wouldn't take long to find out that these are not rebels or Rhuwacs. He's betting that the Union won't want to risk the civilians. Again."

Shri-Lan members seemed to be everywhere. Nova was torn between firing whenever one of the rebels crossed their path and ducking for cover. Besides the hated faces of the Rhuwacs, she saw the higher-ranking rebels of Centauri, Feyd, Magra and Human races wearing Tharron's colors. Not one of them was Delphian.

Greah brought them through a side street and to the recessed door of a low, stone-walled building. He knocked furtively, just once.

Some time passed, during which curtains twitched and whispers were heard, before the door was opened from within. Nova and Tychon both had to stoop to enter a dim, low-ceilinged room, its corners lost in shadow, windows heavily draped. Nova turned back to see someone outside lead the sandrunner away. Then the door was shut.

"Sit on the floor," Greah whispered. "Don't frighten them."

Several people no taller than Greah emerged from other parts of the house and crowded around the new arrivals. Greah pulled the hood from Tychon's head. The little people gasped in unison. One of them, a wizened female, stepped forward to touch first Nova's, then Tychon's hair. She leaned closer, looking into his eyes. At last, she shook her head and said something.

Some of them giggled.

"What?" Nova looked to Greah for translation.

He grinned. "She said that she doesn't know what it is." He turned to explain the disguise.

His introductions seemed to satisfy the group. Some of them nodded wisely and gathered in a corner to discuss the matter. Greah fell into a long conversation with another group of his kinsmen and the old woman took Meta under her wing. Food and drink was brought to the strangers and they were left alone.

Nova sat comfortably on a rug, watching the Shaddallamas, barely registering the bitter taste of their meal. She felt safe here, shuttered away from the enemy behind thick stone and earth walls, the pleasant aroma of smoke and roasted meat mingling with the faint smell of people. The incomprehensible murmur of voices made her drowsy and she sighed contentedly when Tychon pulled her closer to lean against his chest.

Greah returned to them. "They say we can stay as long as we like. But it's best to keep as many of them out of this as possible. You're a risk to them here."

"We'll move after dark," Tychon said. "We need to find a way to get out of here. If we can't get to the Eagle, we'll have to steal one of their planes. We should split up and look around."

"Some of my friends have left already. They know this place better'n we do. I think we'll know in a few hours where they have Kiran."

"I hope they don't get into trouble for us."

"They know how to be invisible," Greah said, unconcerned.

Nova looked up at Tychon. "What if Kiran is locked up in some dungeon? This place is a bloody fortress. It would take an army to get him out."

"They wouldn't put a six-year-old in irons."

"I'm worried about Velani. What if he's done something already?"

"He'll take his time. Kiran's mind is more powerful than his. I wouldn't rush anything if I were Velani. Once we know where he is, it might be wise for us to regroup. We could probably get some of the Vanguard here pretty fast if we can find a way to communicate. Knowing Carras, he's probably put the rest of the squad on stand-by."

"If your plane is here, we'll know that soon, too," Greah said. "My people are quick."

FIFTEEN

Nova's patience was wearing to a fine wire. She barely restrained herself from interrupting the animated conversation taking place among the Shaddallamas. She wanted to pace but, in consideration of the low ceiling, had to dismiss that notion. The thought of pacing on her knees made her laugh nervously.

Four of the natives had gathered around Greah, having returned to this hiding place a few hours after they had left on their errands. There was much gesturing and waving of multi-jointed arms and she could hear their musical laughter—it seemed part of their language with no real connection to humor.

"What do they find to prattle about?" she grumbled.

Tychon half reclined on the floor beside her, carefully testing his wounds. "I think the one in the purple kilt works in Tharron's keep." He flexed a leg. "Looks like he's come up with something."

"How do you know?"

"I've been watching. What's wrong with you?"

"Nervous, I guess. I wish they wouldn't go into so much detail about everything." How she envied his Delphian talent for appearing calm when storms raged all around. The lazy slouch of his body belied the alertness with which he watched their hosts and listened to the sounds of the city outside. She knew him well enough by now to read the deep color of his eyes and the tension in the apparently relaxed pose. But he knew how to channel his resources. While she had waited restlessly for the little people to end their chatter, he had studied and understood their elaborate body language.

Greah finally disengaged himself from the group.

"Well? What is it?" Nova pressed. "Have they found anything?"

He nodded. "Tsegh came just now from Tharron's, ah, home."

"Is Kiran there?"

"Indeed! Tsegh faced some danger in gathering his information. At one point he–"

"Can't you spare us the details?"

Greah leaned closer to Tychon. "Perhaps you will listen."

Tychon grinned. "Forgive her. We're not used to your customs. I'm sure Tsegh acted bravely."

"I can't believe you guys!"

Greah settled beside them on the floor. A few Shaddallamas joined them, their eyes on the speaker as if anticipating the words of a storyteller. Nova was certain that none of them understood their language.

"Tharron's still in the house that used to belong to Neb Hani. Neb Hani was a trader who got very wealthy out on Shad-Lengh and then settled here, in the lowlands." Greah noticed Nova's idly tapping fingers and continued quickly. "Kiran is with Tharron, and so are some of the others you spoke of: Pe Khoja, Comori, Velani. Tsegh overheard their talk. He said that one of Tharron's big battleships is coming. Then Tharron was shouting at Velani a lot."

"He's going to move the boy," Tychon said flatly. "On a battleship."

"Then we'll have to start all over again," Nova said. "Ty, we've got to do something!"

"There are two places with ships here," Greah said. "One

just has a lot of little planes that are kind of round in the back and make a lot of noise when they fly by. Those are on the other side of the town. There are bigger planes on the main airfield. The ones that go straight up. One of those could be yours. But most of them look pretty beat up."

"The Eagle's likely one of those," Nova said. "Sounds like they're keeping the Shrills over on the other side. Not likely to take Kiran up in one of those."

"No, they wouldn't have gear for him," Tychon agreed. "They'll need a cruiser, so that leaves the airfield." He came to his feet, not without a few groans and winces, and twitched a curtain aside to look into the teeming street. "It's just about dark. In this crowd we'll be able to snoop around without being noticed. Nova will take a look at Tharron's keep and work with some of the locals to determine the most likely route they'll take to the airfield and see if there is some sort of ambush point. Greah and I will go to the airfield, find the Eagle and make sure it's available for escape. I'm really hoping we can find a way to contact Adachi and Xi on the other Eagles without anyone noticing. And then we'll see about sabotaging some of the other planes."

"Why?" Greah asked. "I thought the Eagle was fast."

"So is Pe Khoja," Nova said. "We can't risk a chase. We'll be outnumbered. If they get to the battleship, all is lost. They must not leave Shaddallam."

Tychon regarded her thoughtfully. "No, they must not." He took her face into his hands and kissed her softly. "Be careful. Please."

"Don't worry so, Major." She smiled, a little disconcerted by the look he had given her. "I'll meet you at the airfield in three hours. We should know a lot more by then." She motioned to two of the Shaddallama women to accompany her and slipped through the door into the street. Tychon watched through the window as she disappeared into the crowd.

"And what are we gonna do in the meantime?" Greah asked.

Tychon stared at him absently for a moment and then

shook himself out of his thoughts. "Sabotage," he said.

* * *

Nova followed her two guides through the crowded city, dodging rebels along the way, until they reached a compound of structures near the river. The Shaddlamas' gestures made clear that this was Tharron's hideout and then pointed into another direction, likely the location of the airfield. Nova nodded, understanding, but she could not tear her eyes away from the buildings.

A wall, younger than the town, had been erected around an apparently random selection of appropriated houses to serve as Shri-Lan headquarters. Nova could barely see the rooftops beyond the fortification. She circled it, noting two gates, locked from within and closely guarded. Her eyes scanned each house outside the walls, judged distances and counted guards. There were cameras mounted at uneven intervals, but none of them pivoted as they were designed to do and two were overgrown with some clinging plant life.

Her eyes came to rest on a low building a little further along the street. It was decayed and clung to the fortress wall for support. Its crooked roof was high enough to afford a view into the plaza beyond.

Nova motioned to the two women, bidding them to wait, and ignored what were presumably objections to her plan. She crossed the street and ambled toward the shack, stopping often as if to examine the street vendors' merchandise. Even here, close to Shri-Lan headquarters, people converged and vied for living space.

The wooden building stood near the end of the alley where, finally, the traffic seemed to thin out. Two guards patrolled near the wall, looking bored. She waited for them to begin their stroll back to the main gate before darting out from the corner of a warehouse and into the shack.

The climb onto the roof was a matter of seconds. Nova crept over the sloping surface, mindful of the places where the rotted wood had given way to age and weather. She peered over the wall. A lone Rhuwac loitered near a powered-down skimmer in the cobbled courtyard below. The restless noise of the crowded city outside the walls drowned out any sound coming from within, but there was an air of peaceful quiet about the place. This did not look as though Tharron was about to start a trek to the launch.

She considered her options. Down below were windows to be peeked into and conversations to be overheard. Directly to the left of her, a stone staircase led to the top of the wall and onto the roof of the main villa. Escape would be simple. She dropped silently to the ground inside the compound, thankful for her soft Shaddallama leather boots. The guard by the car did not seem interested in guarding anything as she stole past him.

The silence was unnerving. Nova tried a door and found it unlocked. Had everyone left already? Had Tharron, somehow, anticipated their plans and evaded their spies to move Kiran to yet another location? Or was he simply so sure of his safety within Shad-Areen that he could afford to be careless?

The interior of the building, empty and dusty, seemed to have once been an extension of the open market outside. Here the ceilings rose higher than the residential buildings of the town, likely why Tharron, a massive individual, had chosen this place. Hallways led away from the central corridor and newer walls showed where sections had recently been partitioned into rooms. Strangely angled corners and purposeless niches provided her cover as she made her way in the murky light falling through unwashed windows.

She felt a single person's approach before she heard the soft footfalls. A woman hurried past her and turned into another narrow hall. Nova realized that this was the K'lar she had seen on the tape taken from the rebel traitor on Tor Ag. She sidled to the corner, hearing voices. A quick glance confirmed the presence of a K'lar guard by the last door in the hall. The woman spoke to him, laughed, and entered the room. Nova waited a few moments, then inched her gun forward, sighting on the guard. He fell with a dull thud.

She hurried forward and pressed her ear to the door.

"Ghi, Ema," a small voice was heard. "Ghi soma Kiran, oweah!"

Nova closed her eyes. Kiran! He sounded unhappy. She listened for others, but there was only Kiran's plaintive whine and the woman's soothing tones.

Nova adjusted her gun. The woman's voice sounded kind and she had no wish to kill her. She stepped into the room and reached for the K'lar, clamping her hand over her mouth.

Kiran stood close by, his eyes round in surprise. In the dim light and in contrast to the deep blue hair, his face was a ghostly smudge.

"Ema!" he wailed, frightened by the red-skinned woman holding his nursemaid.

"Shh, Kiran," Nova called. Seeing that he was unguarded, she squeezed the trigger. Her captive convulsed briefly and slumped in her arms.

"Ema! Ema!"

Nova lowered the woman to the floor and caught the squirming child. "Kiran, hush," she hugged him fiercely. "It's all right. We're going home."

Kiran stared at her, open-mouthed. "I know you. You're..." he hesitated. "Nova. You were with Dadda at school."

Nova smiled and stroked the long curls. "You are very smart, you know that?"

"Yes, I do," he said and something in his weak smile seemed to make him a dozen years older than his age. "Shan Velani was here but he said he couldn't take me home. Then he showed me things and told me things..."

"What, Kiran?"

"We're gonna go away. He..." Again, his words trailed away. "He scared me. Where's Dadda?"

"He's waiting for us." She went to the window to scan the overgrown gardens surrounding the house. Parts of the wall rose beyond the trees, and she recognized one of the gates. The stairs she had seen would be to the left. "Let's play Skyranch Patrol. We'll climb out the window and then we run across the yard and up the stairs on the wall. Sound like fun?"

He nodded. "I can run fast!"

She unlatched the window and tipped the pane outward, grimacing when some metal part squealed in protest. Kiran giggled when she lifted him onto the sill and then lowered him to the ground outside. It would take her a little longer to squeeze through the narrow opening.

He looked up at her. "Someone's coming!"

"Quick, back inside!"

"No, in there. Behind you. Four of the mean beasties."

"How do you know?"

"I just know," he said, sounding resigned. "Something is different in the air when people move."

"You can stop them," Nova hissed. "If you try."

He shook his head. "No, I can't." He sighed, a strangely adult and chilling sound. "Not yet."

The door behind her slammed back against the wall.

"Run!" she yelled at the boy even as she spun around. At her touch, a blade shot from the handgrip of her gun, ready for close combat. She backhanded her weapon at the first of the Rhuwac guards to enter the room. He reeled backward, his neck slashed ear to ear. She shot a guard at close range and spun around to stab another. Then a Rhuwac grasped her wrist. Enraged, Nova lashed out at his face. He shoved her away, slamming her head against the open door. Stars exploded in front of her eyes and she dropped, feeling blood pour from her nose.

Rough hands pulled her to her feet and shoved her along the corridor. She fought them, but her mind was on Kiran's serious little face. Behind that face she had glimpsed, somehow, so much more than they had feared. Her feet barely touched the ground when two guards manhandled her through Tharron's keep. The fact that she was actually being touched by Rhuwacs did not even register. Kiran's face hung like a vision in front of her eyes, obliterating any thought of escape, robbing her of the will to do so.

They had lost Tychon's son, lost him for good, but she

knew it was not to Tharron.

* * *

"Let's get to work," Tychon whispered to Greah, whom he knew to be somewhere near. Practically invisible, the diminutive Shaddallama had circled the airfield and then reported back. There were guards, twenty at most, but the individual crafts parked here were not manned. They patrolled haphazardly, content to remain at their posts. Only a few overhead lamps illuminated the tarmac in orange pools of light.

Even here, the crowds brought to Shad-Areen infringed on the perimeter of the airfield where they made their camps and confused the sensors. Greah had recruited more of his people to distract the guards enough to keep them from noticing the red-skinned Delphian in the shadows.

They scurried forward, out of the ditch surrounding the parking area. The Eagle stood to the side, away from the small fleet assembled here. Tychon touched its keyplate, wincing when the door slid aside with an audible hiss. Greah darted past him into the ship.

"So this is what your ships look like on the inside!" he said excitedly when Tychon had closed the door again.

Tychon removed his hood and began to search through several crammed storage containers. "Huh? No, this is the cargo space." He nodded toward a door to the main cabin, annoyed that someone had left the normally tightly sealed hatch open. He found a few small transmitters. A rather obsolete jamming device still worked when he tested it.

"Greah, there should be a tool box in that—" He turned. "Greah?"

The sprite was no longer at his side. Tychon found him in the cockpit, taking in the maze of screens and indicators needed when flying manually.

"Come on, we haven't much time. Your nights here are damn short." Tychon fished a shirt out of Eagle Five's camo bin, glad to be back in clean clothes.

Greah turned, a dazed smile on his round face. "It is so

amazing!" He climbed back up to the main floor. "It's like a house! You sleep over there? How long before you have to stop for food and water? How does it fly?"

"I'll tell you later. Let's cause some damage first."

Reluctantly, Greah followed him out of the ship. He moved in a wide circle around Tychon, a shadow again, watching for Tharron's brutish guards while his friend worked.

Tychon sabotaged each of the five planes in a different way. He used his electronic lock pick to gain entry into the first and removed the system starter module. The second plane would not yield to his pick and was instead rigged with a crude explosive, triggered by the slightest taxiing motion. He fused the locks on a passenger shuttle and stole the coolant valves from another. The last of the cruisers would suffer an immediate air supply failure. Greah moved from one plane to the other to smear grease from a ground vehicle into their external sensors.

Tychon ignored the collection of smaller planes. They were not designed to leave Shaddallam's atmosphere and Tharron would not use these to escape.

He did not assume that these were the sum of Tharron's available cruisers, but waiting for another would cause as much delay as repair would. Any of it meant a very small delay but enough of a head start. These hours of quiet destruction had been well spent. He planned to use thrusters upon take-off, perhaps causing even more damage.

He wasted no time wondering what would happen if they failed in taking Kiran back. Their getaway was secured.

Satisfied, he and Greah stole back aboard the Eagle to rest for a while. It occurred to them that Nova's return was long overdue.

* * *

Nova was unceremoniously tossed into a room where she landed hard on her hands and knees. She rose slowly. Her hair obscured her face while she looked around. Rhuwacs between her and the hall. A single window with metal shutters. No other doors.

"Whiteside," she was greeted, her name spoken in a near whisper.

She turned to see Tharron, dressed in a long robe, his head and feet bare, his expression unreadable. A meal was laid out before him; the table set for one. Velani stood nearby, eyeing her nervously.

Tharron snapped something at his men, furious that she had found her way into his quarters. Someone's head would leave his shoulders, of that she was certain. No doubt he would post more guards and seal the building against further intrusions. She was locked in, Tychon and Greah were locked out and chances were slim that there would be any more sneaking into anyone's camp tonight. He stopped shouting only when someone confirmed that the child had been found in the gardens.

But Nova had no thought for that, nor did she pay attention to the thundering curses and commands with which Tharron assaulted his people. No one restrained her when she walked to Velani, her claws bared. "You're dead Velani," she hissed. "You're dead for what you did to Kiran. Pray that it isn't me when your time comes. Someone else might kill you quickly!"

Velani stepped back. "I did not know..." His hands shook when he raised them, appealing to her as if for mercy. Nervous twitches shot across his pale face and the irises of his eyes were nearly white.

Tharron stepped between his Shantir and Nova. "He is a little disturbed by his recent conversation with the boy. Recovering nicely now."

Nova's eyes went to the rebel leader. Had she ever been afraid of him? Why? "You don't know what you're doing."

"Oh, but I do." He scrutinized her, taking in her bloodied, red-tinted face and odd assemblage of clothing. "Those are some interesting uniforms you people wear. But now here you are, finally. You have come back from the dead so many times that I think I'll keep you for a while. I'm surprised you were able to dispatch of the Delphi we left for you. Bets were lost over that."

"It wasn't difficult. Your people beat him so badly that your drugs had him practically finished. I only had to put him out of his misery."

His derisive laughter chilled her.

Nova's attention returned to Velani. The Shantir still stood motionless, staring at some point beyond her. "He looks just about tapped out."

Tharron scowled at Velani. "He will need time to recover. Is that not so, wizard?"

"Huh?" Velani stammered. "Oh, yes, by tomorrow. No later."

Tharron seemed disgusted by the Delphian's weakness. "He will recover enough to deal with the boy. We shall rush into the waiting arms of your miserable fleet." His eyes glinted in the poor overhead light as if with fever. "But I will crush those arms and then their skulls, and I may yet do the same with you!"

Nova blinked. "What fleet?"

"What fleet?" Tharron repeated. "Your fleet. There are two Air Command ships coming this way. I suppose you've been vacationing here for so long that you haven't kept up with the latest news. Not to worry, the young Delphian will deal with your friends."

Nova cursed inwardly. Why was Carras coming here now? On a battleship! What could he accomplish against a city filled to capacity with civilians? She and Tychon were missing in action but that hardly warranted the launching of battleships. Had the rebels taken Eagle One as well? "How can you be so sure of what Kiran can do? Look at Velani! He's falling apart. Looks to me like he doesn't know what he's doing, either."

Velani flinched at the mention of his name. "It takes time," he whispered. "More time than we have, I dare say. But it can be done. Tomorrow, when the boy has rested. I must rest..." He blinked at Tharron. "Must rest..."

"Go!" Tharron roared. "Go! Sleep! Whatever!"

Velani stumbled from the room, and Nova was startled by the brief sensation of pity she felt for him.

Tharron took his seat at the table. "What a fighter you are, Captain. My people tell me you've cost me some of my men today. I don't suggest you try it again while a guest in my house." He appraised her critically. "It is too bad that Tychon is not here to be my guest also. I should have enjoyed taking my enemy's woman in front of him."

"You will not touch me!"

His arm shot out and an iron fist clamped over her shoulder. She found herself on her knees. "I was not asking for permission, Captain." He shoved her some distance away from himself. "Stay on the floor where you belong, Human. Fortunately for you, I still need you. I foresee trouble with the boy. He is unmanageable. Maybe he won't argue with Velani so much if he knows you'll pay for it."

"You bastard!"

"Hm, probably." He eyed her. "You know, I have thought about what would give me the greatest pleasure. I think I will give you to my Rhuwac pets. I have watched their games before and it has been entertaining."

Nova felt her temper rise, a much preferable sensation than fear but, she realized, a much more dangerous one. "Your pitiful army of lizards," she said scornfully. "They can't be trained to even speak properly. For spies and pilots you have to rely on the most despised traitors of our species to join you against us. Your own people on K'lar spit on your name!"

He seemed to find that humorous. "A Rhuwac matures to a fighting age within nine years. Your years. I have a limitless number of foot soldiers. Trained to follow my orders without question. Once I have taken Targon I will own everything else in this sector. I am breeding Rhuwacs by the thousands per month. When the time comes, I will load them onto your carriers and ship them to Centauri. Millions of them! And once every Centauri planet is mine, I will have it all. Even your precious Terra." He roared with laughter. "And all of this will be given to me by a little boy. One little Delphi creature!"

Nova was amazed by the extent of his delusions. "You're a sick man, Tharron."

"Silence!" he roared.

She shrank back against the wall, out of reflex reaching for a gun that wasn't there.

He stood up, glaring at her. His hands were balled into fists. Then, abruptly, he turned and left.

Nova scrambled to her feet while the sound of the door he had slammed still rang in her ears. She searched through the remainder of his meal and laughed with desperate hope when her fingers closed around a knife. It was dull, no more than a butter knife, but she felt better for having it.

No sooner had she hidden it under her shirt than the door opened again. She moved to the far side of the room, expecting some especially brutal Rhuwac sent here by Tharron for amusement.

When she saw who entered, Nova's knees felt like worn springs and only the support of the windowsill behind her kept them from collapsing. Not even her worst nightmare could ever conjure up a moment when she would find herself alone in a locked room with Pe Khoja.

The Caspian entered slowly, looking for her with yellow opaque eyes. She felt as though he was looking straight at the knife she had hidden.

"Nova," he said and smiled.

* * *

Tychon opened the Eagle's door to a barely audible, coded knock. The door hissed aside, admitting Greah and another Shaddallama. He peered into the darkness outside. Nova was nowhere in sight. He closed the door again.

"Well?" he said, joining the other two in the main cabin. He recognized Tsegh.

"There is shouting and yelling going on by the guard house where they keep their radio. I had a look on my way past there. They're all awake now and playing with their machines."

"I know." Tychon jerked a thumb at the cockpit. "It seems

that some of our battleships have arrived. Carras has been trying to reach us. If I answer we'll give our position away. I've just ignored it. I don't want to risk anything until we have Kiran in our sight. What's with Tsegh here?"

"I found him trying to find us. He's come from Tharron's hold." Greah nudged Tsegh, who was craning his neck, staring at the foreign world of the Eagle's interior in silent awe. "Shring bga, adda!"

Tsegh began to speak, his gestures eloquent, as Greah translated.

Nova had been caught! She had gone inside Tharron's walls and they had found her. Now the entire complex of buildings was crawling with guards and more paced the streets. Tharron did not think that Nova had come alone.

Tychon cursed. How could she have been so careless! So stupid! He'd bust her down to Corporal. He'd... "Is she hurt? Greah, ask him if she's all right. Hurry!"

Greah listened to Tsegh's monologue and finally cut him off in mid-sentence when he saw Tychon's anxious face. "He says she was yelling at Tharron."

Tychon smiled grimly at that. She would.

"And then Tharron left. He was mad. They locked her up and then a man with yellow eyes and two thumbs on each hand went in to see her. That's when Tsegh left."

"A Caspian?" Tychon frowned. "Pe Khoja!" A new worry began to nag him. He had seen Pe Khoja's face when Nova had run into them at Shad-Lengh. At the time, Tychon had thought that he had read hatred in the man's face. Thinking about it now, Tychon was certain it had been something else. For just an instant, a flicker of curiosity had crossed the dead features. What was it about Nova that would interest someone like Pe Khoja?

It took every bit of his strength to remain where he was. His entire being screamed out to follow his murderous instincts to Tharron's keep before the beastly Caspian harmed Nova. He could not remember ever feeling as powerless as he was now.

Greah read the pain in his face. "I'll take Tsegh back," he said. "It will be light soon."

Tychon got up to stand with his back to them, leaning heavily on the map table. "Be careful."

"You're bleeding again."

"I know."

"Ty, maybe..."

"Go, Greah. Get him home."

SIXTEEN

The two men were bent over maps, charts and screens in a dimly lit corner of *Teti*'s bridge. It was quiet in the long, crescent-shaped room, both in deference to the high-ranking leaders and the tension that had permeated both battleships since dropping into normal space yesterday. The closest possible jumpsite terminus to Shaddallam was far enough removed from that planet to give Tharron ample time to learn of their approach. His hiding place was well-chosen. They were expected.

Carras traced his finger over a two-dimensional map of Shaddallam. "My last reports show that Major Tychon's final signal originated here, on this plateau near Shad-Lengh. Nothing more after that but we have traced the plane north to the region of Shad-Laika. They flew a direct path, bypassing two towns in these foothills. I would guess from that that they found something."

"You have established Tharron's base to be in the valley, then?"

"Yes, the only area with any significant air and com traffic. Other parts of Shaddallam are far too exposed."

"Have you tried to hail Vanguard Seven?" Baroch asked.

"Of course. There has been no reply."

Baroch nodded. "Consider your team unavailable. You have more Vanguard agents down there?"

"Yes, Captain Xi on Eagle Three and Major Adachi on Eagle One have been monitoring this area for outbound ships for two days now. Nine is on the ground, standing by. Five is now inside Shad-Areen, powered down."

"Good, have someone take me to the *Erato*."

"Sir?"

"I did not choose *Erato* on a whim. Tharron's battleship will arrive shortly, no doubt fully armed. You will intercept and keep them busy while I will deploy the Challenger over Shaddallam."

Carras sprang to his feet. "The Challenger? I protest, sire!"

"Must you oppose me every step of the way?" Baroch asked testily. He lowered his voice after directing a meaningful glance at the nearby bridge crew. Few people aboard were aware that this was anything other than a strike against Tharron's headquarters and a new and treacherous weapon in his possession. "Were you expecting to engage in a duel with the child? We will blanket the entire Shad-Laika valley, including Shad-Areen."

Carras was momentarily struck speechless. The discreetly named Challenger was an anti-personnel weapon designed to capture in-flight ships undamaged. It could clear rebel transports of their cargo of Rhuwacs without having to board and engage in battle. It was a dirty weapon too easily used for other purposes, loathed for its efficiency and utter ruthlessness by all commanders. Here on Shaddallam, the Challenger would not displace a single grain of sand while rendering the entire valley lifeless with a few well-placed volleys. Had this man gone insane?

"Lord Baroch," he said carefully, "perhaps we can wait until Tharron leaves Shaddallam. The valley is densely populated with sentient–"

"Carras, desist, please," Baroch sighed. "We cannot hover in orbit and wait for Tharron to strike first."

"But we don't know if he's been able to access the... weapon. Most likely, he will look to escape. Let me land my troops on Shaddallam to flush him out. If we can get him airborne, he'll be an easy target."

"Or perhaps he'll get on a boat and slip out of the valley. Or use a cave system. Or get on a damn sandrunner and ride out of there! Are you willing to wager on anything that madman might or might not do? And if he does go airborne, are you willing to let him leave the planet, destroy both of our ships and then head into Trans-Targon? What price to pay is Shaddallam compared to the destruction Tharron will cause on other planets? And that is only a consideration if the Tughan obeys him. May the Gods find us all if the Tughan gets loose! I believe that you are allowing sentiment to get in the way of professional judgment. We do not have time for debates. Carry out your orders."

Carras stared after the departing Factor in disbelief. The man was willing to destroy thousands of people and a vast swath of vital forests on what was otherwise a desert planet for the chance of eliminating the Tughan. It was madness. He rose abruptly and strode from the bridge.

Outside, Xi and Adachi waited for their orders. He motioned them along, into the lift shaft to the launch bay where their conversation would not be overheard. Briefly, he explained Baroch's plan. He saw his own fear and disgust mirrored on their faces. But they were lifelong warriors, conditioned to follow orders. Neither commented.

"Xi, take the Factor to the *Erato*. Lieutenant Colonel McDougall is commanding. You will inform him privately that he is to release control of the Challenger to Lieutenant Denier here on the *Teti*. For the record, I believe that, being Delphian, Lord Baroch is not unbiased in this situation. His kinsmen have instilled in him the necessity of killing the Tughan above all else. It is my duty to preserve Shaddallam's civilization. Do you understand?"

Xi nodded. "Yessir."

"Adachi, return to the planet and prepare to intercept

anything leaving the surface from Shad-Areen. Xi will join you there."

"Colonel," Adachi said, "I would fail in my duty if I did not remind you that to undermine a direct order from the Elected Factors is mutiny."

Carras nodded. "Thank you, Adachi. Your rank gives you the authority to relieve me of duty."

Adachi grinned. "I wouldn't presume." The Vanguard commanders left the elevator, not entirely certain which of their leaders was misjudging the situation. One was perhaps mad, certainly obsessed, the other about to destroy his illustrious career.

Carras watched them board their Eagles and returned to the bridge just as an alarm rang through the corridors. "Colonel, the enemy battleship has arrived and is heading for these coordinates, approaching rapidly."

"Move to intercept."

* * *

Nova awoke with a start. How long had she dozed? She looked around her prison, blinking as her eyes adjusted to the pre-dawn shadows. One lamp still cast its light over the table in the middle of the room.

Pe Khoja was using it to read from a musty, moisture-swelled book. "And when Caazin Sovi died," he continued their conversation as if she had not nodded off at all, "Grair Dunn took over, have I got that right?"

Nova sat up on the hard bench, her limbs aching and cramped. "No," she said. "That was later. Grair Dunn was in no position to assume command until they found K'lar Four. There was Sovi's Second, Cre'an Sydd. She created a near mutiny, but by then they had landed on K'lar. Sydd was the only one that knew of the second keyhole past Magra."

"I know that site," he said. "Difficult. Back then it must have been more luck than know-how."

"What time is it?" Nova walked to the small window and peered out into the courtyard. The early light now showed the buildings and the doubled guards.

"I don't know," Pe Khoja said, engrossed in his book.

Nova stared at his richly patterned back in wonder. He had been locked in this little room with her as a favor from Tharron. No doubt the rebel leader had envisioned lively hours of terror for her. Knowing what she did of Pe Khoja's background, Nova had feared the same.

But he had surprised her.

He had searched her and found the dull knife and had cuffed her for her trouble. Then, after kicking the laughable weapon under the door and into the hall, he had swept the table clear of bowls and cups, letting them crash to the floor. Nova's mind replayed visions of Tychon's battered body when the Caspian turned to her.

He had questioned her. At first he had demanded information about Union dealings, which, of course, she refused to answer. For many of his queries she knew no answer. Others she would not disclose even in the face of torture.

Surprisingly, he had not pressed her but had begun to ask about her background and what she knew of the Centauri. They were easy, harmless questions about things that were common knowledge. Astounded, Nova was moved to answer. Soon, she was recounting ancient legend and folklore as well as Centauri's recent history. He had listened well, at times asking intelligent questions to keep her narrative from wandering. Nova had talked eagerly, as much to keep herself from worrying about tomorrow as to keep him from remembering Tharron's 'gift'.

At times he turned from her to study his books, allowing her to doze. Whenever she awoke, he had a new question ready. He had ordered a basin of water to let her clean the blood from her face and the Rhuwac gore from her arms and hands.

She was unable to understand his motives for any of this. He had committed crimes of the foulest nature in Tharron's name and could not be credited with a kind deed for anyone.

But here he treated her with more respect than she would ever expect from a rebel and seemed grateful for the things she told him. He was a scholar of history and she was only filling in a few bare patches in his vast knowledge of fact and mythology. He seemed to crave information and absorbed it like the air he breathed. Something drove this man, and Nova had not the slightest idea of what that might be. It was not the need for wealth or power, for he had both. He seemed to need nothing, not sleep or food, nor whatever amusement he might find with a female captive.

She rubbed her stinging, tired eyes, not daring to go back to sleep. It was nearly morning.

"You would enjoy our information system on Targon," she ventured. "Centauri's entire library bank was brought there for distribution. All of our schools and academies draw on the info center for teaching material. Anyone may access it."

"Any Union member," he said.

"Well, yes," she replied, walking around him and to the door. She heard voices in the distance. Footsteps. Doors slamming. The day had begun. "You don't have to be with Tharron, you know."

His eyes moved away from the book. "I have no wish to join your Union."

"Why not?"

He cocked his head. "You sound surprised. Do you really still think that your fine Commonwealth is something everyone should aspire to? I'd not taken you for a mindless grunt who is told what to think." He studied her face for a few beats. "You know what I'm talking about."

"I do not," she said, perhaps a little too quickly.

He shrugged. "Fine. In any case, I've made my choice. I cannot betray Tharron."

"I can't believe you look to him as he thinks you do."

"Maybe not. I find him amusing. This whole affair has given me great pleasure. Too bad you were too inept to stop him from coming this far. You can't expect me to do your work for you."

"What does that mean?"

"The Tughan is a dangerous thing. Tharron should not be allowed to possess it."

"If you believe that, why didn't you stop him?"

"I tried," he said. "Who do you think sent the K'lar to Tor Ag to give you the video I made? Why do you think you were left in Shad-Lengh? I knew you weren't dead. I know what Tychon is capable of. Just as I hoped one of you would survive the surprise we left for you in the valley. And I may have forgotten to remove your ship's transponder. How neglectful of me."

Nova stared. "You? You led us here? Why?"

"It amused me. I wanted to see you stop Tharron. Or try. I nearly lost you a few times. Who would have thought your old boyfriend was going to take out my courier on Tor Ag. You're lucky he bailed when he recognized you. You have quite an effect on people, Captain."

"You wanted us to find Tharron? But you could have stopped him. You! You could have killed Tharron or taken Kiran away. You could have killed the boy and the whole thing would be done with!"

"Yes, I could have."

"Then why didn't you?" she said, incredulous.

"To what purpose? This is much more fascinating. I'm ready to see what happens next, aren't you?"

"This is a game to you? You've put yourself in harm's way when Air Command gets here. Don't you care what happens?"

"No." He closed his book and placed it on a shelf. "And I've managed to escape your plodding ships before. Now be kind enough to appear mistreated when Tharron arrives."

"Why didn't you?"

"Why didn't I what? Mistreat you? Kill you? You're far more interesting alive."

Nova shrugged, embarrassed. "Tharron threatened to... to take me."

Pe Khoja laughed. It was not an unpleasant sound. "You Humans have strange notions. The man is a giant. He needs you alive."

"But he sent you," Nova said, half-angry at being mocked but strangely affected by his laughter.

"Even if you appealed to me, Human, I would not have touched you. Perhaps you could help yourself to your library on Targon and study Caspian anatomy and mating habits."

Nova had to smile. "Does Tharron know that?"

"Apparently not," Pe Khoja said, still grinning.

Nova remembered his earlier, startling disclosure. "If you're against Tharron using the Tughan, would you consider stopping him? Not for the Union. Stop him for those who will be hurt by the Tughan. Innocent people."

She had misjudged him. He shook his head. "It's too late, Nova." His face assumed a distant, wistful expression. "I, too, am eager to meet this Tughan Wai. I think he could teach me many things."

"But—"

"I hear them coming," he said. "I will thank you for the hours of enlightenment before we return to the business of being enemies."

"I wish it wasn't so," Nova said, meaning it.

"You have reason to hate me."

"Yes. You are a cold-blooded murderer, and you'd see all of Trans-Targon burn before you'd help. I don't understand you. But I see now that not all of you is evil."

He inclined his head formally. "None of us are."

The door beside them opened to admit Tharron and two Rhuwac guards. He saw the remains of his supper on the floor and Nova's tired, disheveled appearance. It did not look as though her stay in this room had been a pleasant one. His eyes narrowed when he saw her standing close to Pe Khoja. There was no fear there, only a serene expectancy that enveloped both of them. What had happened here?

Pe Khoja shoved Nova toward the Rhuwacs. "Is it time to go?"

"It is," Tharron said. "You, Whiteside, will talk sense to the boy. It's his last chance or he will watch you bleed. Am I clear?"

Nova nodded. They would let her talk to Kiran! She began to feel some hope.

An air car was waiting for them outside. She blinked into the bright morning sun, looking to the walls of the plaza. There was no sign of Tychon or her elfin friends anywhere. A Feydan rebel jabbed a gun into her ribs to force her into the car and then took the driver's seat. She saw Tharron, Velani, Pe Khoja and the K'lar woman climb into two other vehicles.

"Nova!" A small body crawled over her backrest to drop into her lap. "I knew you'd come back."

Nova hugged him closely. "Kiran! Are you all right? Did you have breakfast?" She switched to rapid Delphi mainvoice. "Can you handle Velani?"

"I do not know," he said. "He scares me. I think I have hurt him." The corners of his mouth twitched.

Good! Nova thought, but did not say so. She would not ask Kiran to hurt Velani. The boy still believed in good and evil, that fine line between Union and rebel and who was who. If he was to be taught to kill, she would not, could not, be his teacher.

"I'm sure he's just fine, Kiran. Don't let him—" A sharp cuff into her side left her gasping for air. Kiran flinched.

"Shut up with that Delphi jabber, Human," the rebel growled.

She held Kiran tight and watched the town pass by. Was she imagining round little faces peering from windows and doorways as the short convoy passed? Was Tychon planning an ambush in these narrow and crowded streets?

She nudged Kiran, who looked up at her, startled. Carefully, she raised her hand and tapped the neural interface at her temple.

"What if I hurt you, too?" Kiran whispered, understanding her request.

"It doesn't matter. I'm not leaving you alone with Velani."

He reached up to hug her and she felt the contact with his mind as soon as he had placed his small hand over her interface. She nodded and smiled reassuringly.

The air cars reached the first runway of Shad-Areen's makeshift heliport. A guard raised an arm to stop them. Nova peered out of a side window to watch the exchange between Tharron and some of his men. The leader gestured furiously in all directions, finally turning to wave at the waiting cars.

"What's the problem, boss?" Nova asked hopefully when she had climbed out of the vehicle.

"Get them into the hangar and bring me another plane!" Tharron roared. He forced himself not to look at Nova. Doing so might fan his fury to the point of killing her. But Pe Khoja had advised him to let her be. She could well be the lever they needed to deal with the boy.

"All of the planes are sabotaged, sire," a Human at his side said.

Shouts from afar reached their ears. Nova did not hide a smirk when a high-bridged cruiser leaned dangerously. Several people scurried to a safe distance as the all-terrain landing gear buckled and the ship sank to her knees, crushing her undercarriage.

"So you made some friends here," she heard Pe Khoja's voice close to her ear. When she turned, she saw him leaning against her car, looking amused. "Or could it be that Tychon came to his senses, after all?" He smiled at Kiran and lifted him up to sit on the skimmer. Kiran tried to climb on Pe Khoja's shoulders; apparently the Caspian was no stranger to the boy. "I can see that you're not taking any of this seriously, Captain," Pe Khoja said, playfully trying to keep Kiran from succeeding.

"What do you mean?"

He switched languages. "I got you alone with the boy. If you had any idea who this Tughan Wai is you would have strangled him with your bare hands. The driver would not have stopped you." Pe Khoja looked toward his irate leader. "I'd better go and get us another ship." He put Kiran on the ground and climbed into the skimmer. "You are on your own, Human."

Nova could only stare after him as he careened out of the airfield.

"Inside!" Tharron roared, gesturing at the hangar.

The K'lar nursemaid took Kiran's hand.

"Don't you touch him!" Nova hissed and tried to reach for the boy. A strong hand gripped her arm and she saw him led away.

She turned. Fynn Bridger stared back at her.

"Fynn," she whispered.

He stood wordlessly before her, looking like a stranger without his Air Command uniform.

Before she could stop herself, she hauled out with an open-handed slap to his face that sent him staggering backward. It was the only comment she had about the career choice he had made for himself.

She turned away and walked ahead of him to the hangar.

The air around them shifted in a flash of heat and light when a nearby air car burst into flames. Something large moved between them and the sun above. The ground exploded upward in chunks of pavement.

All of them looked up to see the Eagle hover over their heads, its cargo ramp lowered, where, incredibly, a Shaddallama in a kilt was wielding a most deadly weapon.

The K'lar woman picked Kiran up and raced into the hangar. Most of the remaining rebels scattered to return the fire from the ineffective cover of the building.

"Kiran!" Nova started to sprint after them when once again Fynn Bridger stood in her way.

"Get on that plane," he snapped.

"I'm not leaving Kiran!"

He gripped her arm and shoved her toward the Eagle now hovering close to the ground. "Go, dammit! You won't last another hour here."

She saw two Centauri rebels rush toward them, looking confused by Fynn's actions. Fynn aimed his gun and one of them dropped to the ground. "Get on the fucking plane, Nova!" He backhanded his gun across the other rebel's face.

More of Tharron's men now headed their way.

Nova whirled toward the Eagle's cargo bay. Greah stood on the ledge, tethered to the interior by a long rope. He fired past her at the rebels, missing her by nearly nothing. She dove head-first into the bay.

"Kiran!" She turned back to look across the airfield. She saw the hangar door slam shut and lost sight of Fynn Bridger when the Eagle spun and rose from the tarmac. Someone raced out to collect Velani who still stood unmoving beside the wreck of the air car, seeing nothing, hearing nothing.

More armed rebels ran toward them and more skimmers approached from the city. They moved fearlessly despite Greah's well-placed fire. The surprise had worn off; they now remembered how Tharron dealt with cowards.

"Go, go, go!" Greah shouted back into the ship's interior.

Their take-off was dangerously clumsy. Greah was still laughing and shouting at their enemy when Tychon pulled the Eagle up. Nova had to drag him inside so that they could pressurize the cabin. Tychon locked the ship into a wide circle far above Shad-Areen and focused the surveillance system onto its airfield.

"Who was that man back there?" Greah wanted to know.

Nova dropped onto the lounger, stunned by what had just happened.

"Get in here, Greah," Tychon shouted from the cockpit. "Keep your eyes on these screens," he instructed when the Shaddalama hopped into Nova's bench. "If those dots move or blink or if any new ones show up, let me know. Those dots are planes; all that green stuff is people."

Greah nodded earnestly. "And what are those?"

"Robots, hardware, electric toilets for all I know. It doesn't matter. Just call me if anything moves. Also if that turns red. It'll mean they've got something with a range to hit us up here."

He left the Shaddallama in the cockpit and went to Nova.

"I had to leave him," she cried. "I'm so sorry!"

He sat beside her on the lounge and put his hand on her

back. "We'll go back in. As soon as we get some help. I've signaled the other Eagles. Tharron is stuck in that hangar for now."

"He'll murder Kiran before letting us take him. And Carras'll blow that hangar up and us along with it! Why else would he be here now?"

"I'll tell him to stand down. We've still got a chance here."

"I should never have gone into Tharron's hold."

"Probably not."

"Gods, Ty, what he did to Velani!"

"Tharron?"

"Kiran! I guess Velani started to... to change him. But I don't think it's going so well for him. He looked half dead. And Kiran! He looks so..." She shrugged. "So old! It's like he knows things he's got no business knowing. He..." She paused when she felt a gentle contact, like a thought that wasn't her own.

Tychon noted the change in her expression. "What is it?"

"We're in khamal," she said, listening. "Kiran and me."

"You can't! If Velani can't handle it, who knows what it will do to you?"

"I'm not leaving him again, Ty."

SEVENTEEN

"You will do it now!" Tharron hovered over Velani in what was no more than a storage room for old and broken-down equipment.

"I cannot." Velani stared at Kiran huddled in a corner. The boy watched them silently.

"We will never leave here if you don't. We're well outnumbered up there, even if we make it past that woman. And if we wait here long enough, Air Command will land on us with both feet."

The Shantir shook his head.

"Think of what you will accomplish!" Tharron tried. "Your name will live forever! It is you who can change history!"

Velani did not reply. His mind relived again and again the sight of Tharron practically decapitating the Human rebel with his bare hands. What did the woman matter? But Tharron's rage had exploded when he saw one of his own men help Nova escape. At least Kiran had been in this room already and had been spared the sight.

Tharron strode toward Kiran. "Look, boy, Shan Velani is going to have a little talk with you. Then you'll do exactly as he says."

"No."

Tharron crouched beside Kiran, ready to strangle him. "You wouldn't want a whole lot of people to get hurt, would you?" he said, experimenting with a gentler tone. "So, we'll have to get rid of the bad ones. I will show you which planes are the bad ones and Velani will show you how to stop them."

"Stop them?"

"Yes, so they can't fly anymore. Nothing to it."

"I want Nova. Where is my Dadda?"

"You don't think they'd leave without you, do you?"

Kiran shook his head.

Tharron turned back to Velani. "You go in there and do it. Now!" He paced to the door and looked across the interior of the hangar. "If I don't have a plane here soon, your heads will decorate the end of a spike! Where is Pe Khoja?"

He stared at Velani, fuming. The Delphian had explained that, once in khamal, the Tughan would be a tool of his own mind, as easily directed and controlled as a pistol. He would simply take over to lead the Tughan into battle against their enemy.

But something had gone very wrong.

Velani had initiated the khamal easily, delighted with Kiran's capabilities. As a Shantir, he found his exchange with the child most interesting. Even while the Tughan still lay dormant, Kiran possessed a fine mind that would normally qualify him to apprentice to the Shantirate. He would have been a wondrous addition to the guild.

Prodded by Tharron, Velani had begun to show Kiran those things that were new to the child. Certain abilities were genetic, others had been given to him by the Shantirs of Delphi at his first khamal *gzali*. Now Velani fit the pieces into place to create the Tughan for Tharron. He showed Kiran how to turn his perceptions, his intuitive awareness of subspace, into a kinetic force to affect matter or kill an enemy. Most importantly, he showed him how he could absorb the knowledge and experience of those he touched to enrich his own. It was then that something went against the centuries-old dream of the Shantirs.

The Tughan asked: *Why?*

Velani was drawn into a battle of monstrous proportions. He came to understand why the Tughan had to reach maturity within controlled conditions before its release. The boy had thrown a tantrum. Instead of screaming his anger and confusion at Velani, Kiran had directed his fury at the Shantir's mind, unwilling and unable to understand his purpose. Velani had suffered.

Tharron leaned close to the Shantir, his arm stretched toward Kiran. "Do it," he whispered.

Velani came to his feet. He shuffled across the room to sit on the floor beside the boy.

"Kiran," he said, his voice unsteady. "You can be good, is that not so? Your Dadda would be very unhappy if he knew what you did last time. It's not nice."

Kiran's thoughts wandered to Nova. He perceived her surroundings and location and understood that his father was nearby. She acknowledged his presence and he began to feel a little reassured that, somewhere, a grown-up was going to help him.

Velani took his hand.

* * *

"He's so old," Nova whispered. She perched on the edge of the lounger, eyes fixed on some point below the ceiling, seeing nothing. Tychon watched her spellbound face anxiously, torn between manning the cockpit and staying here, beside Nova, where the real battle was about to be fought.

* * *

"*Erato* is in orbit over the valley, Colonel."

Carras nodded. "Newson?"

"Sir?" The engineer looked up from his monitors.

"*Erato*'s Challenger controls will be offline?"

"Yessir, it can be controlled only from here," Newson replied. "By your orders," he reminded him.

"What coverage do we have?"

"The northern half of the plateau and most of the Shad-Laika lowlands."

"Can we reduce that?"

"Certainly. We can narrow our target area down to approximately one square kil from here."

"Good. Do it."

"Which coordinates, sir?" Newson hid his surprise.

Carras turned to the lieutenant near the helm. "What are the coordinates for Eagle Five?"

"Sir?"

Carras nodded. "Tharron knows we have arrived. If he can use his weapon, he will do so now. If my agents are still working, they will be close by. If not, I will assume that Tharron has taken possession of the Eagle. It is a valuable ship and likely faster than anything he has. Either way, Tharron is where the Eagle is."

Newson adjusted the Challenger. "Shad-Areen, then. Ready, sir."

Carras studied a real-vid of the peaceful planet below. The passive signal emitting from Eagle Five, Tychon's borrowed ship, originated within a town with a surprisingly high population compared to other parts of Shaddallam. It could very well be a Shri-Lan stronghold and destroying the city would deal a serious blow to the enemy.

But what if those people were civilians?

The maddening uncertainties of this entire operation irritated him. He must act, and soon. No, he could not wipe out the entire valley. But this city, this one city, might not be too high a price to pay for both Tharron and the Tughan Wai. Carras had simply scaled down an outrage that would never be muted by the Union's public relations specialists and propaganda makers. Gone was the hope to make Brigadier General before his honorable retirement. Gone was the hope of being remembered as one of Targon's more capable commanders. He would be remembered as the man who wiped out thousands of peaceful sentients. And no one would ever know why.

"Colonel Carras! Vanguard One reporting."

Carras rushed to the communications console. "Adachi! Come in."

"I'm over Shad-Areen, sir," came the reply. "Eagle Five is in the air. Holding position over the city at fifteen hundred."

"Are any other planes launching?"

"Negative. Just the Eagle."

Another voice cut into their exchange. "Colonel Carras, this is Baroch on the *Erato*. Please identify the occupants of that craft. If they are yours, order them aside so that we may begin our operation. We have only minutes before you must engage the enemy carrier."

"Yes, sir," Carras said. "Stand clear as well, Adachi."

"Affirmative."

* * *

"Velani!" Nova whispered aboard Eagle Five when she recognized the other presence within Kiran's mind.

The Shantir, in his weakened state, did not notice the intruder. Kiran offered no resistance. Velani put the fuses together, gaining confidence with every step. This, he knew now, the creation of the Tughan, had been his one purpose in life. And it was he, of all Shantirs privy to the secret, who had been given the opportunity to realize the dream. That Tharron was the beneficiary of all of this was a remote point of interest that faded in the light of the whole.

The boy that was the Tughan counted on Nova to stop the Shantir with the blind trust of any six-year-old. And his father was there and would not let bad things happen. Was that not what Nova believed?

But Nova merely watched in amazement, now part of the Tughan. How simple it all was! Could something as infinitely complex as the Tughan Wai be moved so easily? She followed Velani through the blinding maze of Kiran's mind, awestruck by what she saw. She was lost, standing small and insignificant before a power that her own mind could not begin to understand. It was all there! Had they really worried about the Tughan as a mere weapon of destruction? Did no one understand how much more lay dormant here? She was looking into infinity! Here was a creature of unfathomable proportions, waiting to receive knowledge that would give substance to its powers, knowledge it would begin to assimilate once Velani had completed the creation. This creature knew that it was about to be born, and Nova was a mote caught in the vast machinery that drove this endless unknown. She shivered.

"What's that?" Greah yelled.

Tychon looked up at a secondary monitor and leaped into the cockpit to identify the craft now approaching from above.

"They're here, Nova! Vanguard." He hailed them. "This is V7 on Eagle Five."

"Tychon?" came the incredulous reply. "What's going on down there?"

"We've got them cornered for now. Get down here and we'll figure out a way to extract the boy. Are any of the other Vanguard here?"

"Yes, and so is Carras. With his finger on the trigger. And Tharron's got a carrier on the way, too. Get out of there. The place is about to get scorched."

"Tell Carras to stand down!"

"You're crawling with rebels down there!"

"Not as many as you'd think. Those are—"

"Ty!" Nova yelled.

Tychon turned to her. "It's Eagle One—"

"Cut them off! Now!"

Too late. Tychon knew where Eagle One was. Through Nova, Kiran understood. Then Velani knew. He gave the Tughan a vicious mental shove.

Eagle One's signal disappeared from the screen.

"Nova!" Tychon shouted.

Nova knew. The Tughan had risen. Carras would open fire.

* * *

"Vanguard Three," Carras roared aboard *Teti*. "Xi! Return at once. Stand clear!" He slapped at the controls. "Baroch!"

"I hear you."

"Eagle One has taken fire. They've gone down east of the city."

"It was the Tughan, Colonel," Baroch said. "No shots were fired. Your Eagles are useless now. We will fire Challenger on my command."

Carras closed the com link. "Newson, is the Challenger targeted on Eagle Five?"

The engineer nodded. "It'll also affect the ground immediately beyond the Eagle. The city..."

"I'm aware of that," Carras barked. "Fire when he gives the order."

Newson nodded, overriding *Erato*'s signal. "Ready."

* * *

"They've got a plane down there!" Greah gestured wildly at his screens.

Tychon switched the scanners to real-video. He saw people exit the hangar, among them Velani and Kiran, both moving slowly, seeing nothing. They walked toward an air car that would take them up to a cruiser now hovering over the damaged tarmac.

His eyes moved from the screen to Nova. She was immobile, frowning as though she followed some unheard and unpleasant conversation. Like Kiran, she was held captive by the wonder that Velani had unfolded.

"Nova? What do you see?"

Kiran suddenly stumbled over a crack in the torn pavement and fell to his knees. Both Velani and Nova winced at the sharp pain that all of them felt. Startled, Nova was able to tear herself away from the Velani-presence within Kiran.

Kiran had changed! She saw an understanding that had not been there before. Something to do with Eagles and a memory of Centauri.

"Adachi?" Nova gasped. Adachi, commander of Eagle

One, was there. Somehow, he now lived within the Tughan. Or rather, any thought that had ever crossed the man's mind was now part of the Tughan. She gasped when she also recognized a familiar *something* that reminded her of Dylan. And Kiran had grown to accommodate them. He acknowledged their presence, aware, without question.

Velani had seen it, too. Like Nova, he could not break their link.

"There's something happening," Greah shouted. "More planes!"

Tychon turned his attention back to the scene below them. Even as Tharron's new cruiser left the airfield, four Shrills arrived from the city and shot toward Eagle Five.

* * *

"Colonel," Xi reported to Carras from his vantage point on Eagle Three. "Another cruiser has left the Shad-Areen airfield. It's heading toward the enemy carrier and Eagle Five is following."

"Colonel Carras, four fighter planes approaching Eagle Five from the ground."

"Colonel Carras, enemy battleship has launched approximately two hundred fighters."

Carras studied several screens and indicators at once. "McDougall," he advised *Teti*'s captain, "we are launching seven squadrons against the enemy ship. Request that you do the same."

* * *

Aboard Tharron's cruiser, Velani had dropped Kiran's hand and had fallen to his knees. His mouth worked to form words, prayer perhaps, but no sound passed his lips.

Kiran sat small and insignificant in one of the wide chairs of the bridge, his eyes fixed on the Shantir.

"You're not finished," he said, smiling.

"No," Velani whispered.

Tharron tore his eyes away from the screens. "Velani! Take

out that Eagle behind us. Do it now!"

Kiran laughed. Velani died. The Shantir's screams exploded through the rebel ship and even Tharron blanched at the sound.

* * *

Nova's hands flew to her head and she jumped from the couch as if to physically escape her link to Kiran. She moaned when she felt the Velani-presence, like Adachi, now part of the Tughan. The Tughan no longer needed his teacher. His teacher had become part of him. She struggled to back out, frightened by the power she felt, unaware that Union battleships prepared to fire and that four rebel fighter planes slowly caught up with the Eagle. She saw only the Tughan. And now the Tughan saw her. Kiran seemed to remember Nova's presence with some surprise and then allowed her to live. She became a spectator, helplessly bound to this mind that would not release her.

* * *

"Challenger ready," Baroch said, his voice clearly audible aboard the *Erato*, aboard the *Teti*, aboard the Eagles and aboard Tharron's ship. "Fire."

Kiran smiled, having understood the Challenger through Adachi. He turned his attention to *Erato* and deflected the deadly beams as though shielding his eyes from an overbright sun. Most of the blast went wild, out into space where its signal rapidly decayed. Then Kiran followed her output back to the *Erato*. As all life there winked out within seconds, the Tughan absorbed and learned, rejecting nothing and no one.

Nova slumped onto the floor of the Eagle. She had felt Kiran's roar of pain and triumph when the combined consciousness of nearly nine hundred people flowed into him.

"Kiran, please," she begged. "Stop this now."

I haven't even begun! the Tughan returned.

"Ty, he's taken out one of the ships!"

"From here? How is that possible?"

She shook her head. "I don't understand. He's reaching

through subspace without entering subspace. He can touch anything he wants."

Tychon waved a hand to get Greah's attention. "Hang on to something. We're about to leave the atmosphere."

He reached for his headset as the Eagle approached escape velocity. They were still racing after Tharron's ship while in turn pursued by the four rebel fighters. One by one, the planes headed into space, directly toward *Teti*'s dogfight with the enemy Shrills. Tychon held his course nervously, not wanting to lose Tharron's cruiser in the melee. A hit into their deflectors threw the Eagle wild. Greah tumbled off Nova's pilot bench and landed hard on the steps up to the main cabin. He touched his head and cursed when his hand came away bloodied.

"Nova, there are four Shrills on our tail," Tychon said. "I'm going to have to let the cruiser go."

Kiran had perceived Tychon's predicament through Nova. His attention moved only momentarily to their pursuers. All four Shrills disintegrated. Tychon stared at his screens. They were gone! "What is going on? Did Kiran do that?"

* * *

Kiran no longer existed. The being that now inhabited the young body gazed around Tharron's ship to find the K'lar leader. "Tharron," he said.

Tharron stared at him in wonder. "Well done, boy," he managed. "But those Shrills are mine. I want you to do away with that second battleship now. You hear me? And the cruiser behind us."

Kiran regarded him for a moment. He felt Nova's warning. Did she not want this man dead? "The Eagle?" he said. "The one with my father on it? Will you give me candy if I do it? Come here, Mighty Tharron. Take my hand so that I may know you."

Tharron backed off. "You listen, boy..."

Kiran slid out of his chair.

"Sit down!" Tharron commanded.

"You know," Kiran said, his cherubic face smiling happily at the rebel leader, "I don't even need to touch you. I can feel you through the floor we're both standing on."

Tharron recoiled from the child and found himself backed into a corner of the cockpit. Suddenly, the K'lar's eyes widened in understanding. There was a moment of vertigo as he floated between life and death. Then there was nothing.

Kiran shook himself in disgust when Tharron's being had become part of the Tughan. *I see what you mean*, he said to Nova. He turned to the pilot, the only rebel still alive on this ship.

Pe Khoja had watched Velani die and had marveled at the ease with which their leader had been dispatched. They were gone now, their bodies littering the floor, their minds living on inside this child.

Kiran's hand moved to Pe Khoja's wrist.

"Can you fly this ship?" the rebel asked.

"Yes."

"The Eagle's right behind us." Pe Khoja felt no fear. Neither did he underestimate this boy. "If Tychon doesn't shoot us down, the battleship will. They'll destroy both of these ships."

Kiran shrugged. "They'll try. I can handle the *Teti* and I can handle Tychon." He dropped his hand. "Perhaps you shall live, Pe Khoja. There is something you want to know, isn't there?"

Pe Khoja nodded, his eyes on his screens. "I have many questions."

"And you want answers for all of those?"

Suddenly Pe Khoja was no longer sure. He looked into the Tughan's eyes and knew that all of the answers were there. The child had absorbed the conscious and subconscious, the knowledge and the memories of almost a thousand people and had learned. But did he, Pe Khoja, really want to know? Did he really?

"Well?" the Tughan demanded. "Shall I tell you a few things?" He climbed into the co-pilot's seat. His child's fingers brushed back the long blue curls and the eyes in the youthful face regarded him mischievously. "Didn't you always want to know where we all come from? You always thought that our origin might have been something quite extraordinary, didn't you? That, just maybe, we are all the same species, after all? Should I tell you how right you are about that? Do you really want to know?"

Pe Khoja gripped his controls. "No!" he said, his teeth clenched.

"How about our future? Do you want to have a look at what's ahead? By understanding all those people that have joined me, I know what happened and why, so very long ago. You would, too, if you could see all of us at once. But I can also see where we're all going. For the same reason. Nothing is coincidence if you know the math, Pe Khoja, nothing! It's just more tangled than you were led to believe." Kiran paused for a moment. "And did you know that I can change it all? I can do anything!"

"You can also die." Pe Khoja flipped his plane to rush directly at the Eagle behind them. Tychon would either shoot them down or let them crash into him. It would mean the same, either way.

Kiran shook his head. The ship assumed a mind of its own and veered away from the Eagle. Pe Khoja suddenly saw into the Tughan and knew. For an instant, his life's search for understanding had come to fruition, and he saw all of it. Then he died for it.

* * *

"What was that?" Tychon looked after the receding ship. For an instant, it had seemed as though they had been on a collision course with the rebel cruiser. "Nova? Talk to him! Find out what's going on!"

"The Tughan," Nova managed. "He killed Tharron. Killed Pe Khoja..."

"He's flying that plane alone? I'll tan his hide!"

* * *

271

"Eagle Five, come in," Carras called again. "Eagle Five!"

He reached for another channel. Who was aboard? Why was it chasing the last of the rebel cruisers? The Tughan was on one of those ships. But which? He glanced at the screens in front of him, unwilling to take the time to wonder why *Erato* had fallen silent. One problem at a time, he thought.

The bridge behind him was a frantic, noise-filled hive as operations officers conducted the external battle with the enemy Shrills.

"Hullo? Battleship up there?"

Carras frowned. "Identify."

"Um, this is Greah."

"Who?"

"I'm from Shaddallam. We're on the Eagle. Nova is sick or something."

"Who else is aboard?"

"Ty."

"Not the boy?"

"No, he's on the other ship. He's killed everybody!"

"Let me speak to Tychon."

Someone shouted in the background and Greah shouted back something equally unclear. Then Greah was back. "Uh, he's busy. Something broke."

Carras swore. "Tell him to get out of the way!" He turned to his helmsman. "Destroy the rebel ship. Go through the Eagle if you have to."

"But, sir, what about our fighters? The battle—"

"Go!"

* * *

"No!" Kiran screamed into Nova's mind when he saw *Teti* streak after them. The blow knocked Nova backward, stunned.

Tychon hailed the rebel ship. "Kiran! You will not harm that battleship!" he said firmly, as he would at any other time when Kiran misbehaved. He is just a little boy, he told himself, knowing better. Just a little boy. "I know you can hear me. Let Nova go. You're hurting her. I want you to turn your ship back to Shaddallam. I'll be right behind you."

The Eagle shook like a horse bucking its rider when a hit from the *Teti* glanced off the shields. Another volley passed the Eagle and found its target to blast Kiran's ship off course.

Tychon watched in horror as the small craft righted itself and came about as if to make a stand. He waited for the final blow from the *Teti*.

Kiran had other plans. Tychon swerved around *Teti* and followed as the rebel cruiser dove past Carras' battleship, dodging her fire, and raced toward the dead *Erato* drifting at some distance. He did not hesitate to follow Kiran when his ship dove into *Erato*'s open launch bay, where it skidded as it touched down and crushed its landing gear. Tychon set the Eagle down close to the crippled vessel. The massive bay door lowered behind them, even as deadly volleys from the *Teti* slammed into *Erato*'s shields.

* * *

Nova dragged herself to her feet and staggered toward the cockpit. Tychon tossed his headset aside and jumped from the pilot couch to catch her.

"Kiran..." she mumbled. Why did everything seem so foggy?

"You stay here," Tychon said to Greah. Greah didn't seem inclined to do much else. He stared speechlessly out of the cockpit and through the transparent wall that separated the launch from the pressurized decks where the bodies of pilots and crew lay where they had dropped. No one here had been prepared for the Tughan's rage.

Tychon walked Nova back to the lounger. "Lie down. I'll–"

She snatched his hand and held it to her interface node, allowing him to see the Tughan through her khamal with the child. Tychon's eyes widened in horrified surprise when he perceived what Kiran had become. Like Nova, he felt the presence of the people now dead and the terrible intelligence that made up the Tughan Wai. "No," he breathed.

"Gone now. He's broken our khamal. He doesn't want you

273

to see him like this." Nova struggled to sit up. "He's taken control of the battleship. Leaving Shaddallam now. So fast... Carras is following. Kiran plans to jump. No idea where to."

Tychon nodded, slowly, as if to himself. Wordlessly, he pulled his gun from its holster and left the Eagle.

"Ty, don't," Nova cried. She groped for the edge of the lounger and lurched to her feet, her mind clearer now that the Tughan had released her. She stumbled to the cargo bay door and into *Erato*'s landing area, stopping only to snatch a gun from its storage.

Kiran stood near the rebel ship's ramp, coughing, his face smudged and very pale. Acrid smoke still seeped from the ship. No one else had exited.

He stared up at the gun in his father's hand.

"Dadda?" Regardless of the lives he had taken and the vast power awakening within him, his face was that of a small boy, frightened and confused. He backed away from Tychon and fell over a body on the ground. Some small part of him recognized the lifeless thing and he shook his head in horrified comprehension. "I did this? Why did I do this? Why is this happening?"

"You can still stop this!" Tychon said urgently.

Kiran came to his feet. His expression turned to rage as if someone had switched one mask for another. "I cannot! Your own people were shooting at you to get at me. Can't you see what they've done? Can they lock me away? Can they ever live without fear of me? They will kill me, Tychon. They were prepared to destroy the whole planet to get at me. Baroch is here with me. I know what happened!"

"You're just doing what you were designed to do. You'll have to learn some things."

"I know everything!" Kiran's words were an accusation. "I have touched this ship and I know every Union ship ever built and some you haven't invented yet. I have touched nine hundred and twenty-two people and I know things that no one will ever know. And that is only the beginning! They will not let me touch them. They will kill me if I let them."

"You are still Kiran Tar Phera and heir to Delphi."

"I am a monster locked in the body of a child and I have no place to go!" The fury emanating from the Tughan was palpable.

Tychon gripped his gun with both hands. It shook in his grasp with the unfathomable effort of leveling it at his son's head. The agony on his face was not something Nova had ever encountered. "Why won't you stop me?" he pleaded, forcing the words through gritted teeth.

Kiran shook his head, his anger dissipating as quickly as it had appeared. "I don't belong here, Father. I don't want this. End this now." He closed his eyes and lifted his arms away from his body. "Do it! Before I change my mind."

Nova glanced at the setting of her own gun, aimed, and shot Tychon twice.

She heard Greah's scream from inside the Eagle when the blast forced Tychon aside to stumble onto a conveyor, dazed and unable to move.

Stunned, Kiran looked from his father to Nova and the gun in her hand.

"You have destroyed enough people," she said. "I won't let you destroy him, too. I can't!"

This was not Kiran, she reminded herself, feeling the setting on her gun adjust under her finger as she turned it onto the boy. This was a creature without equal, one who had killed to feed itself and would kill again to become even more powerful. Tharron was within him, as was Velani and Pe Khoja and so many others. All of them furious, all of them grieving. Already, these entities were fighting over dominance in shaping Kiran's new personality. This *thing* had to die.

Or did it? When the fury settles, when the grieving ends, would what remained not also have the right to live? Would the Tharron-presence inside the boy guide his future, or would reason prevail? Would Pe Khoja's thirst for knowledge lead the Tughan to kill, or would he use this powerful new mind for greater things? How would all the others that died here today shape this creature?

Her eyes shifted to Tychon. "I'm sorry," she said, offering her apology to everyone and no one. "I have no choice." She lowered her gun. "Take the Eagle. It'll outrun Carras. Go!"

"Why are you doing this?" Kiran whispered.

"I am doing this for him!"

Something moved across Kiran's face and shifted into the sum of the elements that made up the Tughan Wai now. It was ancient and in motion and still incomplete, but it was no longer a boy. "Maybe that is what makes you human, Human," he said.

He looked at the man who had given him life and had nearly taken it away. Greah crouched beside Tychon now, speechless in wide-eyed bewilderment. "Would you have done the same for her, Father?" Kiran said. "She can keep teaching you if you let her."

"Kiran..." Tychon rasped.

Kiran cocked his head, listening for something that was noiselessly approaching. "I'm still here, somewhere, Dadda. Please know that I loved you and that I wanted to be like you. I won't get that chance now, but for a little while it was a good dream." He looked up at Nova. "Look after Tychon. You are worthy of each other, I think. He needs you."

"None of this is your fault, Kiran," she said. "We won't blame you, ever."

He took her hand. "Don't let them hunt me, for their sake. Tell them I've left Trans-Targon. And tell them I shot Dadda." For a moment, Kiran's mischievous grin reappeared. "That way you'll dodge the court martial."

"Where will you go?"

"Shaddallam, at the moment. Your colonel's planes are losing their fight. There are still people dying because of me. It's got to stop."

She touched his cheek. "You are not a monster."

"Not all of us are evil," he said, an echo of Pe Khoja. "I won't be back, don't worry. I need time to find out who I am, perhaps work on my survival instinct. You won't have a second chance to point a gun at me." He stood on his toes to kiss her and then paused for a brief moment. A smile lit his tired face. She gasped when he raised his small hands and pressed them to her belly. For an instant, she felt every cell in her body react to his touch. "You can give him a daughter, if you wish," he whispered.

Nova watched him climb into the Eagle and then hurried to where Tychon was struggling to get up. Greah did his best to help when they hauled him up and maneuvered him into the landing bay's control room. There they waited silently for the bay to depressurize.

From inside Eagle Five, Kiran relinquished his mental control of the battleship's functions and allowed her to drift. Watching through the control room's window, they saw the Eagle lift off and out of *Erato*, leaving the bay doors open. It moved only a short distance away before it vanished as if it had taken only a second for Kiran to open a keyhole and slip into subspace.

"Whoa!" Greah shouted. "What was that?"

"What have I done?" Nova said tonelessly.

Tychon leaned heavily on the edge of a control panel, suspecting that a few days in a clinic lay in his future. "No regrets now," he said. "You promised him as much."

"You agree with what I did?"

He thought a moment. "No," he said. He pulled her close to himself and she moved into his embrace, hiding her face in the warm curve of his neck, wishing to stay there for a very long time. "But I am grateful that you did it."

"He may never forgive me for letting him go," she said. "But I have to believe that he won't make me regret this." She reached up to trace the lines etched into the handsome face where he should not have had any for years. A sickle-shaped scar below his eye would always remind him of this day. "You've lost so much, Ty."

"But not everything. And he's alive because of you." He smiled but she saw the pain behind the Delphian facade and the grief he would not examine until there was time and space for these things.

"Look, look, look!" Greah shouted. Unable to stand still in his excitement, he bobbed up and down in front of the observation window. "Look at this!"

Teti had come into panoramic view outside the bay door, the hundreds of lights from her windows shining in the cold dark like a distant city. The mammoth ship slowed to approach the *Erato* with caution. Her maw opened to issue a few fighter planes.

Voices burst through the open com, wanting to know. Tychon peered at the unfamiliar controls around them and then poked experimentally at a likely one. Several of the overhead screens came to life, among them a view of *Teti*'s crowded control room. Greah waved eagerly.

Carras' face loomed over them. "What is going on over there? Where is… where is the boy?"

Although Nova tensed when she saw the colonel appear on the screen, Tychon did not let her pull out of his embrace. "At ease, soldier," he said mildly.

She turned her head to look at Greah. The Shaddallama answered her unspoken question by nodding. She looked into the camera. "I'm sorry, sir. He is gone. We do have Tharron and Pe Khoja. They're dead, sir."

Carras' eyes narrowed, even as some of the people on his bridge broke into a cheer. He glanced at nearby officers before he replied. "Stay where you are. I'm coming over there." He shut the com link down.

Greah stood on a chair for a better view of *Teti*. "So what are you gonna tell him?"

"Depends on what he asks us," Tychon said.

They watched silently from the control room while a runabout entered *Erato*'s landing area and settled to the floor. Nova found the controls for the massive door and the mechanism to re-pressurize the bay. Red lights overhead dimmed and the shuttle's doors opened. Tychon leaned on Nova's shoulder when they left the control room to meet Colonel Carras.

Two others had arrived with the colonel, one of them in

civilian clothes. He immediately entered the disabled rebel ship while the officer went into the control room, leaving Carras alone with his agents and the Shaddallama.

The colonel looked around the hall and beyond the transparent walls into the adjoining space. "All dead?"

"I assume so, sir," Tychon said.

Carras regarded them for a long, silent moment. Tychon's arm was around Nova's shoulder and both looked drained, disheveled and strangely reserved. His eyes traveled down to the diminutive Shaddallama who returned his gaze with a broad smile. "The Tughan escaped?"

"Yessir," Nova said. "With the Eagle. We saw him open a keyhole just outside. At least I think that's what it was."

"There are no breaches near here."

"None that we can detect, sir. He could be anywhere now."

Carras gazed at the corpses littering the passage around the launch. "I'm sorry about your son, Tychon," he said finally.

Tychon took a deep and not quite steady breath. "He's alive, Tal. Somewhere."

"Did he... harm you?" Carras asked. "You look terrible."

"No, sir. I was shot. It's not serious."

The colonel nodded slowly, as if not quite believing him. "We have a Shantir aboard *Teti*, if you prefer that to our medics."

"Thank you, sir."

"He will not want to discuss the Tughan with you. No one on Delphi does. Ever."

"Understood, sir."

The engineer returned from the control room to join them by the shuttle. "No life signs aboard, sir," she said.

Carras stood with his hands on his hips, surveying the bay. He pursed his lips and pondered for a while. "Clearly, Tharron was experimenting with some sort of radiation, maybe even something similar to our Challenger. No doubt he then got in his own way. He was not a cautious man."

"No doubt, sir," Nova said.

"You three are very fortunate to have arrived here after the initial blast. Too bad that you were overwhelmed by one of the surviving Shri-Lan rebels and lost the Eagle during his escape."

"Indeed, an expensive loss."

Carras gestured at the overhead surveillance system. "That kind of radiation can wipe out entire recording systems. Isn't that so, Captain Zuira?"

"That is correct, sir. I will take a look." She walked back through the control room and into the hallway beyond.

The colonel searched their faces. "Is there anything else that we need to discuss before we bring in a crew?"

"Tamotsu Comori is also in Shad-Areen," Nova said, her eyes still following the engineer, once again amazed by the efficiency with which the Union's military dealt with inconveniences. "Along with several other high-ranking Shri-Lan. The native population will cooperate if we extract and remove them." She gestured at Greah. "I'd like to request compensation for this man and his people. They sustained some losses."

Tychon winked at Nova. "And I'd like to request a leave of absence, sir. To recuperate. From being shot. It's very painful."

"I got shot, too," Nova protested.

If it had been in the colonel's nature to roll his eyes heavenward, he would have done so now. "You three get into that shuttle before you fall down. I recommend isolation until we determine the nature of this… radiation. And until everything has been sanitized. A month at most, Targon time. Am I clear?"

"May we be isolated on Delphi, sir?" Nova inquired.

"Delphi? The base?"

"No," Tychon said. He pressed his lips to Nova's cheek before turning them both toward the shuttle. "Home."

* * * * *

*

ABOUT THE AUTHOR

Chris Reher is a first generation Canadian currently and out of necessity residing on planet Earth (which, in the general and interplanetary scheme of things, could *really* use a catchier name. Imagine heading past Proxima Centauri and someone asks you whence you came and you tell them "dirt". All theological implications aside, that just won't do.)

When not finding ways to defy the laws of physics or torture her subjects or entice them with inter-species hanky-panky, she designs web sites or writes about designing web sites. She enjoys long walks on the beach or, given the local beach shortage, writes about beaches far beyond Proxima Centauri.

www.chrisreher.com

Sky Hunter
The Catalyst
Only Human
Rebel Alliances
Delphi Promised

Quantum Tangle
Terminus Shift
Entropy's End

www.ingramcontent.com/pod-product-compliance
Lightning Source LLC
Chambersburg PA
CBHW061551170626
46811CB00001B/168